SPELLS & STITCHES

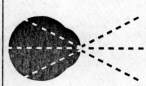

This Large Print Book carries the
Seal of Approval of N.A.V.H.

SPELLS & STITCHES

BARBARA BRETTON

THORNDIKE PRESS

A part of Gale, Cengage Learning

 GALE
CENGAGE Learning·

Detroit • New York • San Francisco • New Haven, Conn • Waterville, Maine • London

GALE
CENGAGE Learning®

LIBRARY OF CONGRESS CATALOGING-IN-PUBLICATION DATA

Bretton, Barbara.
  Spells & stitches / by Barbara Bretton.
    pages ; cm. — (Thorndike Press large print romance)
  ISBN-13: 978-1-4104-4740-1 (hardcover)
  ISBN-10: 1-4104-4740-5 (hardcover)
  1. Women merchants—Fiction. 2. Mother and child—Fiction.
3. Knitting shops—Fiction. 4. Magic—Fiction. 5. Vermont—Fiction.
6. Large type books. I. Title. II. Title: Spells and stitches.
PS3552.R435S67 2012
813'.54—dc23   2011051250

Published in 2012 by arrangement with The Berkley Publishing Group, a member of Penguin Group (USA), Inc.

Printed in Mexico
1 2 3 4 5 6 7 16 15 14 13 12

For my husband, Roy.
For everything. Forever.

ACKNOWLEDGMENTS

Special thanks (and much love) to Angela Cairns Bretton, R.N., for her help.

1

SUGAR MAPLE, VERMONT — STICKS & STRINGS

Do you know the recipe for crazy?

Take one picture-postcard New England town with a magickal secret, add busloads of crazed yarnaholics on a mission from Elizabeth Zimmermann, fold in a steady stream of walk-in knitting groupies seduced by the "30% Off" sign in the window of the most popular knit shop in the Northeast, then mix them all together with a hormonal sorceress-in-training, and trust me when I say that anything can happen.

I'm Chloe Hobbs, the very pregnant owner of Sticks & Strings, and, believe me, I was knee-deep in crazy and we were still five hours away from closing. I'd been up since the crack of dawn, rearranging stock, fixing displays of knitted garments, entering new prices into the computer, and riding herd on runaway magick. In the old days,

9

before magick and pregnancy took over my life, I looked forward to our Black Friday sale the way a kid looked forward to Christmas. With nothing but Red Bull and Chips Ahoy, I juggled runaway yarn and crazed customers from all points on the compass, and still managed to keep Sugar Maple's secrets safe from prying eyes.

Who knew that pregnancy and magick would be such a volatile combination? My half-human hormones were running amok while my sorceress-in-training magick followed right behind. I cried crystals during an episode of *Mad Men.* I hiccuped soap bubbles. I accidentally locked a platoon of pixies in the freezer and had to warm them up in a nest of orphaned toe-up socks. And there was the time I broke out in spells and sent two customers from Idaho on a wild ride up the Green Mountains clinging to a giant yarn swift. I won't tell you how many favors I had to call in that night to undo the mess, but the ladies went home to Boise with nothing more than a slight headache and five pounds of six-ply cashmere.

The trick today was to stay calm and count on my inner Zen master to get me through the chaos of our Black Friday sale without sending any more customers on unscheduled sightseeing trips.

But after eight months of putting out mag-ickal fires I was exhausted and the urge to curl up in the corner, any corner, and catch forty (or four hundred) winks was down-right irresistible.

"Don't even think about it," my friend Lynette Pendragon said as she bustled past with an armload of swirly-soft angora in saturated Easter egg pastels. "You can nap later."

I shot her a fierce look. "I thought you were a shapeshifter, not a mind reader."

"Honey, you know your face gives you away every time. You were looking at that sofa the same way you looked at Luke when he first came to town."

Luke was the man responsible for the baby girl due to join our family on January first. He was not only the love of my life, he was also our chief of police and only resident full-blood human, a fact that still kept some of our villagers looking over their collective shoulder.

Over three hundred years ago my ancestor Aerynn had led the exodus of magickal creatures from Salem to Sugar Maple to escape the all-too-human devastation caused by the infamous Witch Trials. Before she pierced the veil many years later, she cast a protective spell around her beloved town that would shield it from human mischief as long as one of her descendants walked the earth.

This time last year it had looked like that moment was about to arrive. Without a daughter to continue the Hobbs lineage, the buck stopped with me and so would our one-of-a-kind security system. Sugar Maple's true nature would be revealed for the entire world to see and we all knew that would be the end of us.

Let me spell it out for you: I was a tall, skinny, single, half-human, half-magick cat lover who hadn't been on a second date since high school. Grim didn't begin to cover my prospects.

The residents of Sugar Maple cast a wide net that pulled in every unattached vampire and werewolf, selkie and troll in our dimension. Who would have thought there could be so many Mr. Wrongs in one little town? When my closest friends started hinting that Fae bad boy Dane might be the answer to my prayers, I was ready to join a convent. Forbes the Mountain Giant was a better choice.

Their best attempts at hooking me up with someone — anyone! — had only sent me deeper into *Top Model* reruns and embarrassing encounters with boxed wine and

Cherry Garcia as the town spiraled closer to disaster.

And then Luke walked into my life and in an instant, everything changed.

I loved Luke and he loved me back. The magick I had waited my entire life to possess was growing stronger. The town I cherished was once again at peace and thriving. My baby girl shifted position inside me and I smiled. As far as I could see, our future was golden.

But that still didn't mean I could take my eye off the ball. Magick was all well and good, but sometimes you needed a little hands-on human intervention.

"Not so fast, Lynnie." I reached over and plucked a fluffy yellow feather from her shoulder. "Fourth time this week."

Lynette blew out a sigh. "Now you know why I never wear black."

Although she refused to admit it, Lynette had a slight problem with transitioning. She was a brilliant shapeshifter but not so terrific when it came to reclaiming her natural form. If I had a dollar for every time Lynette had landed on my stovetop or in my sink during the final stages of transition, I'd be driving a new Rolls-Royce instead of a last-century Buick. Her husband, Cyrus, had been trying to convince her she needed

13

glasses but she was having none of it. I was afraid nothing less than singeing off her tail feathers in a Samhain bonfire would convince the vain shapeshifter that it might be time to embrace middle age.

At least, I thought she was approaching middle age. In Sugar Maple, age was anybody's guess. We had adapted to the world of humans but we still weren't part of it. Our internal clocks followed a very different schedule. In human years, one of our preschoolers might be eligible for AARP.

Poor Luke was still having trouble with that and so was I. Up until recently I had been aging on a human scale, but now that my magick had finally kicked in, my life span was anybody's guess.

Lynette thanked me, then disappeared back into the crowd of shoppers. She and Cyrus owned the Sugar Maple Playhouse and were currently in rehearsal for their annual production of *A Christmas Carol*. The fact that she'd given up part of her holiday weekend to help out at Sticks & Strings meant the world to me.

In fact a lot of my townie friends had volunteered to lend a hand. Lilith, a gorgeous Norwegian troll with a heart of gold, helped me open before she dashed across the street to unlock the doors to the library.

Paul and Verna Griggs, a long-married werewolf couple, sent their strapping teenage sons over late the previous night to move the Dumpster behind the shop in order to free up a few more parking spaces. Fae innkeeper Renate Weaver's married daughter, Bettina, was tucked away in a corner with her glorious harp, playing music so beautiful it could charm the credit card from the tightest purse. Even vampire matriarch Midge Stallworth, who never showed her plump and rosy face before dark, promised she'd come by at four thirty to help me close.

They weren't my family by blood but they were definitely my family of choice.

My sentimental reverie was interrupted by a piercing yelp, followed by the cry, "Put down that fleece, beyotch, or I'll —"

If you're a knitter, you'll understand why I wasn't going to wait to find out what she had planned. Even crocheters know bloodshed and fiber don't mix.

A spinner I recognized from one of last summer's classes was in a standoff over a scruffy but luscious Bluefaced Leicester fleece I had yet to clean or card, much less price. Unfortunately she wasn't in that standoff with another spinner; she was going mano a mano with Elspeth, our houseguest from hell. The woman looked flushed and frantic as she clutched the filthy fleece to her capacious bosom while Elspeth tried to pry it away from her.

You remember what Benjamin Franklin said about houseguests? "Guests, like fish, begin to stink after three days." He must have shared a house with a troll like Elspeth.

Elspeth didn't stink in the literal sense (even though Luke said she smelled like stale waffles), but before she'd been in town a month, the aged troll had managed to alienate everyone in town and most of my customers. Believe me, I would have sent her packing from Sugar Maple if I could, but she was surrounded by some seriously powerful magick that rendered her untouchable. When Aerynn's mate Samuel, the father of our clan, pierced the veil, his last wish had been that Elspeth see me through my pregnancy, aka the longest nine months of my life.

So Elspeth pretty much did what she wanted whenever she wanted to, with no thought for the rest of us. Mild-mannered Bettina had suggested that perhaps we could pool our magick and render Elspeth speechless for a month or two, but Samuel, my ancestor and her protector, had apparently considered the possibility of combined

16

forces when he set the spell in motion and so we were reduced to wearing headphones and cranking up the Led Zeppelin to drown out her endless complaints.

You can imagine how much Luke enjoyed sharing our cottage with her.

"Elspeth!" I barked like a rottweiler.

"I claimed it first," Martha, my customer, announced as I approached. "This . . . this Betty White lookalike came out of nowhere and tried to get it away from me!"

I thanked the gods Elspeth had remembered to show herself in human form, because the sight of a three-hundred-something-year-old troll might not be good for business.

"Let go, Elspeth," I said, trying not to sound as crazy as I was feeling. "Martha's one of my favorite customers."

Not that Elspeth would care about something as mundane as commerce, but I could hope.

"This weren't for sale," Elspeth said, her bony jaw jutting forward. "She opened one of those cupboards and swiped it sure as I was standing there." She pointed at my not-for-sale closet near the workroom. "Saw her with my own eyes I did."

"Maybe I did, maybe I didn't," Martha said. "That didn't give you the right to assault me."

Oh, great. That was all I needed. An assault-and-battery charge leveled against the shop.

I had to think fast. I flashed Elspeth a look that could stop a buffalo in its tracks.

"This was tucked away for a reason, Martha," I said, running my hand along the dirty fleece and making a face. "Do you really want to deal with cleaning and carding?"

"It's Bluefaced Leicester," she said. "How often do you find a BFL fleece this size?"

"I have a cleaned BFL tucked away that I was saving. It's thirty percent larger." I paused for effect. "What if I offered it to you for the same sale price as the dirty one?"

She dropped that fleece so fast I almost laughed. "I'd say you had a deal."

It wasn't the Helsinki Accords, but I had learned to take my victories where I found them. I wrote up a sales ticket and sent Martha marching off to the register. Then I wheeled on Elspeth.

"What are you doing here?" I demanded. "You said you were going interdimension to visit friends today." Both Luke and I had been looking forward to a day without her constant grumbling and griping.

"My comings and goings be none of your

18

business, missy."

"You lied!" I'm not sure why that came as a surprise. "You had no intention of going anywhere."

She maintained an aggressive silence, which pushed me the rest of the way over the edge.

"When I tell you to stay away from the shop I mean it. You don't get into arguments with my customers. That's not exactly good for business."

"She be nothing more than a thief."

"Martha is not a thief. She's . . . enthusiastic." Fiber lovers were a fierce group who believed possession wasn't just nine-tenths of the law, it was everything.

"She went where she had no business going."

Look who was talking. I wasn't going to try to explain Black Friday mania to her. It would be like explaining a DVR to a box turtle.

"You can't stay here, Elspeth."

"You need keeping after."

"What I need is for you to go back to the cottage and quit picking fights with my customers."

"I take no orders from you, missy. I was sent here to stay the forces of doom."

I was about to remind her that I wasn't a

big fan of the doom talk, but to my surprise she turned on her heel and melted away.

Damn her. I'd warned Elspeth about using magick in public, but she knew better. I supposed I should be grateful she hadn't shown up at the shop looking like the three-foot-tall, butter-yellow-haired troll she actually was. Okay, so maybe the Betty White disguise was a little much, but fortunately nobody seemed to notice.

I tucked the fleece away where marauding spinners wouldn't find it, then went back to sorting through my remaining stock. Penelope, store cat and Hobbs clan familiar, peered up at me from her usual spot atop my basket of self-replenishing roving. Penny had been with me all my life and with my mother and my grandmother before me, all the way up the line to Aerynn, the mother of us all.

"Everything's under control." I bent down as far as I could and gave her a skritch behind the left ear. "Go back to sleep."

The Noro was all gone and so was the Malabrigo. We still had a box of Tilli Tomas, some Debbie Bliss, and a fair amount of Cleckheaton and Jamieson's. Even the splitty acrylic I refused to list on our website was flying off the shelves like fugitives from maximum security. Unless I missed my guess, we'd be out of sale stock long before closing time.

I had barely settled back down to tagging more stock when Janice Meany popped up at my side. Janice and I had always been close, but after the adventure in Salem last spring our bond was unbreakable. She owned and operated Cut & Curl, the full-service salon and day spa next to the library, and in her spare time took care of a husband and growing family.

"Don't look now," she whispered in my ear, "but you're being stalked."

I groaned and slapped a price sticker on my next-to-last skein of Noro Silk Garden. "Believe me, if you can't knit me, spin me, or felt me nobody in this shop is interested." The only thing being stalked was the legendary Wollmeise I had hidden inside the shop refrigerator behind the turkey sandwiches.

"No, really," Janice said, angling her body so her back was turned to the selling floor. "This gray-haired chick has been standing over there near the Ashford wheels for five minutes and I swear she hasn't blinked once."

I slapped a sticker on a sparkly skein of Disco Lights. "People zone out in yarn shops." I grinned up at my red-haired friend. "Personally I think it's the fumes, but don't tell our dyers I said so."

Janice didn't laugh, which definitely caught my attention. Anyone who says tenth-generation witches don't have a sense of humor has clearly never met any of the Meany women. Besides, I could always make my friend laugh.

"Okay," I said, putting down my roll of stickers and giving her my full attention. "What makes you think she's stalking me?"

"Because she's looking at you like you're two hundred grams of qiviut, that's why."

"She probably never saw anyone this pregnant and she's about to text the Guinness World Records."

No joke, I looked like I was carrying a football team. I mean, I was huge. Luke thought I looked womanly but I was reasonably sure that was a euphemism for fat.

Not that I minded. I loved being pregnant. Okay, so maybe I didn't love that I found out I was pregnant from a bad-tempered troll who had dropped into our lives the way Dorothy's house dropped on the Wicked Witch of the West or that the morning sickness lasted all day, but I definitely loved the knowledge that every day that passed brought me twenty-four hours closer to meeting our daughter.

And, let's be honest, bigger boobs didn't

hurt, either.

Janice, who had five kids of her own, wasn't interested in my musings on motherhood.

"You're going to think I'm crazy," she said, "but I'm pretty sure I've seen her before."

"That's because you probably have," I pointed out. "Sticks & Strings has the most loyal clientele in the Northeast." I was going to say "in the world," but I figured I'd save the hyperbole for my next e-mail blast. On second thought, who needed hyperbole when your in-store workshops are booked a year in advance and you're known across the Internet as the shop where your yarn never tangles, your sleeves always match, and you never, ever drop a stitch.

Janice shook her head. "She's not a regular customer." She paused for a moment, brow furrowed. "Damn, where have I seen her?"

"Don't ask me," I said with a shrug. "I'm eight hundred months pregnant."

But Janice had piqued my curiosity and I cast a quick glance toward the woman she had spotted lurking near the Ashfords. She was maybe five-two, small boned with a comfortable amount of cushioning. She wore a shiny purple down vest over a fancy navy jogging outfit, and dark green clogs, all the better to show off her yellow argyle socks. Her gray hair was cut in a no-nonsense bob. Her only jewelry was a plain gold wedding band and a pair of pearl studs in her ears.

All things considered, a short, gray-haired white woman in a northern New England yarn shop wasn't exactly a blue whale sighting in Snow Lake, but I had to agree with my friend.

"You're right," I said. "She *does* look familiar."

"And she can't take her eyes off you."

Right again.

The woman nodded and smiled at me. I nodded and smiled back at her as a tiny prickle of apprehension moved between my shoulder blades.

"Salem," Janice said. "That's where I saw her."

The prickle of apprehension spread to my spine. "I wish you hadn't said that." Our trip to Salem had tested all of us in ways I never wanted to be tested again. I wracked my brain in an effort to place the woman in time and space. "Maybe she was the desk clerk at the motel."

Janice shook her head. "Luke checked us in. We stayed in the car."

Across the room, the gray-haired woman's

smile widened and she started pushing her way through the crowd of yarnaholics as she headed straight for me.

"Oh, crap," I said. "She's coming this way."

The magick side of my DNA equation was up for anything, but the human side was screaming for me to get out of Dodge. Adrenaline could be every bit as powerful as a major spell.

"Watch the shop," I said to Janice as I struggled to slide my currently enormous butt off the stool where I'd been perched. This had trouble written all over it. The thing to do was run.

Unfortunately I was too late.

"Chloe?" The woman looked at me the way my cats did when I brought out the Fancy Feast. "It *is* Chloe, isn't it? Luke mentioned you owned a yarn shop and I was hoping —" She stopped as her gaze moved down from my face to the ginormous belly that not even an industrial-strength workbench could hide.

"Oh!" It was amazing just how much you could pack into one tiny word.

For a crazy second I considered whipping out the magick and wiping her Chloe-specific memory bank clean, but with the store this crowded, that would be asking for trouble. I was still learning my way around the world of spells and potions, and even though I had developed into a pretty darn good sorceress, I had a long way to go. One little slip and the entire shop could find itself turned into a clan of quilters who were allergic to wool.

"Eight and a half months," I said before she had a chance to ask. "And no, I'm not carrying twins." I paused for a moment, but she was still transfixed by my bump. You would have thought I had a flat-screen TV strapped to my belly. "And you're — ?"

She pulled her gaze away and struggled to regroup. "I'm Fran." She said it as if that should mean something to me, but I hadn't a clue. "Fran Kelly. We met back in April when you and Luke were up in Salem." She paused while I wracked my brain for the missing data. "Walmart . . . near sporting goods."

This was getting more embarrassing by the nanosecond.

"I worked with Luke when he was with the department." She forced a short laugh as she cast a sneaky glance toward the Welsh gold circlet I wore on the middle finger of my left hand. "Not that I want to take credit for this or anything, but I'm the one who told him about the job opening here."

The entire awkward encounter in the center aisle of the discount store came rushing back to me. Not only had Fran worked with Luke in Boston, she was also good friends with his brother Ronnie, the Realtor, and probably the rest of the MacKenzie clan as well. Luke had been ducking dinner invitations from his family for months with lame excuses about his workload and my store hours. Even worse, he hadn't shared our good news with anyone beyond the Sugar Maple town limits.

I'd warned him repeatedly that we needed to let his family know about the baby before she started college, but he did that guy thing I hated and went selectively deaf every time I brought it up. He had his reasons, but even I knew you couldn't keep a secret like this from your family forever.

"Fran," I said with a great big smile that I hoped covered my embarrassment. "Luke will be so sorry he missed you."

She laughed merrily. "We didn't expect to find him in the yarn shop. We'll pop into the police station next door and say hello after we leave here."

"He's not there, either," I said, feeling my cheeks burning red-hot. I gestured toward Janice, who was hanging on our every word, and heard myself babble something about helping Lorcan Meany weatherize their boat. Which was, of course, a total lie, but telling a human that her old friend was seeing a selkie off on his annual aquatic renewal wasn't an option. "He won't be back until late afternoon, but if you'd like to hang out here and wait, you're welcome to stay."

Okay, somebody stick a cuff-down sock in my mouth. The last thing I wanted was for Luke's nosy human pal to stick around and observe the proceedings. I'd rather be trapped in a wind tunnel with Donald Trump's hair.

You wouldn't think things could get any worse, but you would be wrong.

"Wait a second." I struggled to keep my heart rate under control. "Did you say *we?*"

Fran's eyes cut to her left and I followed her gaze. "Bunny had the feeling Luke was hiding something, but I don't think she figured on this. We thought we'd combine some shopping with a little snooping."

Bunny was Bernadette MacKenzie, a.k.a. Luke's mother. The same woman he had been ducking since the plus sign appeared on the pregnancy tester. Bunny and I had spoken a few times, your basic chitchat about the weather and Luke's whereabouts, and each time we did, I hung up feeling like a rat for not telling the woman that I was carrying her grandchild.

It seemed to me that was the kind of thing you shared with the people who loved you. The people who brought you into the world and guided you through infancy and childhood and the wild waters of adolescence.

But then, what did I know? To me, family was a mystery wrapped in an enigma buried in kettle-dyed merino. I had spent most of my childhood wishing Cliff and Clair Huxtable would adopt me. I probably stood a better chance of understanding quantum physics than the workings of your average human family.

A sixtyish blond woman of medium height was slowly making her way toward us. Her eyes swept the displays on either side of her with metronomic precision. She paused once at a gathering of lace-weight suri alpaca, dallied momentarily over a basket of angelic angora, exchanged commentary with two bodybuilder types who had been looming over some mohair for at least a half hour.

She gave off a kind of sugar-cookies-with-a-gin-chaser vibe that I could sense across the room. She wore neatly pressed jeans, Skechers, and a simple top-down raglan in teal blue. Her arms were piled high with Cascade 220 and a sprinkling of Madelinetosh and she had that *don't mess with me* air some women grew into as they got older. Deep grooves of worry bracketed her wide mouth, but they were offset by the spray of laugh lines at the outer corners of her dark green eyes.

She scared me more than any army of Fae warriors ever had.

If I knocked Fran down, then scrambled over the worktable, I stood a fifty-fifty chance of making it out the door before she zeroed in on me. But I was eight and a half months pregnant and barely mobile, so I did the next best thing.

I set her yarn on fire.

2

I didn't mean to do it, but I guess the shock of seeing Bunny MacKenzie in Sticks & Strings blew away the last shred of control over my magick and set the whole thing in motion.

Flames shot from my fingertips like Fourth of July fireworks gone wild and headed straight toward Luke's mother. I shrieked. Janice knocked the yarn out of her arms and began jumping up and down on the smoldering skeins. Bless sheep and the wool they provide. Wool doesn't burn, it only smolders, but the sight of smoke ignited hysteria just the same. Fran yanked a half-empty bottle of water from her bag, uncapped it, and flung the contents at her friend.

All in all, not the way you want to meet his mother.

The good news was that the humans among us had no idea I was the resident firebug because Aerynn's protective charm had done its job and cloaked the source.

The bad news? The baby secret wasn't a secret anymore.

The fire, the unexpected shower, everything fell away the moment Bunny MacKenzie's dark green eyes settled on my big round belly. I watched in a weird combination of terror and fascination as her expression slid from shock to joy to *I'm going to kill him!*

I opened my mouth to speak, but no words came out. A weird, prickly feeling exploded beneath my skin, like burning needles trying to work their way out. My lungs felt tight and I struggled to pull in a deep breath. My heart started pounding triple time, my vision tunneled down, and the next thing I knew Bunny MacKenzie was helping me over to one of the overstuffed sofas near the fireplace.

"We need more water," Bunny barked as she settled me into the cushions. "Now!"

Janice dashed off toward the kitchen while poor Fran stared at me, eyes wide.

"Should I call 911?" she asked, rummaging through her purse again as Luke's mother took my pulse.

Bunny met my eyes. "Anything hurt?"

I shook my head.

"Any contractions?"

I shook my head again.

"That's what we want to hear." She checked my pulse with sure fingers. "So far, so good."

I found my voice. "Are you a nurse?"

"Thirty-five years. Cardiac intensive care. I retired in May." Her tone was matter-of-fact but the look in her eyes was anything but. "When are you due?"

"January first."

A wry smile tilted the ends of her mouth. "And when did he plan on telling us?"

I managed what I hoped was a wry smile of my own. "January second."

She spun out a few choice phrases that made me laugh in spite of myself, the gist of it being that Luke was a stubborn know-it-all idiot who had no business locking out his family at a time like this.

I couldn't disagree. Happily I was saved from saying anything to that effect when Janice swooped in with two more bottles of water, a banana, and a towel for a very soggy Bunny.

Some people break out in a sweat when they get nervous. These days I break out in magick. The mini firestorm was only the beginning. My entire body shook with the effort to keep more spells from exploding all over my yarn shop like the contents of a crazed piñata.

Bunny apparently noticed the tremors rocketing through me. (I had the feeling not much escaped the woman.)

"Holy Mary," she murmured as she lifted my right wrist and took my pulse again. "Honey, your pulse is way too fast for me."

"I'm fine," I managed as my words swirled around her head in white-hot neon. "It's nothing to worry about."

"This has happened before?"

I waved my hand in what I hoped was a casually dismissive gesture and a flotilla of traveling pixies with attitude appeared on Bunny's right shoulder. Ever get a mosquito bite in the dead of winter and wonder how in the world that happened? You have a pixie infestation. They have sharp little teeth and a wicked sense of humor that usually involves drawing blood. They also smell like a bad tomato when they're drunk, but you didn't hear that from me.

"Ouch!" Bunny glanced at her shoulder, then over at Fran. "I hope we didn't pick up bedbugs at that miserable diner this morning. I told you I saw something crawling on the back of your seat."

A column of dancing sprites was spiraling down from the ceiling, bouncing off her

34

head, tugging on her ears, waltzing across the bridge of her nose. A second column spiraled down and wreathed Fran's forehead.

Fran started scratching her temples. "I wish you hadn't said that."

The two women started swatting the air and scratching their heads in an attempt to dislodge the unwelcome visitors, who were now eyeballing each other as they assumed battle positions.

A turf war over Bunny MacKenzie? I don't think so. But my magick was running amok and I was afraid I might sneeze a call to battle. I flashed Janice a *help me* look and curled my hands under my butt, praying I didn't singe anything vital.

I'd heard the stories about the great pixie wars of the last century. First the pixies, then the sprites, and if you didn't broker a peace between them quickly the trolls would step in and try to take over. If that happened, we'd all be in big trouble because nobody can tell trolls anything. Trust me. Not even trolls want to live with another troll. We'd been living with Elspeth for eight months now and had the battle scars to prove it.

Janice made a show of rubbing my hands. "You're freezing!" she said, flashing me a covert wink. She whisked a huge big-needle afghan from the back of one of the hearth-side sofas and draped it across my shoulders. Bless friends with wicked good powers. She had infused the afghan with spell-retardant properties that instantly cooled my fingertips and sent my magick into a low-energy rest period.

Janice then turned her attention to the pixie-sprite battle brewing on Bunny Mac-Kenzie's left shoulder.

"I can't believe this!" Bunny was saying as she knocked a pixie into a pile of Malabrigo. "I don't know why they call them bedbugs when they're everywhere."

Poor Fran was practically dancing a jig as sprites tumbled to the ground at her feet.

"Let me take a look," Janice said. "I have five kids. I've pretty much seen everything."

"Janice is an herbalist," I offered. "She knows all sorts of natural remedies for things like this."

Bunny wasn't impressed, but Fran looked like she would try just about anything at this point.

Me? I felt like I was having an out-of-body experience as I watched my closest friend paw through Bunny's hair like a chimpanzee grooming her mate.

"Nothing there," Janice said in a casual

36

tone of voice. She checked Fran out next. "You're fine, too."

"Nothing?" Bunny shot her a look. "I felt like I had an entire community running around on me. There had to be something."

"There was, but not the way you think," Janice said, gesturing toward a towering pile of roving in a basket next to Fran. "Cochineal dye. Sixty-three percent of fair-skinned females have a negative response the first time they're exposed to it." She sounded so convincing I almost believed her. "Fortunately it's a one-time reaction and it won't happen again."

I'm not sure if Bunny actually believed the explanation or had other things on her mind, but either way I decided it was time to make an exit. I slid the afghan from my shoulders and stood up. "I need to —"

"Sit down," she ordered. "We're not finished here."

Another woman might have balked at her *I'm the boss* motherly command, but to me it felt like a hug. My parents died when I was very little and sometimes I think I've spent my entire life looking to replace what I lost.

I sat back down on the sofa and motioned for Bunny to sit next to me. Janice, being Janice, instantly saw what was happening and whisked Fran off in search of coffee and doughnuts so we could talk.

"Sorry we can't use my office, but I need to keep my eye on things out here." I gestured toward the thick crowd of customers shopping, laughing, and comparing pattern ideas.

She leaned over and took my left hand in hers. "Let's see how you're doing."

"I'm fine," I protested, "really, I —"

She raised a brow and I fell into silence as she checked my pulse against her watch. "Much better, but still a little fast." She patted my hand then released it. "Let's phone your doctor just to be on the safe side."

How many roadblocks could a fifteen-minute relationship encounter anyway? I didn't have a doctor. At least, not the kind of doctor recognized by the AMA. I posed special problems that a nonmagick doctor would be helpless to handle. (I tried not to think about the special human problems a magick practitioner might find beyond her powers.)

In this Twitter/Facebook/YouTube world you couldn't be too careful. I've had more than my share of nightmares about what could happen if Sugar Maple's story ever spilled out into the world of humans. Although I was half human, I had opted to follow the same basic path that my mother and all the other Hobbs women had followed. A Quebec healer/midwife named Brianne was working in tandem with Lilith to see me safely through my pregnancy and delivery.

And how could I forget Elspeth? I still wasn't sure what her role was in the journey, but there was no denying the fact that she was definitely on board for the duration.

"I appreciate your concern, Mrs. MacKenzie, but —"

"Bunny."

"Bunny," I repeated, "but I'm fine. I'll tell the doctor about it next week at my regular appointment." It was a lie but a necessary one.

She whipped out her phone. "Give me his number," she ordered. "I'll call and fill him in."

"No, really. I swear to you everything is totally fine."

"Are you on any medications?"

I shook my head. "Nothing."

"And you're taking prenatal vitamins."

"I'm doing everything I'm supposed to do, Bunny." I sounded defensive and I guess I was. The things I was doing hadn't been covered in her nurse training.

"I'm sure you are, honey. I always push

too hard." She smiled and my remaining defenses began to crumble. "My kids say I'm a pain in the ass."

"I'd say you're concerned."

"A concerned pain in the ass." She placed a hand on my bump. I'm not usually big on strangers feeling up my occupied uterus, but to the baby, she was family. "A girl?"

And here I was supposed to be the one with powers. "How did you know?"

"I was hoping." A shadow crossed her face and I knew she was thinking about the daughter Luke and his ex-wife had lost a few years ago. "Do you have the sonogram handy? I'd love to see her."

We don't do sonograms in Sugar Maple, but I couldn't tell Bunny that. Instead I babbled on about spilling a cup of coffee on my copy and needing to ask my doctor for a new one.

Bunny nodded, but I wouldn't blame her if she thought I was a flaming nutcase. I definitely sounded like one.

Bunny, however, still had more questions.

"You're wearing a wedding band," she said, gesturing toward the circle of Welsh gold I wore on my middle finger. "Are you and my son married?"

"No," I said. "It's a family ring."

"So why aren't you and my son married?"

Luke had asked me to marry him so many times that I had lost count before the end of my first trimester, but I said nothing to Bunny. It seemed the safest option.

And, to be honest, she scared me!

Bunny, however, was undeterred. "I raised my son to take responsibility for his actions."

"And he has," I shot back. So much for the safest option. "He's every bit as excited about the baby as I am." In some ways, maybe even more excited since he knew how precious a child's life was. "I definitely think you should talk to him about this."

"You bet I will," Bunny said, "but that doesn't mean I don't want to hear what you have to say. After all, you're the one carrying my granddaughter."

The baby answered with a powerful kick. I reached for Bunny's hand and placed it back against the spot. "I think she wants to offer an opinion," I said as another kick made us both laugh out loud. Strange how natural it felt to share this moment with her.

"A true MacKenzie woman," Bunny said, her eyes tearing up again. "Opinionated and strong."

"Same thing can be said of a Hobbs woman."

"I have no doubt." She patted my belly

then leaned back against the sofa cushions. "So do you love my son?"

She said it the same way a knitter would say, "Do you love cashmere?" Clearly there was only one right answer.

"I love him very much."

"Does he love you?"

"Yes." I doubted many things about humans and their world but Luke's love wasn't one of them.

"So what's the problem?"

"There is no problem. Right now we're concentrating on the baby."

"A baby who deserves two parents."

"She has two parents."

"I mean a real family."

"We *are* a real family."

"Not in the eyes of God or Vermont."

She didn't add "or the MacKenzies," but I heard the words loud and clear.

"I disagree, Bunny."

She gave me a long, measuring look that had me praying the protective charm around Sugar Maple could keep me safe from wannabe mothers-in-law. "In our family we marry first and have children second."

"We didn't plan it this way, Bunny. The pregnancy was a happy surprise for both of us."

"So you do plan to marry later on."

"I didn't say that." In fact, I wished I hadn't said anything at all. "You really should talk to Luke about this."

"You're right," she said with a nod of her carefully coiffed head. "I need to talk to Luke."

She whipped out her iPhone and pressed the Prodigal Son speed-dial button while I prayed for an attack of Braxton-Hicks contractions.

Poor Luke. He wouldn't know what hit him.

3

LUKE — SHADOW BEACH, SOUTHERN NEW HAMPSHIRE

The next time a six-foot, six-inch, two-hundred-twenty-pound selkie asked me to drive him to the ocean so he could start his winter retreat I'd say no.

Chloe tried to tell me I might be in over my pay grade, but I liked Lorcan Meany, and after all that his wife Janice had done for us in Salem, I figured I owed them one. So when the guy asked me for a lift I figured how tough could it be.

Like a lot of things in life, it had seemed like a good idea at the time.

I'd stand there on the shore and watch as Lorcan walked into the waves then disappeared beneath the swells. Then I'd gather up his clothes, his wallet, his iPod, and his battered copy of *On the Road* and be home with Chloe in time for Thanksgiving leftovers.

The first clue that I was in for a wild ride came when I swung by the Meany house to pick him up. He was waiting in the driveway with a body bag and three giant coolers at his feet.

"Should I be worried?" I asked. "I'm your friend but don't forget I'm also the chief of police."

I'd worked homicide in Boston before moving up to Sugar Maple. Body bags and coolers weren't usually a good sign.

He shot me the kind of look I usually got when I told a New Yorker I was a Pats fan. "It's my pelt."

"Your pelt?" I sounded like English was my third language.

"Sealskin," he said. "What did you think, I grew a new one every year?"

"Uh, yeah," I said. "That actually is what I thought."

"Without the pelt, I couldn't go back to the sea."

"And that's a big deal?"

"If I didn't go back, I'd be dead by Christmas." Normally he took his annual retreat at Snow Lake, submerging himself beneath the ice for two long, safe winter months. But every five years he needed to return to the ocean or face extinction.

I stared at him. "You're shitting me."

"Chloe didn't fill you in?"

"She tried, but I told her I had a handle on it."

I was wrong. So the body bag held a dark, gleaming sealskin that he would wear into the sea. My imagination conjured up some kind of zip-up-the-front coat that he could slip on and off at will, but I wasn't even close to reality.

And that was just the beginning.

"Holy crap," I said when he flipped open the cooler a half hour later. "Smells like dead fish."

Some people bring Cheez Doodles and doughnuts to snack on. Lorcan Meany brought trout. I knew the guy liked fish — nobody grilled fresh trout the way Lorcan did — but there wasn't a grill in sight. The guy was downing the frozen trout ice chunks and all, tearing the heads off then swallowing the damn things tail end first.

"Fish-loading," he said between mouthfuls. "Sometimes I go a week before finding food when I first go back. Gotta be prepared."

By the time he started on the third cooler he was making weird snuffling noises and snorting fish bones onto the dashboard.

"C'mon, man!" I protested as fish guts flew past my nose. "Gimme a break." I'd

46

spent quality time with corpses that smelled better. I buzzed down the window and stuck my head out in an attempt to keep from puking up my breakfast.

The closer we got to the ocean, the weirder it got inside the Jeep. Lorcan polished off the last of the trout, then seemed to drop into something close to a food coma. The capacity for human speech seemed to have been supplanted with random squeaks and periodic gasps for air.

When he poured two sport bottles of Poland Spring over his head, I considered tossing him the keys and hitchhiking back to Vermont, but he'd probably drive my Jeep into the ocean.

My cell rang and I let it flip over to voice mail. No way was I taking a call from my mother with seal boy next to me, barking his ass off. Besides, it wasn't like I didn't know what she was calling about. This was the third year I'd been AWOL at the Thanksgiving table. That alone was enough to merit at least two calls.

Chloe had been pushing me to tell the extended MacKenzie clan about the baby, but so far I'd resisted her best arguments. They'd swarm all over us like picnic ants, darting into every nook and cranny of our lives. Chloe's magick had been haywire lately. All we needed was for her to literally nail Great-Aunt Brigid's butt to the wall and all hell would break loose.

Besides, what if the baby wasn't exactly human? I'd spent a few sleepless, whiskey-fueled nights mulling over that question. I mean, I was sitting next to a guy who was about to spend the winter in a seal suit. Nothing seemed impossible to me anymore. Waiting until the baby was here in this world to introduce her to the human side of her family seemed the wise way to go.

The phone rang again. I ignored it again. Whoever came up with the idea of personalized ringtones must've had a mother like mine.

The ringing stopped, but that didn't mean my mother had given up. For all I knew she was on the phone with Chloe right now, detailing chapter and verse of my failings as a son. So far Chloe had gone along with my decision to keep her pregnancy our secret, but with the holiday season under way and her third-trimester emotions running high, there was the very real possibility she might blurt out the news the second my mother said, "How are you?"

But I'd deal with that later. Right now I had a selkie to deliver.

The last five miles were tough going. Lorcan ran out of trout and stared at me with big, sad brown eyes until I stopped at a Long John Silver's for a bucket of fish and chips. He'd given me a detailed map before we started and I followed it off-road until we reached the secluded beach that was our ultimate destination.

"Okay, bud," I said as I climbed out of the truck. "Let's get this thing rolling."

The agitation that had marked the trip down here vanished as a sense of peace seemed to encircle Lorcan. Even I could see he was changing right before my eyes. I unlatched the back of my truck, then he reached in and unzipped the body bag.

I'd be lying if I said I didn't have a couple of bad moments when I got a good look at his pelt. I'd grown up on Disney's fairy tales and this made the murder of Bambi's mother a walk in the park. The pelt wasn't exactly coat-ready. It was big, hot, moist, almost breathing with life. It stank from fish and brine and something else. Something my blood recognized but my brain refused to process. The head was sleek, the nose long and whiskered. The teeth were marbled brown and yellow, the incisors sharp and angled for business.

This was Lorcan Meany, same as the human form I'd come to call friend.

He donned the pelt, letting it settle over his form like exactly what it was: a second skin. So far it was a lot like old adventure movies where the hunter shielded his human essence from his prey by donning a bear skin and slipping through the woods unnoticed.

And then it got really weird.

He dropped to his knees a few feet from the water's edge. and toppled over on his right side just as Chloe's ringtone erupted from my jacket pocket.

No way was I letting that call roll over to voice mail.

I pressed on as I ran toward Lorcan's rigid form.

"You okay?" I barked into the phone.

"Fine, but —"

"Contractions?"

"No, but, Luke —"

Lorcan was white, pasty, sweating profusely beneath the heavy skin. "He's flopping around on the sand. Is that normal?"

"I don't know. I've never —"

"Shit, he's having trouble breathing. Do selkies need air or water? CPR? I need help here."

"Luke, listen to me. Your —"

"I'll call you back."

The guy was going down for the count.

Or at least I thought he was. Nothing in my training had prepared me for this. It occurred to me that maybe he needed oxygen, the kind you found in water. I bent down to roll him toward the surf, but he was five hundred pounds of pure muscle and I couldn't budge him even an inch. The lines between human and seal were blurring, Lorcan's features melting into the lines of the pelt. Was this the way it was supposed to go down or did he need help?

Chloe's ringtone sounded again. "You're gonna have to hold, Chloe. I've got a situation here."

"That makes two of us, Luke William Aloysius MacKenzie," a familiar voice stated, "because you've got yourself a situation here, too."

What the hell had I done to piss off the gods?

"Ma, I've got to go." A dozen sea lions bounded onto shore, barking loudly as they thumped their way toward Lorcan. One of the sea lions was the size of a pickup truck. His muzzle was dark gray, his whiskers white. He stood back from the others as they circled Lorcan's prone form and watched me with huge brown eyes that seemed to take my measure.

"Where are you?" my mother demanded.

"What's all that barking?"

"This isn't a good time, Ma." I was being herded toward the water by two sea lions who seemed to think I was a long-lost cousin. "I'll call you back."

"I find out you're about to be a father again and you're going to hang up on me? I don't think —"

"Ma, seriously, this isn't a good time. I'll call you back as soon as I can."

"I've heard that story before, mister. You owe your father and me an explanation and I want —"

"You're breaking up, Ma. Can't understand a word you're saying."

"I wasn't born yesterday. Your sister Meghan pulls that nonsense, so don't you start. You're just lucky I have to drive Fran back home or I'd take Chloe up on her offer and spend the night."

Elspeth our bossy houseguest and my mother under the same roof. What the hell was Chloe thinking?

"Hello! Are you there, Luke? Say something."

Hard to talk when you're running from a monster sea lion looking to head-butt you into the next county. Damn, he was fast. He caught me on the right hip and sent me flying.

"Luke! Hello? Did you hang up on me? I don't think this is very —" Those were her last words as the cell slipped from my hand and was swept into the Atlantic.

As it was, I barely had time to roll out of the way in time to avoid being crushed by a gathering of sea lions marching Lorcan into the sea. Everything else faded away — the icy water, the fierce wind, my mother's voice — as their massive bodies disappeared beneath the waves, taking my friend with them.

4

CHLOE — BACK IN SUGAR MAPLE

We all stood in the doorway of Sticks & Strings and watched as Bunny and Fran drove away.

"She didn't wave back," Janice noted as I flipped the Open sign to Closed. "That's not good."

"You think?" The baby kicked and I placed my hands against my belly. "Luke's going to be fielding calls from every Mac-Kenzie between here and Seattle."

"I'd put a spell on her," Janice said. "Make the two of them forget what happened here."

"If I was going to put a spell on them, I would've done it while she was here."

"Send a reverse thought probe with an ionizer," Lynette suggested. "Works like a charm within a two-hundred-yard radius."

"I'm better at scattershots," I said. "I can't seem to get the hang of thought probes."

"That's because you're pregnant," Janice

54

said. "The hormones screw with your concentration."

"You're not pregnant," I said to her. "Why don't you do it?"

Janice had been magick from the day she was born. Wiping out a few memories was as easy as brushing her teeth.

"You know I'd do anything for you, Chloe."

"Then you'd better hurry."

"You didn't let me finish," she said. "I'd do anything for you, but I can't do that."

"It's not like we'd be doing anything terrible to them. I mean, so they find out tomorrow that I'm pregnant. That isn't going to change the course of human events, is it?"

"Don't go all *Star Trek* on me," Janice said and everyone laughed. "I'm not worried about the course of human events." Dynamic, self-assured Janice Meany was looking downright sheepish as she whispered in my ear, "Elspeth has me on spellfast while I'm under her tutelage. She says abstinence will heighten my abilities. I'm forbidden to cast spells or charms or enchantments until the new moon."

I groaned. "You actually listen to what that awful creature has to say?"

"When it comes to skills, she's actually

55

pretty amazing," Janice said, looking even more sheepish than before, if possible.

"She's the most annoying creature I've ever met."

"No argument there," Janice said, "but trust me when I say she's a walking Book of Spells."

I allowed myself a minor eye roll. "Then maybe I should ask Elspeth to put a spell on Bunny MacKenzie."

Now that got everyone's attention.

"You don't want to put a spell on your mother-in-law," Rosie from Assisted Living said sternly. Rosie was a world-class eavesdropper. "You end as you begin. Remember that."

"She's not my mother-in-law," I reminded the vampire retiree.

"She's your baby's grandma," Rosie said, dentures clicking madly inside her mouth.

"Listen to Rosie," Midge Stallworth chirped. "She knows."

Rosie was right. Midge was right. They were all right. I had to declare Bunny a no-spells zone and stick to my guns.

This was between Luke and his mother and I was going to stay so far out of it I might as well be in Bermuda.

"Look at this place," I said with a groan. "It looks like an army marched through." I began gathering up empty cups and crumpled napkins.

"You go sit down, honey," Lilith said. "We'll all pitch in and have it done in two shakes of a lamb's tail."

"Of course we will," Renate said. "Many hands make light work."

"Enough with the clichés!" Janice pleaded. "You're making my ears bleed."

Everyone ignored her.

"Luke should know you never hang up on your mother," Midge Stallworth trilled as she went in search of a broom and dustpan. "No matter how old you are, you have to listen to your mother."

I loved mother talk. These days I soaked up every word.

"Amen," Renate Weaver said, suddenly shrinking down to her natural Fae size. "I blueflamed Bettina last week and she claimed the pixel resolution was weak, but I wasn't buying that hogwash." Blueflame was our community's answer to the BlackBerry and iPhone but instead of a tiny screen we used life-sized holograms to communicate. "I knew she was out there having lunch with her hotsy-totsy human harp friends and didn't have time for her mother."

Even eternally sweet Lilith, our township librarian/historian, was foursquare on the side of maternal indignation. "You're right, Renate. According to studies done by the Institute of Magick and Alchemy, blueflame is the most reliable form of communication in the dimension. There's no excuse."

"Of course there isn't," Renate said. It wasn't easy to strike fear in a daughter's heart when you were currently the size of a field mouse, but Renate gave it her all as she glared over at her eldest, Bettina.

"Fair warning, Chloe: if human mothers are anything like the Fae, then poor Luke is toast," Bettina deadpanned as she fitted her harp into its travel case.

"Bunny will get over the dropped call," I said as I retrieved another used paper plate, "but she's never going to forgive Luke for not telling her about the baby."

"His family's old-school?" Lynette asked as she wiped at a smudge on the display counter.

I nodded. "The MacKenzies are an until-death-do-us-part clan. They still can't believe two of their kids are divorced."

"Luke's superstitious," Verna Griggs said as she settled down on one of the sofas with the log cabin afghan she'd been knitting for the last six months. "Paul said he knocks wood every time he talks about the baby. That's why he didn't tell his family. He

58

wants to wait until she's here and he can count all the fingers and toes."

Luke had struggled to make peace with his daughter's death and he had finally achieved his goal not long before we found out we were pregnant. He claimed he wasn't superstitious, but I knew he wouldn't relax until our baby girl was born.

Which was all well and good for us, but families didn't think that way. When it came to babies, nothing less than full disclosure would do.

Lilith nodded vigorously. "Archie saw him throw salt over his shoulder at Fully Caffeinated when someone asked when you were due."

"And gods forbid a black cat crosses his path," Midge said with a cackle. "He turned paler than my last customer."

Midge and her husband, George, owned the town's only (and rarely used) funeral home and she never missed a chance for a little mortuary humor.

"Hey!" I protested. "There's nothing wrong with a little charm to keep the evil forces from your doorstep, is there?"

"That's exactly what's so puzzling about humans," Lynette said. "They have no trouble believing in magick when it suits their purposes, but parade the truth right in front of their eyes and they're blind as bats."

Which sounded like a very good thing to me. Sugar Maple's existence was predicated on our ability to hide our magick in plain sight.

Midge frowned at Lynette. "Dumpling, I really wish you'd stop bringing bats into the conversation. You know how I feel about those cranky old stereotypes. This is the twenty-first century."

"Not everything is a vampire reference," Lynette shot back. "I can talk about bats without you getting your Spanx in a twist."

We all pretended not to hear the rogue giggle that erupted from somewhere in the room. There wasn't a pair of Spanx in the universe big enough to accommodate Midge Stallworth's double-wide butt.

"Are there any more cupcakes left?" I asked Janice. This seemed as good a time as any to change the subject.

"At least a dozen," she said. Not to mention some cranberry muffins and blueberry scones.

"Are you thinking what I'm thinking?" I asked.

"Baked goods get stale so quickly," Janice said with a straight face.

Lilith winked at me. "I'd say their shelf life is pretty limited."

"Minutes," I agreed. "I'd hate to see them go to waste."

"I'll brew the tea," Lynette said, heading off to the minikitchen in the back.

"I'll get the cupcakes," Bettina said.

"And I'll call the traveling house sprites to do the cleanup afterward," I said, to cheers all around.

"This feels like the old days," Rosie said as we settled around the crackling gas fireplace with our snacks and our knitting. "We haven't had a knit night in forever."

"Blame me," I said, casting on a tiny six-color stranded cap I'd been dying to start. "I think I've done nothing but eat and sleep since I found out I was pregnant."

A round-robin of knowing looks were exchanged.

I patted my belly. "Hello, people. I *am* with child. Don't tell me you haven't noticed."

"Honey, it's not your pregnancy changing things, it's that troll you and Luke are living with," Midge said, patting my knee with one plump, perfectly manicured hand. She lowered her voice to a stage whisper. "She is — you should excuse the expression — a real beyotch."

My pals nodded like a gaggle of bobblehead dolls.

"Midge is right," Verna said. "I know that Elspeth is one of your distant relatives, Janice, but the woman is a bigger buzzkill than Prohibition."

"Don't blame me," Janice said. "She's here to midwife Chloe. When the baby arrives, she'll go back to Salem."

"She's not here to midwife me," I protested. "She's here to make me crazy." At least that was the way it felt.

"She's a troll," Verna persisted. "You don't have troll in your background, Janice. I've been meaning to ask how she fits in your family tree."

Janice sighed. "Witch on her mother's side, troll on her father's."

"His looks, her powers," I observed with maybe a tad more snark than I had intended. Janice's eleventh cousin four times removed was a toothache you couldn't get rid of.

"I know the type all too well," Renate chimed in. "She'll never leave. Mark my words on that."

"If she doesn't leave, I will," I said as my fingers deftly maneuvered the brightly colored strands of fine merino. "The way she creeps around, all cloaked up and hidden —" I gave a mock shiver. "It's a good thing Luke and I got pregnant before she got here because it sure couldn't have happened after."

"I hear you, sister," Janice said as everyone laughed. "Lorcan's mother came to live with us after his father pierced the veil and it was the longest seven years of my life."

"She was there eight weeks," I corrected her with a grin. "It only seemed like seven years."

"It couldn't have been that bad," Rosie said. "You and Lorcan managed to pop out five kids in four years."

Janice laughed louder than anyone. "Safety in numbers," she said with a wide grin. "I figured if we outnumbered the in-laws we might have a chance."

"Don't get me started on in-laws," Midge said. "George's folks were from the old country." She rolled her saucer-sized eyes for emphasis. "Out every night hunting, sleeping all day while I was homeschooling the kids. Bloodstains everywhere. They're the ones who got the boys involved in that whole retro-feeding movement, but that's a whole other story. It wasn't until I made Ina Garten's roast chicken with forty cloves of garlic five nights straight that they decided it was time to get their own place."

"You should thank your lucky stars Luke

isn't a mama's boy," Lilith said as she nibbled the edges of a cranberry muffin. "Archie doesn't change his socks without consulting his mother."

"Get out! That's impossible. Archie's way too —" I stopped midsentence before I insulted the woman's husband.

"Oh, go ahead," Lilith said with a good-natured chuckle. "He's a troll. I know he's a troll. You know he's a troll. We all know he's a troll." Her smile widened. "And I don't just mean his lineage."

The thought of the gruff, disagreeable TV/electronics repair shop owner calling mommy before he made a wardrobe decision had the group of us giggling like schoolgirls.

"Here's my rule of thumb," Verna Griggs said as she rounded the corner of her afghan. "The louder the husband, the more powerful the mother-in-law."

"Don't let the quiet ones fool you," Midge said. "My George makes our customers sound noisy, but when she was here, his mama ruled the roost."

"You've been lucky up until now," Bettina said to me. "You and Luke have been living in fantasyland."

"We have a three-hundred-year-old house-guest who has been living with us since

April. If that's your idea of fantasyland —"

"She's not his mother," Rosie said. "That makes all the difference."

"Remind me next time I bump into her in the hallway at three in the morning."

"What were you doing in the hallway at three in the morning?" Lynette asked.

I pointed toward my belly. "Take a guess."

"Family changes everything," Janice said. "Mostly in a good way, but it takes time to claim your turf and learn how to hold on to it. A man's family is a force to be reckoned with."

"You make it sound like a war council," I said, my knitting forgotten. "So maybe Bunny was pissed off with Luke for not telling her about the baby, but that's understandable. She has every right to be pissed off. I would be, too."

"This is just the start," Rosie predicted. "Mark my word, Bunny is setting her trap right this very minute."

"Totally," Lynette agreed. "Before the weekend is over, Big Mama is going to call and invite you to a command performance."

"Attendance mandatory," Janice confirmed.

Attendance mandatory? Here I was, about to be handed the family I'd always wanted, and I felt like throwing up for the first time that trimester. "Maybe I should've watched less *Cosby* and more *Desperate House-wives*."

"Screw the housewives," Janice said to general hilarity. "You need to borrow my copy of *The Art of War*."

"What I need is an unlisted phone number." Evil Fae warriors, kidnapped souls, disappearing towns — those I could handle. But the thought of dealing with a real live human family instead of the fantasy one I'd imagined was enough to send me into a serious tailspin. "I don't think I'm ready for all this drama."

A simple beginner's spell and Bunny's phone calls would go bouncing back like a boomerang. Luke had wanted to keep his family at a distance and this would be the perfect way to grant his heart's desire a little while longer.

But I couldn't do it.

"I'm disappointed in you, honey," Midge said as I tamped down the magick. "You waited all your life to get your powers and really be one of us and now you're siding with your human bloodline again."

"I'm not siding with the humans," I protested, "I'm doing what's right for my daughter."

"What's right for your daughter is making

66

sure the truth about Sugar Maple stays hidden."

"I know that."

"So why are you hesitating? Grandparents come for visits, Chloe. Long visits. Are you sure you're ready for that?"

"I'm not even ready for the baby," I said in a surprising burst of candor. The past year had been one life-changing event after another. I was exhausted! "All I know is that the MacKenzies are her family and I'm not going to do anything that will keep her from knowing and loving them."

And although I didn't say it out loud, maybe I wanted to get to know and love them, too. Although I had embraced my hard-won magick and all it entailed, my blood was still half human and that fact wouldn't be denied.

For all that I loved my adopted family of friends in Sugar Maple, there had always been an empty space inside me that they couldn't fill. It wasn't until I met Luke and found myself drawn to his very human warmth that I began to understand what was missing.

I never met my human father's family. I'm not even sure he had any at the time I was born. All I knew about him was that he was young and handsome and worked with his hands and that he loved Guinevere Hobbs. His life before he met my mother, the family he left behind to be with her, had all disappeared into oblivion, never acknowledged by Sorcha the Healer, who had raised me after my parents' deaths.

That wasn't what I wanted for Luke and our daughter.

Sorcha had believed that interaction with humans could only lead to disaster, and the death of Guinevere was proof of that fact. Although my powers didn't kick in until I was almost thirty, I had been raised according to my heritage as one of Aerynn's descendants with the expectation that I would be the one who took Sugar Maple well into the twenty-first century and beyond.

"It could be worse," I said, shaking off the bittersweet sense of longing that thoughts of my parents always evoked.

"Darn right," said Lilith. "If you'd fallen for Gunnar or Dane, you would've ended up with Isadora as your mother-in-law."

Janice shivered dramatically. "There's a scary thought."

Isadora was the banished leader of the Fae warrior faction that had been dedicated to pulling Sugar Maple and all its residents beyond the mists into a different dimension. She had been the cause of every terrible thing that had ever happened in my life and not a day went by when I didn't reinforce the spell I'd cast to keep her far away from us.

Gunnar and Dane were her twin sons. Dane was his mother's child, a beautiful creature with a twisted soul, while Gunnar's beauty manifested itself inside and out. We had all pretty much grown up together and once upon a time I had come close to falling under Dane's dark spell. When Fae turned their sexual magick on someone, especially someone with human blood, the game was over. Outrageous beauty combined with otherworldly magnetism made for a dangerously irresistible lover. Danger, of course, being the operative word. Sex was only part of the agenda.

Thankfully reason had prevailed before I succumbed to Dane's advances, but the experience had turned him into a formidable enemy. Like I said, not many females said no to him. He was gone now to whatever hell existed for all things evil, but the memory of danger would be a long time fading.

Gunnar had been sunshine to his shadow, a spirit of pure light. For a time Sugar Maple had lobbied for a match between my dear friend Gunnar and me, but that wasn't meant to be. In the end Gunnar had sacrificed his life to make my life with Luke possible.

I had loved Gunnar as a friend, but my heart belonged to Luke and Luke alone and always would. Hobbs women fell in love just once during their lifetime and they bore only one child: a daughter who, as a descendant of Aerynn and Samuel, would continue to keep Sugar Maple safe from danger.

But I would be lying if I said Gunnar wasn't in my thoughts every single day. I missed his laughter, his warmth, his steadfast friendship. This probably sounds crazy, but I missed all the things we would never share. I never once imagined that he wouldn't be here with me to celebrate the birth of my daughter, but the fates had had other plans.

I couldn't change our daughter's future — it had been preordained by magick far greater than mine — but I could make sure she didn't walk this world alone. She needed to know her place in the world. Both worlds.

She needed to know her family.

5

LUKE

My cell phone drowned. That was the bad news.

The good news? My cell phone drowned.

Somewhere out there my mother was leaving endless voice mails threatening me with everything from disinheritance to eternal damnation if I didn't call her back immediately, but thanks to the Atlantic Ocean only Verizon knew for sure.

Unfortunately somewhere out there Chloe was taking the hit for me.

Damn. Why didn't I listen to her and spill the beans months ago? The shock of finding out I was going to be a father again had knocked me back for a while. The memory of my daughter Steffie's death overshadowed the joy and I had to fight hard to let go of my fears and believe that this time would be different.

Of course, there was the Chloe problem

71

to contend with. She was smart and funny and kind and talented and beautiful and a sorceress. A flames-shooting-from-her-fingertips, sparks-flying-from-her-eyes, turn-you-into-a-newt sorceress who lived in a town crammed with vampires, werewolves, trolls, ghosts, sprites, and a sleeping giant.

Try explaining that to a seventy-one-year-old woman who thought an Episcopalian son-in-law was a walk on the wild side.

And while you're at it, try explaining why the town was populated with preternaturally gorgeous specimens who bore more than a passing resemblance to stars like Julia Roberts and Catherine Zeta-Jones. Try explaining why an outsider couldn't book a room in the seemingly empty Sugar Maple Inn or why there were no birth or death records after 1703.

And that was just for starters.

My family didn't believe in boundaries. They dropped by without calling. They snooped in medicine cabinets. They offered opinions on everything from your sex life to how much fiber you should be eating. If my mother didn't pick up on the Sugar Maple vibe, one of my sisters would, guaranteed.

Hell, she was probably sitting in our cottage with Fran right now, the two of them eyeballing everything from the number of litter boxes to Chloe's naked ring finger. When it came to my mother, two plus two always equaled more than four.

The last thing we needed was more houseguests. If they were still there, I was going to offer a night's stay, all expenses paid, at the nearest Ramada.

I rolled back into Sugar Maple a little after six o'clock, tired, hungry, and stinking from dead halibut and seaweed. The only thing on my mind as I turned down Osborne Street was a hot shower and some alone time with Chloe. Elspeth, our troll houseguest from hell, had beamed herself up to Salem to spend Thanksgiving with some of her friends, leaving us with privacy for the first time in almost eight months.

Or maybe not. The old bat could disappear at the drop of a denture, only to reappear smack in the middle of what you thought was a private moment.

Yeah, *those* moments.

Chloe had planned to shutter the shop around three o'clock and head home to get some rest, and the thought of crawling into bed with her made me hit the gas pedal a little harder.

Hell, I was the only cop in town and I wasn't about to pull myself over for speeding.

By the time I showered and grabbed a bite to eat, it would be seven thirty or eight. My mother was a morning person. She usually went lights-out around nine and was up before the sun. If I played it right, I might be able to avoid saying more than "hello" and "I was going to tell you next week" before I had a chance to dream up a good story.

I was gliding to a stop at the stop sign when my eye caught a blaze of lights in the side mirror. What the hell? Unless I missed my guess, the lights were coming from Sticks & Strings.

The shop that should have been closed almost three hours ago.

I hung a U-turn and headed back up the empty street, then whipped into my spot in the alleyway between the police station and the yarn shop. Laughter blasted through the walls. Loud, raucous, the kind of uncensored female laughter men never get to hear.

How the hell many people were in there anyway? I was able to pick out at least eight separate sounds. Chloe's full-bodied laughter rang out above the chorus. I listened more closely. My mother had a distinctive laugh, kind of a cross between a cackle and a chuckle, but I didn't hear it or Fran's smoker's rumble in the mix.

The laughter got louder when I walked through the door.

"Don't worry," Janice said the second she saw me. "They left two hours ago."

"Will you look at his face?" Rosie from Assisted Living cackled. "Bet you were hiding around the corner!"

"Your mama is on the warpath," Renate Weaver said with a self-righteous shake of her head. "What were you thinking, Luke? You can't keep secrets from family."

"Actually you can," Chloe said to her with a wink in my direction. "Didn't you keep your QVC addiction secret from Colm until he found your stash in the attic?"

Renate didn't miss a beat. "Apples and oranges. Hiding a pair of knee-high red suede boots isn't the same as hiding a pregnancy."

The Fae innkeeper had a point. "So how mad is she?" I asked Chloe.

"Hard to tell exactly," Chloe said, "but I'd say your ass is grass."

More laughter.

"You really shouldn't have hung up on her, Luke." Lynette made a tsk-tsk sound. "Bad move."

"I didn't hang up. I was being chased by a gang of sea lions and the phone went flying into the ocean."

Janice started to laugh. "You mean the welcome party."

"You stink," Midge Stallworth said, holding her snub nose with two pudgy fingers.

"Good grief!" Lilith delicately fanned the air around her. "You might want to consider a new aftershave, Luke."

Rosie and Verna buried their noses in a mountain of bright green yarn.

"Thanks for the heads-up, Janice," I said as Chloe laughingly dodged my kiss. "Your old man trashed my truck with his halibut happy meal. You could've told me what to expect."

"It was trout and if I had, would you have volunteered?" Janice retorted.

I shot her my best dead-eyed cop look. "Now I know why every cat in town has tried to break into your minivan."

Her expression softened. "Did he get off to a good start?"

I told her about the group of gigantic sea lions who'd encircled Lorcan and escorted him into the cold waters of the Atlantic.

"Was there one big guy with a gray muzzle and enormous dark eyes?"

"That's the one who tried to kick my ass," I said.

"He's Lorcan's father and he wasn't trying to kick your ass. He was thanking you."

Okay, I'll admit the thought of Lorcan Meany being the son of a sea lion threw me for a second, but I reminded myself I was in Sugar Maple, where things like that made perfect sense.

"I have his stuff in the truck," I said to Janice as she jammed her knitting into a bright red tote bag. "I was going to drop it off at the house, but since you're here . . ."

She nodded and I saw beneath the wisecracks and the laughter to the wife who would worry all winter long until her husband came back to her. Chloe squeezed my hand and I knew she had seen it, too. Not even magick could guarantee your life would turn out exactly the way you hoped it would. In a hell of a lot of ways, we were all flying blind.

"We were taking bets on how long you'd hide out there," Verna Griggs said as she fiddled around with the big yellow and orange blanket on her lap.

"According to my calculations, the odds were twenty-to-one you'd sleep in the truck tonight rather than face your mother," Bettina Weaver Leonides said, needles flashing as she knitted something lacy and pink that I'd bet the shop was for my baby.

"And it was hard to get any takers," Rosie from Sugar Maple Assisted Living informed

77

me. "Who'd want to bet against a sure thing?"

"Thanks a lot for the vote of confidence, ladies." I was starting to get pissed off. "I can handle my mother."

"Honey, I've met your mother," Renate said to more laughter, "and there's no contest."

"You might have been some muckety-muck down in Boston," Rosie elaborated just in case I didn't get the point, "but that doesn't butter any parsnips with your mother."

"I'll keep that in mind," I said, struggling to maintain a straight face.

Chloe reached for my hand and I helped leverage her up from the sofa. "No offense, Luke," she said, "but Midge is right: you *do* stink."

CHLOE

An hour later Luke and I were home, curled up by the fire eating huge leftover turkey sandwiches with all the trimmings. Elspeth, to our mutual delight, was nowhere to be found.

"Now you smell like cranberry sauce," I said as he leaned over to swipe one of my pickles. "Definitely an improvement."

He smiled, but I could see his mind was

somewhere else.

"Tell me," I said.

"Tell you what?"

"Whatever it is that's keeping you so far away."

He was quiet for a moment. "Have you ever seen what happens when a selkie returns to the ocean?"

"I saw Lorcan dive into Snow Lake a few years ago, but there wasn't a whole lot of drama involved." I took a bite of my sandwich and chewed thoughtfully. "If you forget about the big seal suit, that is."

"Gotta tell you, I wish I'd had a heads-up about that seal suit."

"You've heard the selkie legends. It shouldn't have been that big a surprise."

"Cut the human a little slack, Hobbs. Lorcan didn't get that at Men's Warehouse."

"You're right," I said, putting my plate down and curling up closer to his warmth. "He probably didn't."

We were quiet for a while, then Luke spoke again.

"How much danger is he in out there?"

"Lorcan?" I shrugged. "I never really thought about it."

"He's out there in the Atlantic Ocean with fishing boats and tankers and who knows what the hell else."

"Janice never mentioned any danger."

"I saw her face," Luke said. "She's scared shitless."

"Janice isn't afraid of anything."

"She's afraid of this," Luke said. "You never noticed?"

"Mostly he's wintered in Snow Lake. I guess I was caught up in my own worries and wasn't paying attention." An embarrassing admission, but the truth often is. I had never once considered the possibility that Lorcan Meany wouldn't return to his family each spring.

Now I wouldn't be able to get that thought out of my mind. It didn't take much these days to send my thoughts racing down some dark and scary paths. The closer I got to my due date, the more I worried. Everything seemed like an omen of potential disaster. A storm on its way, bad news about a customer, if Luke was two minutes late from running an errand, anything about a baby gone missing — that was all it took to throw me into a tailspin that invariably ended in hysterical tears.

And Elspeth didn't help matters. She saw doom waiting around every corner and didn't hesitate to share her foreboding. If only I could turn her off the way I turned off the nightly news. I'm a world-class worrier in the best of times. Now that I was pregnant, hormonal, and living with Elspeth my imagination was definitely in overdrive.

The world was a dangerous place. That was a given. Both the world of humans and the world of magick held terrors that rose up in the middle of the night when my guard was down and made me wish I could keep our child safe inside my womb forever. I wasn't afraid of childbirth. I didn't worry about the pain. It was what would happen after our baby drew her first breath in this world that scared me.

They said it was normal for a pregnant woman to be overwhelmed with fear and worry for her unborn child and I was no exception. Only when Luke was with me and I could smell his skin, feel the warmth of his body against mine, did the worry fade.

At least for a moment or two.

He ate his sandwiches and what was left of mine while I dozed briefly to a rerun of *Miracle on 34th Street.* The original version, with Maureen O'Hara, which was the only one that counted.

"He's real, you know," I murmured into his shoulder during a commercial. It was time he knew the truth.

"Who is?"

"Kris Kringle."

There was a long silence. "And I suppose he lives here in Sugar Maple."

"Don't be ridiculous. Last I heard he was still at the North Pole."

"Building Nintendos in his toy workshop with nonunion elves."

I gently head-butted him. "You sound cynical."

"And you sound like you're yanking my chain."

"He's one of us," I said. "He fled the Old World around the same time Samuel's family did. They say he charmed the frightened children with handmade toys during the journey and that's how it started."

"The reindeer, the elves, Mrs. Claus — ?"

"He's a philanthropist."

"A three-hundred-something-year-old philanthropist-slash-wizard who happens to live near the North Pole."

"Actually he's a shifter."

"A shifter."

"Like Lynette and her family."

"And he morphs into what — Rudolph?"

I started to laugh. "You don't believe me."

"Hey, I want to. It's a great story."

"And it's a true story. Would you have believed me yesterday if I'd told you Lorcan's father was a grizzled old sea lion or that his brothers would escort him into the ocean for his renewal?"

"Point made."

I took a deep breath and seized my moment. "That's the thing about family. They're always there for you whether you want them to be or not."

"You set me up." This time it was his turn to laugh.

"I seized an opportunity." I leaned forward and grabbed a potato chip from the open bag on the coffee table. "We're a month away from becoming parents. I think it's time I met your family."

"They live too far away to invite them over for dinner," he said, "and we sure as hell can't put them up for a weekend."

The thought of Elspeth and Bunny together in one dimension made me shiver. "I see your point."

"We're not driving down there again."

"One of my indie dyers is part owner of a fancy brunch place on the north shore of Lake Winnipesaukee. It's kind of halfway between them and us, if you don't get too technical about it."

"Neutral territory," Luke said. "I like that idea."

"We meet, we eat, we talk. You'll make your mother very happy."

He met my eyes. "This is what you want?"

"Very much," I said. "I want our daughter to have the family I always wanted."

"Families are a hell of a lot more complicated than you think."

"I'm willing to risk it."

"We won't be able to keep them away once the baby arrives."

I kissed the side of his neck at the place where his blood beat quick and hot just beneath the skin. "I don't want to keep them away. They're her family."

"They could be yours, too."

"I know that." We had become experts at the marriage proposal dance.

"How many times does this make: nine, ten, eleven?"

"Fourteen," I answered. "Not that I'm counting or anything."

"I love you, Chloe. I want to build my life with you and our kid."

"We are building a life."

"We're not married."

"Look at what happened to my father. Why rock the boat?"

"Nothing's going to happen to me if we get married."

"Hobbs women don't have the greatest track record when it comes to happy endings." The men we loved usually paid a steep price.

"I don't believe in that crap."

"Maybe you should. If anything happened to you because we married —" I couldn't bring myself to finish the sentence.

"We're not going to end up like your parents," he said, pulling me into his embrace.

"I hope we end up like *your* parents." Married over forty years and still together, watching their children and grandchildren grow. I couldn't imagine anything more wonderful.

"Tell me that after you've met my old man."

"I'd like to have that chance."

He gave me a rueful smile. "Got any magick for the prodigal son?"

"You don't need magick," I said. "Just hit speed dial."

"You have a lot to learn about humans and their families."

"I know," I said, handing him the phone. "And it's time I got started."

6

MEGHAN — PRINCETON, NEW JERSEY
"Sorry to do this to you, Meg, but I need someone to close for me tonight."

Meghan MacKenzie paused her game of Angry Birds and smiled at the older woman leaning against the reception desk.

"No problem, Amy. Another one of those migraines?"

"The worst yet," Amy said, looking appropriately green around the gills. "That last session almost killed me. I'm going to go lie in traffic somewhere and pray a truck drives over my head."

"A little drastic, don't you think?" she said with a small laugh. "I hear there's medication that can help."

"Been there, tried everything," Amy said. "Everyone's gone home except the two women with the trial memberships and some guy in blue sweats. Far as I know they're in the locker rooms."

"You mean that hunk with the icy blue eyes?"

Amy stared at her blankly. "I don't know what color eyes the guy in blue sweats has."

"Believe me, you'd remember this guy," Meghan said. "Six feet, four inches of pure fantasy." He had an aura about him that would make him stand out anywhere. Well, in Meghan's fantasies, at least. It wasn't often your private go-to dream guy stepped into your life. Even if it was only a walk-on part.

"If you say so," Amy said with a sigh and pushed a heavy set of keys toward Meghan. "He just looked like a guy to me. Anyway, you know the code for the alarm, right?"

Meghan nodded. "No problem. It's not like I'm in a rush to get home."

"The first six weeks are the hardest," Amy said.

"It's been seven since Mark and I split."

"Okay, so maybe the first seven weeks are the hardest. What do I know? I've been married since I was in the cradle." She leaned over and gave Meghan a quick hug. "You're young. You're cute. You'll find someone new."

Amy was the nicest of all the instructors at Hot Yoga off Route 1 in Princeton. When Meghan first hooked up with Mark the plan had been to drive down to Florida and set up shop as personal trainers, yoga a specialty. She wasn't exactly sure how they landed in New Jersey, but first the car broke down, then Mark broke his toe, and next thing Meghan knew she was working part-time at Hot Yoga while he screwed the girl in the apartment across the courtyard.

So there she was, working the front desk and teaching six classes a week while she wondered what to do next.

Maybe she should just pack up her crap, toss it in the back of her Toyota, and head down to Florida on her own. Half the people she'd trained with under Yogini Sirubhi were down in the Miami area. It wouldn't be hard to find a place to stay and pick up some part-time work while she came up with a plan.

And if she didn't come up with a plan in Miami, she'd hop over to Nassau in the Bahamas and get a gig dealing blackjack on Paradise Island until she did.

She would land on her feet. She always had. If she didn't teach yoga or deal blackjack, she could always parlay her prelaw studies into some temp work until something better came along.

Maybe she would start calling some of her Miami friends tonight and get the lay of the land, so to speak. She'd pour herself some red, fire up the laptop, and start making lists. Miami friends. Job skills. Short-term goals. Long-term goals. What she wanted for Christmas, even though nobody had asked lately.

Christmas. Just the thought of it made her feel like she had a migraine, too.

Her mother had been all over her the last few days, spamming her in-box with crazy messages about Luke and some knitting chick he'd supposedly knocked up, but she hadn't gotten around to answering any of them yet. She and Luke were close. He would have told her if he'd found someone.

Bunny tended to go off the deep end anytime one of her kids went off the reservation and start imagining all sorts of nutty stuff. Despite making detective with the Boston PD, Luke had been the black sheep of the family for most of their lives, but Meghan liked to think she was in the running for the title.

Then again, if he had secretly started a new family up there in snow country, maybe she had her work cut out for her.

She added Luke to the list of phone calls she planned to make, then walked back to the ladies' locker room to light a fire under the stragglers.

"We close in ten," she said to the two women who were blow-drying their hair in the bathroom, "but if you need a few more just let me know."

"No problem," said the younger of the two, "but thanks."

She paused in front of the door to the men's lockers and rapped twice. "Ten minutes to closing," she called out.

She waited for a response and when there wasn't any, she rapped again, harder.

"Ten-minute warning!"

It had to be him. Only one guy had taken class today and he was romance-novel-cover hot, all chiseled and sweaty and borderline dangerous. Everything she loved in a man over and over again.

She pushed the door open a crack and listened. It was as quiet as a church in there. Not that she had been to church lately, but she had a good memory. No sounds of water running. No blow-dryer. No radio blaring sports or, God forbid, talk radio.

Maybe he was gone. He probably left while she was in the ladies' locker room, slipped right out when she wasn't looking.

But she'd wait a few just to be sure.

She went back to the desk, gathered up her stuff, and tossed it all into the big leather tote she'd been carrying since college. The two women waved good-bye on their way out the door, but there was no sign of Fabio.

The easiest way to lose her job at Hot Yoga would be to lock a paying customer in the studio, so she slung her bag over her shoulder and marched into the locker room to make sure there were no bodies slumped over a bench or circling the shower drain.

Better safe than unemployed.

THREE HOURS LATER

His kisses were slow and wet and deep and if they went on any longer Meghan was reasonably sure they'd kill her.

Pleasure could kill a woman if she wasn't careful, and she was anything but careful when it came to love.

Which this wasn't, of course. Not love. Not now. You didn't fall in love with a total stranger in three hours even if the total stranger walked straight out of fantasies you'd never told another living soul.

Everything about him was perfect. She could get drunk just looking at him, touching him, breathing in the smell of his golden skin.

"I have to close the studio," she whispered, coming up for air. "I can't afford to lose my job."

"You won't lose your job." He did something with his tongue that made her forget
her own name.

"We shouldn't."

His hands dipped lower.

"What if someone walks in while we're
—"

His fingers began their magic. "They
won't."

"The door is wide open. Anybody could
—"

"I know," he said. "That makes it even
more fun."

Oh, God, he was right . . . so right. . . .

She moved against his hand, straining for
the ultimate pleasure that he kept just out
of reach. A cry was building up in her throat
and she sank her teeth into his muscular
shoulder to keep from making a sound.

"Bitch," he murmured into her hair,
spreading her legs wide with his knee. "You
know what I like."

She bit him again, harder this time, hungry
for something she hadn't known existed
until that moment, with that man. He filled
her to the breaking point, taking her to the
outer edges of madness, until there was
nowhere left to go.

She stopped caring if someone walked in
and saw them. She stopped caring if she

lost her job or what was left of her sanity. If he had asked, she would have walked across fiery coals to be with him.

Suddenly all that mattered was his hands on her body, his mouth on hers.

He took the keys and threw them across the room. The sound as they hit the floor made her jump. Her heart slammed her rib cage hard and she felt sweat break out on the back of her neck.

"Scared?" He stood over her, filling her line of vision.

"Should I be?"

"Depends on what you're afraid of."

Spiders. Snakes. Spending another long dark night alone.

She knew the answer he wanted to hear.

"You," she said and suddenly she wasn't lying. "I'm afraid of you."

"Good," he said. "That's a start."

7

CHLOE

"Maybe this wasn't such a bright idea after all," I muttered a few mornings later as I sat at the kitchen table with my laptop and an enormous glass of orange juice.

Bettina Weaver Leonides was watching the shop so I had until two o'clock to sit around in my maternity sweatpants and Luke's old shirt. I had a basket of yarn samples to swatch, designs to format and convert to pdf's, and enough paperwork to keep me busy until the baby arrived, but the phone wouldn't stop ringing. Indie dyers, a shepherdess from Brunswick, Luke's mother.

"Hope I'm not calling too early, honey," Bunny MacKenzie said briskly, "but I wanted to get you before you started work."

"Not too early at all," I said, glancing at the clock and wincing at the hour. "Actually I'm not going into the shop until this afternoon."

"No problems, I hope."

"Only if you consider paperwork a problem," I said with a laugh. "Sometimes I get so busy with knitters at the store I can't get anything else done."

"You work too hard," she said with maternal certainty. "I saw you bustling around that shop."

"More like waddling around the shop."

"You're carrying beautifully, honey. I wish I'd carried like you, but I blew up like a hot-air balloon every time."

We chitchatted pregnancy for a few minutes, then she got down to the reason for her call.

"I lost the name of the restaurant we're meeting at on Sunday."

"Carole's Lakeside Inn." I spelled out the name of the town. "North shore of Lake Winnipesaukee."

We chatted a few seconds more, then I hung up, feeling very smug. That wasn't hard at all.

Ten minutes later she phoned again. This time it was to find out if children under twelve were welcome at the buffet.

Five minutes after that it was to tell me Luke wasn't answering his cell phone and would I please tell him to phone home immediately.

After the third "tell Luke" call I turned off the ringer and let Bunny roll into voice mail. It had to be done.

"And what have I been telling you, missy." Elspeth, our unwanted houseguest, suddenly appeared by my side, a three-foot doughnut of a woman with hair the color of a yellow cab. "Nothing good comes from truck with humans. All those foolish contraptions ringing and buzzing day and night just so they can keep an eye on each other's business. Best to keep them at a distance, I say."

"I'm half human," I reminded her, studiously ignoring the fact that Elspeth lived to spy on everyone's business. "My baby will be three-quarters human. I want to meet her family." I wanted her to *know* her family.

"There will be a time for that." She had a way of making a simple statement sound darkly threatening. "This weren't it."

Grammar aside, even I had to admit that traipsing two hours away from home in the last few weeks of pregnancy probably wasn't my brightest idea, but I had checked with Brianne, the Quebec healer who would help deliver my baby, and she had okayed the plan so long as we did it this week.

"There be too many of them," Elspeth

said as she peered over my shoulder at the computer screen. "I've seen rabbits with smaller litters."

"Don't you have anything that needs doing?" I asked, glancing over my shoulder at her. "You're in my space."

She made a sound somewhere between a grunt and a Bronx cheer, then disappeared. I was about to send up a cheer of my own when she reappeared, doll sized, on my touch pad.

"Hey!" I yelped as the cursor danced across the page.

" 'Tis Samuel's fault plain and simple," she said, stomping across the keyboard. "I am here to see your child safely into this world of yours and then good-bye."

It probably shouldn't have bugged me that she didn't want to be here any more than I wanted her to be. I mean, I would have given away all my qiviut, with a baby camel chaser, to get her a one-way ticket back to Salem, but Samuel's last wish was immutable.

Aerynn's mate, the man who had fathered her only child, had been a powerful sorcerer who had gathered up every micron of magick left to him at the end of his earthly life and wrapped it around me and the foul-tempered troll with the yellow hair, binding us together until the next generation of Hobbs woman had safely entered this world.

Believe me, I had tried every spell I knew (and a few new ones I invented) to send Elspeth back to the lighthouse where she had kept house for Samuel all those years, but nothing worked. Worse, they left an intradimensional trail that told her exactly what I had been up to.

Last week I did manage to conjure up a charm that afforded Luke and me a zone of privacy where Elspeth was concerned. Without it she would think nothing of marching into our bedroom at five a.m. to complain about the birds singing outside the window.

And without it, Luke might have walked into the Atlantic with Lorcan.

"You're blocking the screen, Elspeth." I didn't mean to send her flying over to the caps lock key when I hit the backspace. It just happened. The fact that she also disappeared was a very lucky break.

Over time Sugar Maple had developed a system for living as magick in a nonmagick world. Many of our children ended up going away to top-notch schools in the human world. (Janice, for instance, went to Harvard.) But without birth certificates, medical records from a licensed practitioner, and valid SAT scores that education couldn't happen, so we improvised.

Okay, so we lied. We had a close call a year ago when the powers-that-be in the state capital became very interested in our "missing" birth and death records, but with Luke's help we had managed to dodge that bullet. But I considered it a wake-up call.

If we were going to continue to live in the world of humans, we would have to at least pretend to play by their rules. My human side might have felt guilty, but my magick side didn't bat an eye at translating our own meticulously kept records into something viable for the world beyond Sugar Maple.

Usually we didn't worry about this sort of thing until the child reached high school, but Brianne believed earlier was better, so I had a list of dates and info I needed to e-mail back to her. That was what I should have been doing, but you know how it is. I love me some Internet in the morning.

I logged on to Ravelry, checked for messages, then headed straight for my Gmail account.

TO: Chloe
FROM: Bunny and Jack MacKenzie
SUBJECT: brunch

We MapQuested Carole's Lakeside Inn and it's an easy ninety-minute drive for us. Jenny and Paul will try to make it. Kimberly and Travis are a definite. Ronnie and Deni are bringing the grand-kids. Kevin and Tiffany will drive up from Rhode Island the day before and spend the night with Danny and Margo (cousins). Patrick said he'll try but it's his weekend with the kids. And Meghan if she can tear herself away from her latest beau.

TO: Bunny and Jack MacKenzie
FROM: Chloe
SUBJECT: re: brunch

Sounds great. We have a one o'clock reservation for sixteen people. Carole says we can push it to twenty if we need to, okay?

I knew Luke came from a humongously big family, but seeing all of those names listed in Bunny's e-mail made me break out in a cold sweat. I was usually pretty good with names — it's part of a knit shop owner's skill set — but pregnancy brain had muddled up my neurons to the point where even my own name slipped my mind.

Bunny had written from a different address this time, one she shared with her husband. I reopened the e-mail, scrolled down, and noted a link to Ronnie's real estate website. A click brought me to MacKenzie Homes and I gasped as Luke's face filled the screen.

But it wasn't Luke. It was an older, slightly heavier, more polished version of the man I loved. Big brother Ronnie's hair was perfectly groomed. His fair Scots-Irish skin sported a light tan. A spray of crow's-feet bracketed hazel eyes that leaned more toward green than blue. He looked like what he was: a happy, successful man in his early forties.

An array of links presented itself along the sidebar: Check My Listings, How Much Can You Spend, Our Towns and Why We Love Them, and All about Me.

You know which one I clicked on.

It took three seconds for the page to load. I'd seen family albums with fewer photos. In fact the only thing missing was the white picket fence. Even the family dog, a handsome golden retriever named Lucky, merited bandwidth.

I started scribbling names and basic info on the back of one of the questionnaires.

Ronnie — oldest brother
Denise (Deni) — wife m. 1978
Jessie b. 1980
Susan b. 1982
Kit b. 1983
Samantha b. 1990

Ron Jr. and Susan were both married with children. Kit was clerking for a law firm in Virginia. Sam was at Bowdoin up in Maine studying forestry. The other two were married with children.

I hunted around and found a Facebook icon on the listings page and launched myself deeper into MacKenzie mania. I bounced from Ronnie's real estate page to his personal page, where I finally learned what TMI really meant. Here is some free advice: never visit a teenager's Twitter account. And no, you don't want to know why.

Sticks & Strings had its own presence on the social networking site so I knew my way around. Find one friend and pretty soon you've found everyone you've ever known. Luke's family were heavy users, which only made my job easier. The page quickly filled up with names and basic info.

"You should print out the photos." Bettina's hologram blueflamed into the room. "That's what I do before a big wedding. It makes it easier to match names to faces. People love it when the harpist knows their names."

"Great idea." I flipped my printer on. "What's up?" Bettina was a Fae Luddite with an aversion to blueflame so her appearance definitely had my attention.

"Your voice-mail box is full. I need a sig faxed over ASAP on the KFI order."

"I'll get right on it."

"And Elspeth is here. She's driving away the customers, telling them why they should be home taking care of their families instead of buying wool they could spin themselves if they weren't such lazy —"

I groaned out loud. "I get the picture." The only thing worse than making me crazy was making the customers crazy. "She loves to work. Put her in the stockroom and let her count Brown Sheep. I'll be there as soon as I can."

"No, no!" Bettina's cheeks reddened through the bluescreen haze. "Everything's fine. I just wasn't sure how to handle her. I figured I'd better check first."

"She's cranky, not dangerous," I reassured

the gentle-natured harpist. "Just tell her what to do and be firm about it." And then pray.

Bettina glanced around as if to make sure no one was listening. "She told me she hates the Fae. Can you believe she would say such a thing to me?"

Unfortunately I could. Bettina was beautiful like all Fae, but she dressed like she belonged to a magickal subset of the Amish. Her skirts were long. Her sweaters were roomy. She wore her long dark hair pulled back into a low ponytail. Her demeanor was soft-spoken and unassuming. She did nothing to call attention to herself when she sat at her harp or went about her daily chores, but nothing could dim the sheer radiance of her amazing face and luminous violet eyes. I mean, the plainest of the Fae can stop traffic anywhere in the human world.

What I'm trying to say is Bettina was everything that would make a short-tempered troll apoplectic.

"Ignore her," I said. "That's what Luke and I try to do."

Try, of course, being the operative word.

Bettina's blueflame guttered and I was alone again. Or as alone as you can be with four spoiled cats. EZ meowed for my attention, poised to leap onto my lap but puzzled because my lap no longer existed.

"Not much longer," I told her, leaning over the best I could to give her a skritch behind the ear. "I won't be lapless forever."

The look she gave me was highly skeptical and who could blame her. I was at the point in my pregnancy where my feet were a distant memory and the thought of sleeping on my stomach sounded like a fairy tale.

I printed out photos of Luke's brothers and sisters. All except Meghan, the youngest, who didn't have a Web presence that I could uncover. I knew she was Luke's favorite, but beyond the facts that she was single and moved around a lot, I didn't know much else about her. I was about to start on nieces, nephews, and extended family when Luke exploded through the back door like his hair was on fire.

I shrieked. The cats scattered. At least three or four hidden pixies probably reached for their worry beads.

He was at my side so fast you would swear he had magick, pulling me into an embrace that took my breath away. Literally.

"Luke!" I struggled to put a little space between us so my lungs could inflate.

He kissed me like one of us was going off to war. "I thought —" He stopped, then kissed me again.

Silvery white sparks flew everywhere. They ricocheted off the microwave, bounced off the walls, pinged my laptop, sent shivers up my spine. We'd been striking sparks from the moment we met and I hoped it would go on forever.

I placed my hand on his chest and leaned back. "What's going on?"

"My mother." He was doing that cop thing he does, eyes searching everywhere for signs of danger.

I started to laugh. "Your mother?"

"She's been trying to call you. She said she left a few messages, then got the voice-mail-full message." Some of the tension left his voice. "She decided you'd gone into early labor and were lying on the kitchen floor alone and dilated."

"Oh, crap." I gestured toward the cell phone on the kitchen table. "I turned it off after the third time she called about Sunday brunch. It never occurred to me she'd worry about me." Why would it? She barely knew me.

"World-class worrier," Luke said, "and family is her specialty."

"But I'm not family."

"Yeah," he said, stroking my hair. "Like it or not, you are now."

I didn't have a chance to ponder that

106

statement because Luke's cell emitted three long, three short, then three long beeps. Bunny MacKenzie's SOS.

"She's fine, Ma," he said by way of hello. "Her phone ran out of juice is all."

I suppressed a giggle as he rolled his eyes in response.

"She was working from home this morning . . . yes, we have a landline . . . why didn't you try that number?" Long pause. "D'you have a piece of paper and a pen? It's —" He recited it into the receiver twice, just to be sure. "She's got a lot to do, Ma . . . no, she's right here . . . okay." He pushed the cell in my direction. "She wants to talk to you."

"No!" I mouthed, backing away, but even two hundred miles away, Bunny was formidable. "Hi, Bunny . . . yes, I'm fine . . . sorry about the phone . . . I will . . . promise . . . okay . . . see you on Sunday." We said goodbye and I clicked off.

I handed the phone back to Luke, then rested my head on my laptop's keyboard. "All of this drama is exhausting."

"They mean well, but they're serious pains in the ass."

I gestured toward the pages scattered across the kitchen table. "There are an awful lot of you MacKenzies."

He picked up one of the pages and started to laugh. "Family crib notes?"

"It's either that or make them wear name tags."

"We don't have to do this. I'll tell them you have to work or something."

"I have to do it."

"Not for me."

"For me," I said. "For the baby."

"There's plenty of time for that after she's here."

"I want to do it right, Luke. I want her to have all the things I didn't have growing up."

"You were loved," he reminded me. "Everyone in town parented you."

I shook my head. "But it wasn't the same." Sorcha the Healer had loved me most of all, stepping into the yawning emptiness where my mother used to be, pouring all of her love and skill and wisdom into me until I overflowed. But a tiny part of me was always aware of the fact that Lilith was her daughter by blood while I was her child by circumstance.

Luke glanced around the room again. "Where's the she-beast? I don't smell any brimstone."

I didn't have to ask whom he meant. "She's at the shop torturing Bettina."

"So we're alone."

His smile was so hopeful that I fell in love with him all over again.

"Almost," I said, pointing toward my bump. "In case you forgot, I'm extremely pregnant."

He pressed a kiss to the side of my neck and I shivered. "In case you forgot, I'm extremely inventive."

And for the next forty minutes he set about refreshing my memory.

8

CHLOE — THE FOLLOWING SUNDAY
"Terrible, terrible," Elspeth muttered from the backseat. "Nobody listens to me and now the die is cast."

Luke glanced at her through the rearview mirror. "You want to pipe down back there? I'm trying to keep us alive long enough to get to brunch."

Not exactly words I wanted to hear as he maneuvered his way around a fender bender on the hill leading up to Carole's Lakeside Inn. I tried not to look at the rear-ended minivan or the crying kids peering out the side window as we inched past.

"It wasn't supposed to snow," I said for probably the eightieth time since we'd left Sugar Maple a few hours earlier. "The forecast was for cold and sunny all the way." So far we'd driven through at least five inches of sunny with more to come.

"Humans," Elspeth said with a snort of

derision. I had never actually heard a derisive snort before, but, trust me, you'll know one when you hear it. "Don't know which way is up if you stand them on their head."

Luke grunted something unintelligible. I had stopped asking for translations before we even left the Sugar Maple town limits. Elspeth didn't bring out the best in him.

Or anybody else for that matter.

"Remind me why she's here," Luke said as he adjusted the defroster.

"Because she doesn't take no for an answer," I whispered. "At least she promised me she'd stay away from the brunch." I didn't know what she would do with herself while we were with the MacKenzie clan, but as long as she stayed quiet, invisible, and in a different dimension we had a fighting chance.

"I hear ye," Elspeth said. "I'm here because Himself wanted it that way, but there are many places between heaven and earth where I would rather be."

Tell us something we don't know.

"You need to work on your attitude," I said to her over my shoulder. "All of this gloom-and-doom talk is getting on my nerves." I had had a terrible nightmare the night before, not for the first time, that left

111

me shaken and weepy. I was trapped in a dark room and I could hear the baby crying, but no matter what I did I couldn't find her. I wasn't a big fan of those dreams.

"Truth is like chicory," Elspeth said. "It leaves a bitter aftertaste in an unwilling mouth."

Luke and I locked eyes for a second, then we burst into laughter.

" 'Tisn't funny," Elspeth declared, her rubbery round body vibrating with outrage. "You have no business being here today, I tell you, no business."

"You know," Luke said to me, "she's probably right."

"I heard that," Elspeth said with more than a note of triumph in her nails-on-a-blackboard voice.

"It's the snow," I said as I tried to squeeze in one more row on the hoodie I was making for the baby. Road trips, even short ones, had dwindled in the last few months and everyone knows knitters love their road trips. "Everything was okay until it started to snow."

"You should be home where you belong." Elspeth continued as if I hadn't spoken at all. "There be a reason for all things, missy, and the spells of containment weaken with every mile you travel away from the center."

"Spells of containment? You're making that up." I'd never heard anything about a spell of containment, and I was the hotshot sorceress.

"The spells of containment nurture the babe until the time is right to be born and not before." She gave me one of those troll looks I hated. "There be no early births in Sugar Maple, not now or ever."

I thought back through years of baby showers and Presentation ceremonies. "She's right," I said to Luke. "I can't recall any premature births."

"And there won't be one now," Elspeth said. "Not so long as ye stay where ye belong."

Which I hadn't. We were at least one hundred miles away from Sugar Maple and those spells of containment. Despite the warmth from the heater, one of those weird chills rippled through me. I tried to shake it off, but a sense of unease lingered.

"Back off," Luke warned Elspeth. "I don't want you bugging Chloe with any of your crap."

"It's not crap," I said, placing a warning hand on Luke's forearm. "Trolls tell the truth. It's a congenital thing."

In the backseat Elspeth was downright preening. "Ah, so you admit I might know a

113

thing or two beyond your ken, do you now, missy?"

"You're a thousand years old!" *Give or take a couple of centuries.* "If you don't know a thing or two you've been wasting your time."

"Doom is on the horizon," she intoned, "and I can only hope my magick can —"

"Shut up." Luke's voice was low, steely, borderline threatening.

"Luke . . ." My own voice held a soft note of warning. Never piss off a troll. I thought everyone knew that.

"He senses it, too," Elspeth said, still undeterred. "Even the human feels it in the air."

"I don't feel shit," Luke said through gritted teeth, "and magick or no magick, I swear to God I'll leave your sorry yellow-haired ass on the side of the road if you say one more thing about bad luck or containment or one goddamn word about our baby."

Elspeth opened her mouth but apparently thought better of it and stayed silent. But it wasn't a good kind of silent because I could hear her bitching in three other dimensions. The tension in the truck made my teeth ache and I was about to ask if Luke would dump my sorry yellow-haired ass on the side of the road when he said, "There it is."

I put down my knitting and looked out the window.

Carole's Lakeside Inn looked exactly the way I had hoped it would: a sprawling stone and wood structure with lake frontage and a view of the White Mountains visible through the swirling snow.

"The parking lot's jammed," Luke observed as we inched our way up the hill. "I'll let you out at the door and search around for a spot."

"We can walk," Elspeth said. "No need to coddle the missy because she's carrying a wee one."

"Coddle me," I said to Luke. "My center of gravity is changing by the minute." I was the tall, gangly girl who tripped over her own feet in the best of times. Add an icy walkway and an enormous baby belly to the mix and I'd be courting disaster.

"Walking is good for you," Elspeth persisted. "Best way to prepare yourself for what's to come."

"Why don't you mind your own business?" I shot back. "Talk to me after you've had a baby."

"So much you know, missy. I birthed eleven, with three pairs of twins in the bargain."

"You carried eleven babies yourself?" I was trying to pin her down. Elspeth was a tricky one, capable of all manner of verbal sleight of hand.

"And what was it I just said? Who else would be carrying my babies?"

I wasn't about to start a discussion of in vitro, surrogacy, or donor eggs. Besides, wasn't she the one who criticized the MacKenzies for being prolific?

"Must've been a long time ago," Luke muttered.

"I heard that," Elspeth said.

"Good."

"Luke, stop it." I placed a hand on his forearm. "I want to hear about your kids, Elspeth." I had imagined her as the ultimate spinster, content to live her life in service to a powerful but needy male: Aerynn's mate, Samuel.

"Eight have pierced the veil; three went beyond the mist to live amongst the Fae."

"Are you in contact with them?" I asked.

"They are as dead to me."

The lightbulb inside my head went on. "So that's why you were so rude to Bettina the other day." It seemed as if the war with the Fae would never end.

She made a particularly ugly face at the mention of Bettina's name. "A foolish woman, that one, not worth the time it takes to think of her."

"Why did your children go beyond the mist? Did they marry into Fae families?"

She narrowed her eyes in my direction and I swear I could feel her annoyance burrowing its way into my skull.

"They were weak boys, easy prey for hungry Fae priestesses in need of new blood. They were helpless to fight it."

The sexual power of the Fae was the stuff of legend. When a member of the Fae turned his or her full power in your direction, you were pretty much toast. I counted myself lucky that my experience with the Fae Dane had resulted in nothing more than emotional whiplash.

It seemed another lifetime ago.

I peered out the window at the rows of parked cars. "I see a few Massachusetts plates," I said, trying to keep the quaver from my voice. "Anything look familiar?"

"Parents. Ronnie. One of the sisters."

"Oh, gods . . ."

"It's not too late to change your mind," he said.

"Yes, it is," I said. "Someone's waving at us."

"What was that?" Luke swiveled his head toward me. "I can't understand you."

"I said someone's waving at us."

"Ohhhh." Elspeth emitted a long, keening sound. " 'Tis starting . . . 'tis starting and it cannot be stopped."

"Nothing's starting," I protested as Luke waved back at a smiling middle-aged couple then made another loop around the small lot. "I just have butterflies."

The second I said it, a swarm of butterflies spilled out of my mouth and filled the truck.

"What the hell — ?" Luke barely missed slamming into a parked Saab when a monarch landed on the bridge of his nose.

" 'Tis the spell of containment loosing its hold," Elspeth said. "A bad sign . . . a very bad sign."

"Stop with this spell-of-containment stuff, will you, Elspeth? You're making me crazy!"

"You're speaking French," Luke said. "When the hell did you start speaking French?"

The butterflies disappeared and tiny silver shooting stars took their place. Unfortunately they were shooting out of my ears and straight toward Luke and the troll in the backseat.

"Ow!" Luke swatted at them as they buzzed his head.

"I'm sorry!"

A flotilla of stars knocked Elspeth against

the door.

Okay, so it wasn't all bad.

"Do something," Luke shouted as a shooting star dinged the windshield. "These damn things hurt."

"Tell me about it," I said. Possibly in French, but I wasn't sure.

We rolled past another car with Bay State plates as it angled into an empty spot. The parents were too busy shouting at the gaggle of kids in the backseat of their Jeep to notice the fireworks in ours.

I should have listened to Lilith when she recommended a gentle yoga regimen to smooth out the rough edges of my frazzled nerves. Maybe then I wouldn't be speaking French and shooting butterflies and electric stars from various orifices.

One thing was certain: I couldn't meet Luke's family in this condition.

I took a deep breath, centered myself, then dived deep into the *Reader's Digest* version of the Book of Spells that I hoped would span the distance between Sugar Maple and Lake Winnipesaukee.

It took three tries, but my command of English returned and the butterflies and shooting stars disappeared. Now all I had to do was remember the blend of spells in case I started spitting gold nuggets over brunch.

"Last chance," Luke said as a spot right next to the entrance miraculously opened up.

"Nothing good will happen here, missy," Elspeth reminded me. "Let the human aim this contraption back where we come from."

I should have. In retrospect I wish I had listened to Luke and to Elspeth and said, "Let's go back to Sugar Maple as fast as we can."

But I didn't and that was my first mistake.

9

MEGHAN

His name was James Whelan and he owned a cabin in Massachusetts. A secluded cabin far from nosy neighbors and busy roads where they'd spent the last five days in bed getting to know each other. She couldn't remember exactly how they got there. She drove. Or maybe he drove. Maybe nobody drove and they were teleported by Scotty and the crew of the *Enterprise.* All she knew was that the world could go to hell. He was the only thing that mattered.

She knew he was mercurial, up one minute and down the next. She knew he had a temper, which meant hot sex, which was followed by slow, sweet makeup sex. She knew she felt alive when she was with him. She knew that it would never last.

In rare lucid moments she understood that the whole thing was crazy. Sane women didn't toss their jobs and their lives aside because a man smelled like starlight, but from the moment he walked into Hot Yoga her life had been out of her control.

She told herself it was his eyes; those icy blue eyes with the frame of thick dark lashes had been her undoing. One look and she was under his spell.

"I'm sex crazed," she said, curled on her side with her mouth pressed against his warm, hard belly. "I literally can't get enough of you." She trailed her tongue down lower, then lower still, until his body reacted.

He told her what he wanted and she gave it to him. They both knew he would teach her things no mortal should know existed. Deliciously sinful things that made her blush in the darkness when she had never blushed before. This was way more than good sex. This was sex you would die for, do anything for, and it was starting to scare her.

Early on the sixth morning she caught sight of herself in the bathroom mirror and a chill rippled through her body. She looked wild and hungry, feral. Like a woman who had been raised by wolves instead of a traditional, churchgoing Irish American family.

She tried to imagine strolling into Carole's

Lakeside Inn to toast Luke and his new whatever and the thought made her laugh out loud. Could you say intervention? Her mother would think she was strung out on drugs — heroin, maybe, or crack — and drag her off to one of those rehab centers that promised miracles in thirty days or your money back.

She loved Luke, really loved him. He was the only one of her siblings who got her. Steffie's death had sent shock waves through the entire family, dragging her brother down into the kind of grief she prayed she would never know. If he really had found someone and was starting over she wanted to be there to cheer him on.

She took another look at her reflection. The glazed look in her eyes. The lips swollen from hours of kissing. Her mother would nail her to the wall in an instant if she walked into brunch looking like this. Still she wondered if maybe she should give it a try. The idea of bringing James along with her was just wrong enough to be irresistible.

"What would you say about driving up to Lake Winnipesaukee for brunch with my family?"

He was sprawled across the bed, all muscular limbs and broad chest. It took every

ounce of her willpower to keep from strad-
dling him.

His smile was lazy and amused. "In this
weather?"

She crossed the room to the window,
deliciously aware of his heated gaze on her
body. She was surprised her bones didn't
melt.

The amount of snow startled her. The
sloping landscape of trees and gentle hills
had been obliterated by at least eight inches
of powder.

"I guess we're not going to Lake Winnipesaukee," she said, walking slowly toward the
bed.

"Disappointed?"

She smiled her own lazy smile. "That
depends on you."

He reached for her wrist and pulled her
down on top of him and it was a long time
before either one of them said anything else.

Hours later she opened her eyes in time to
see him pulling on his jeans.

"Don't get dressed on my account," she
said as he reached for the beautiful Aran
sweater he had worn on the drive to the
cabin.

"They'll be closing the roads. If I don't
bring in more supplies now, we'll be cold

and hungry by this time tomorrow."

"Wait," she said, stretching as she sat up in bed. "I'll come with."

"I like you where you are." He leaned over and pinned her to the mattress with the weight of his body and kissed her until she forgot everything but how much she wanted him.

"I used to be a productive member of society," she said as lust, sweet and urgent, filled her senses like wine.

"You taught yoga," he said, cupping her breasts with his enormous hands.

She arched against him. She couldn't get close enough. "That's an honorable profession."

"There are better things to do with your time."

"No argument there."

He stepped just out of reach. "There's wine on the counter. I tossed the last three logs on the fire. I might be a while depending on the roads." He grabbed the keys to her beat-up Toyota.

"You're taking my car," she observed.

He grinned down at her. "Like you thought I was going to walk?"

"What if something happens?"

"Like what?"

125

"I don't know. An emergency . . . something."

"You have your phone," he said with an offhand shrug. "Call somebody."

He was out the door before she had a chance to ask him for his cell number.

She was too mellow to worry, too well used to think about protesting the fact that if he didn't come back she would be stranded.

For the moment she was exactly where she wanted to be.

10

CHLOE

"She's not going to stay put," Luke said as Elspeth melted into the snowfall and vanished. "Mark my words, she's going to turn up at the omelet station looking like Betty White's evil twin."

"She's not a big fan of humans," I reminded him. "I think she'll stay away until we're ready to drive home."

"Where do you think she went?" Luke asked, peering into the snow.

"Don't know and don't care. As far as I'm concerned, let sleeping trolls lie," I advised. If I ever put down my knitting, I would embroider that sentiment on a throw pillow.

"I just wish she didn't smell like waffles," Luke said and I laughed. "She's ruining breakfast for me."

"Come on," I said, hanging on to his arm. "Let's go before I lose my nerve."

"They're standing in the doorway," Luke

said as we made our way along the snowy path. "Are you ready for this?"

I took a deep breath and straightened my shoulders. "No," I said and we both laughed.

"There you are!" Bunny leaped forward, arms outstretched, and enveloped me in a hug. The glittery Christmas tree pin on her left shoulder dug into my chest. "When we saw the snow, I was afraid we'd have to postpone."

"I'm a hearty New England girl," I said, wriggling away from the brooch of death. "It takes more than a little snow to slow us down." Which was, of course, a total lie since I was a wimp who wouldn't drive between October and May and lived in fear of slipping on the ice.

Next to us Luke and his father did that male chest-bumping thing that passed for hello, but I saw real emotion in their eyes. As far as I could figure, they hadn't seen each other in at least two years, although neither one referenced the fact.

"Dad," Luke said, reaching for my hand, "this is Chloe."

Jack MacKenzie considered me for what seemed like forever. "So you're the reason he's moved way up to snow country."

"My job is the reason I moved up there,"

Luke interjected a tad testily.

"Yes," I said with what I hoped was a saucy grin, "but I'm the reason he stayed."

Hello. That was a joke, people. There should have been laughter, but instead I heard the silence fall like a ton of bricks dumped on my inner wiseass.

Luke stared at me. His mother's cheeks reddened. His father's eyes narrowed and then, just when I figured there wasn't enough magick in the universe to undo the mess I just made, Jack MacKenzie threw back his head and roared with laughter.

"I can see why," he said, then pulled me into a gigantic bear hug that left me gasping for air. "My son knows a keeper when he meets one."

I wasn't so sure about the "keeper" remark but decided to let that go for another day. My inner wiseass was officially on a time-out until we got back to Sugar Maple.

"I'm happy to meet you, Mr. MacKenzie."

"Mr. MacKenzie was my old man. Call me Jack."

Another assault-and-battery kind of hug.

"Dad," Luke said, "ease up. She's breathing for two."

"Aw, jeez!" Jack turned bright red and backed away like I was on fire. "I was just —"

"I'm fine," I said, reaching out to pat his beefy forearm. "Luke is a worrier."

A shadow passed between the MacKenzies and I knew it was the memory of the granddaughter they'd lost.

"Worrying is good." Bunny's tone was brisk, but the look in her eyes gave her away. I felt my jagged nerves begin to settle down. "If you don't worry about your family, then something's wrong."

"You look familiar, like some actress," Jack said as we turned to stroll into the dining room. He turned to his wife. "You know the one I mean, Bunny. Tall, blond, real skinny —"

"Uma Thurman," Bunny and Luke said in unison.

"Tell me which one she is," Jack asked Bunny.

Bunny mimed the twist scene from *Pulp Fiction.*

"No," said Jack, "that's not the one. I said blond."

"She was wearing a wig, Jack. Uma Thurman *is* blond."

"Trust me, Dad," Luke said. "Chloe's a ringer for Uma ten years ago."

"Hello," I said. "Unless Uma's carrying around twenty-eight pounds of baby weight, I just don't see it."

That got Bunny's attention and she was by my side in an instant. "Twenty-eight pounds?" She looked me up and down. "You're what? Maybe five-ten?"

I nodded. That was close enough.

"I'm thinking you could use another five."

I took in a deep, steadying breath and prayed I would say the right thing. Just my luck my baby's grandmother was a retired nurse.

"So far I'm right on target," I said as evenly as I could manage.

She arched a perfectly feathered blond brow. "And your doctor agrees?"

I had hoped to postpone the lying part of the program a little longer, but we were off and running. "So far."

She linked arms with me. "How's your appetite?"

"Terrific."

"You're a good eater?"

I started to laugh. "Five veg and three fruit every day." Not to mention Chips Ahoy, Ben & Jerry's, and a side of grilled cheese, but there was no need for full disclosure.

"We're a nosy tribe," she said. "Give it a few years. You'll get used to us."

She talked about the future like it was a sure thing, like she could see down the years straight through to the happy ending no

Hobbs woman had ever managed.

But I didn't have time to dwell on that. Bunny MacKenzie was a human question machine. She lobbed them at me the way the pitching machine lobbed softballs at the Sugar Maple Driving Range and Batting Cage.

"So who was that you were talking to by your truck?"

I stared at her like English was my second language. "What?"

She gave me a patient smile. "That woman you were talking to near the truck. Was she a friend of yours?"

Crap. Had she actually seen us talking to Elspeth? There was no way I could explain the existence of a three-foot-tall troll with hair the color of a yellow cab.

"A business acquaintance owns the inn," I said, stumbling all over my words. It wasn't an answer, but maybe Bunny wouldn't notice.

Fat chance of that.

"So she's the owner?"

"One of the workers."

"I feel like I've seen her before."

I shot Bunny a look. "Have you been to the inn before?"

"Never, but there was something very familiar about her. I actually thought she looked a bit like Betty White." She gave a little laugh. "Oh, well. That's what happens when you get to be my age, honey. Sooner or later everyone looks familiar."

Luke and I were surrounded by a mob of people the second we stepped into the dining room, most of whom bore at least a fleeting resemblance to the father of my baby. Tall. Good-looking. Gregarious. And did I mention loud?

They were also the huggingest bunch I'd ever met. I was passed from one pair of arms to the next like a giant stuffed toy as faces and names flew past at the speed of light.

Ten seconds and already I was in family overload. All of the prep work I'd done on Facebook flew right out the window. They could have been the Trapp Family Singers or the Brady Bunch for all I could comprehend. Score another one for pregnancy brain.

I looked toward Luke for support but he was equally surrounded by MacKenzies of varying ages and sizes, most of whom were reading him the riot act for staying away for so long. He caught my eye and gave me one of those *I told you so* looks that would have made me laugh if I hadn't been drowning in questions.

I started throwing answers out there like Frisbees, hoping against hope the right MacKenzie would catch them.

"I'm in my ninth month . . . a girl . . . no, we don't have a name yet . . . we're not married . . . no, we're not engaged . . . yes, we're totally committed . . . I don't know . . . I don't know . . . *Help!*"

I didn't actually scream "help," but I came close. I'd chaired contentious town hall meetings with ghosts, vampires, werewolves, shapeshifters, witches, and a sleep-deprived mountain giant that were easier.

Not to mention a whole lot quieter.

A pregnant woman around my age put her arm around me and leaned close. "I don't know about you, Chloe, but if I don't eat something in the next thirty seconds I won't be held responsible for my actions."

"I don't know who you are," I said, "but if you lead me to the Belgian waffles, I'll send your kid to Harvard." Even if the waffles did smell an awful lot like Elspeth.

"I'm Kim Davenport, Luke's older sister and I just might take you up on your offer."

I looked down at her moderate bump. "April?" I asked.

"Tax Day." She rolled her eyes. "How's that for timing?"

"I can beat that," I said. "Try January first."

She burst into laughter. "I love it! Little brother misses out on a big deduction."

"You're the financial analyst, right?"

"Guilty."

She led me toward a table groaning with waffles, pancakes, scrambled eggs, bacon, sausage, and every baked good you could possibly imagine. An omelet station occupied the far corner of the room, right near an open bar serving delicious-looking mimosas.

"I'd kill for one of those," Kim said.

"I'm a wine-in-the-box kind of girl myself, but I could definitely use one or three of them."

"Tell me about it."

I arched a brow in her direction. "At least you don't need name tags to keep everyone straight."

"Want to bet?" she tossed back. "This is maybe half the clan. Just wait until you experience a MacKenzie Thanksgiving."

"I'll be happy if I survive this MacKenzie brunch."

"We're loud, pushy, and opinionated, but we mean well."

"If you're trying to calm me down, it's not working."

"Seriously," Kim said. "We all know you're the only reason Luke's here today."

Dangerous territory. I wasn't about to risk stepping on a familial land mine. "I'm glad we came," I said carefully.

She grinned and a look passed between us. I sensed I might have made a friend. Then again, I couldn't be sure. I was the outsider here, in ways she couldn't imagine. Still, we were setting up the boundaries, writing the guidebook on the fly. My loyalties belonged first and foremost to Luke and to our baby, but it was good to know I might have an ally in the family.

Not that I was thinking in terms of alliances, but, like I told you before, I watch a lot of television and from what I'd observed, families were as much about conflict as they were about coming together. And big families even more so.

Luke and I were never going to fit into the fabric of the MacKenzie tapestry the way his brothers and sisters and their families did. Sooner or later we were going to disappoint Bunny and Jack and that was when we'd need someone in-house to plead our case and I was pretty sure Kim would be the one.

Actually I had expected the baby of the family, Meghan, to be our advocate. I knew she was Luke's favorite, but she'd phoned Bunny and claimed they were delayed by the snow but would try to make it.

And we all know what that means.

"Probably that boyfriend of hers," Bunny said with a sharp look of disapproval. "I wish she would meet a nice young man and settle down. Is that too much to ask?"

"Leave her alone, Ma," Luke said. "Keep pushing and she'll end up living with a rock star in Vegas."

"Maybe you know somebody she could go out with," Bunny said to me. "Some handsome, unattached boy in your charming little village."

I choked on a bite of waffle and had to wash it down with a gulp of juice. The thought of Luke's sister hooking up with any of Sugar Maple's unattached males made me break out in hives. Our secrets would be on the Internet before we knew what hit us.

"So where is this little village of yours?" big brother Ronnie asked as we settled down at the huge table.

"You know where it is," Luke jumped in. "You've been on my ass about it since I took the job."

"I'm making conversation," Ronnie said with a wink in my direction. "I've been told

I'm very good at it."

Clearly Luke wasn't in the mood for fraternal banter. "Let her eat first," he all but growled. "We've been on the road since eight this morning."

"You can talk with your mouth full," Ronnie said to me with a wicked grin very much like Luke's. "I don't mind."

"Northern Vermont," I said, forking a piece of ham and a wedge of golden waffle dripping with syrup. "A really tiny village called Sugar Maple."

"You should see the town," Bunny enthused. "It's a quintessential New England hamlet."

"Quintessential! Listen to her." Luke's sister-in-law Tiffany elbowed the man next to her. I assumed he was her husband Kevin. "Breaking out the multisyllables for Luke's —" She stopped dead, clearly uncertain what to call me.

"Lover," Jen said, raising her mimosa in a toast. "I think that's pretty evident."

An uncomfortable silence fell across the table. I felt heat moving its way up my throat and spreading across my cheeks. I looked over at Luke and noted that one of those little muscles in the side of his jaw had begun to twitch. Yes, we were lovers, but there was something else in that statement that neither of us liked.

"I prefer partner," Kim said, reaching for her glass of orange juice sans champagne.

"I don't go for that partner stuff," patriarch Jack said with a disapproving glance our way. "You have a husband. You have a wife. That's the way it should be."

"Or you can have two husbands or two wives," Kim said with a wink.

"What's wrong with you, Kimberly Marie? You know better than to get him started on that," Bunny chided her oldest daughter, to applause from the rest of the family. "Let's all just agree to disagree with your father and be done with it."

Personally I was all for a rousing discussion of gay marriage and civil unions. Anything to take the spotlight off the subject of Sugar Maple, but the MacKenzies were back on topic.

Me.

"So you were saying you were born in Sugar Maple," Bunny prodded me while I prodded my waffle with the tines of my fork.

I gave her my best smile. "Almost thirty years ago."

"Where are your people from?"

My *people?* Now things were about to get tricky. I didn't have any people.

"My mother was born in Sugar Maple also."

"How about your father?"

"C'mon, Ma," Luke broke in. "You sound like a prosecuting attorney I used to know."

"Not that awful David Devaney," Jen said with a shake of her head. "I dated him before I met Paul. The man had a comb-over you could hide Donald Trump under." She shuddered and everyone laughed.

"You're being rude," Bunny snapped. "All of you. We're getting to know Chloe, not talking about old boyfriends." She shot her daughter a meaningful look, the kind meant to bring a grown woman to her knees.

I didn't know about Jen, but it definitely worked on me. I was moving swiftly into a state of high anxiety and I knew what that meant. My fingertips were starting to tingle and I hoped I wasn't about to spontaneously flambé Jack's omelet.

I'd managed to explain away the flamethrowing incident during the Black Friday sale at Sticks & Strings, but there was no way Bunny would buy it a second time.

"And your father?" Bunny persisted. "So where was Mr. Hobbs from?"

Mr. Hobbs? There was no Mr. Hobbs. Why hadn't I thought this through? I had been so busy memorizing MacKenzie photos and mini bios that I had totally forgotten to get my own highly edited bio in order.

"He . . . uh . . . my father wasn't Mr. Hobbs." I told myself there was no reason to be embarrassed, but I felt exactly the way I had during my brief enrollment at BU. A half human, half sorceress with a size nine foot firmly planted in both worlds and unable to explain my position in either one.

"Your mother married twice?" Bunny kept her eye on the ball.

"Only once," I said. "Guinevere kept her own name when they married."

"Guinevere," Kim said with a theatrical sigh. "That's a beautiful name."

I flashed a grateful smile.

"So what's your father's name?" Jen asked, spooning oatmeal into the mouth of the very small child who had suddenly appeared on her lap. "I'm guessing Arthur."

"Ted Aubry," I said, maybe a tad more harshly than intended, but the stress was definitely getting to me. I wasn't sure if I had imagined the note of snark beneath her playful words.

"Where was he from?" Bunny asked, leaning forward.

"Maine."

"Are his people still up there?"

I could feel the air leave my lungs on a whoosh of surprise. "What?"

"His people," she repeated. "Brothers, sisters, cousins. You must have relatives up there, right?"

Suddenly English was no longer my first language and I struggled to make sense of her question. All the planning, all the years of parroting the same story over and over again, and here was the one question nobody had ever asked me.

I could feel myself coming apart like a poorly knit sweater, loose ends flying everywhere. I was a Hobbs woman through and through. My memories of my father were sweetly fading shadows compared to the vibrant light cast by my magick heritage. No Aubry had ever shown up in Sugar Maple searching for Ted or the little girl he left behind.

Years of longing rose up in me like some monster wave and brought with them memories I thought I'd managed to bury with newer, better ones. I was the one who was different. The girl who never quite fit in anywhere she went. The angry teenager with a chip on her all-too-human shoulder. They were all there, all gathered inside my heart and mind, and probably always would be.

"My mother was a spinner. My father was

a carpenter from Maine. They met, they fell in love, they married, and when I was six they died in a car crash. I have no one left." I took a deep breath and tried to quell the tingling in my fingertips. "Any more questions?"

Sister Jen aimed her electric blue eyes in my direction. "So are you Catholic?"

I was out of there.

11

LUKE

"What the hell is wrong with you?" I exploded the moment Chloe cleared the doorway. "Couldn't you see she was upset?" I was surprised they hadn't noticed the smoke beginning to pour from her fingertips. We were lucky she hadn't activated the sprinkler system.

"All we did was ask about her family," my mother said, spreading her hands wide. "I ask everyone about their family. What's so terrible about that?"

Where do I start?

"You could have at least warned us," my brother Ronnie said as he crunched into a cream-cheesed bagel. "How were we supposed to know her parents died in a car crash?"

"Ronnie's right." Now my brother Kevin was adding his two cents to the discussion. "If you weren't holed up in fucking Ben &

144

Jerry land all these months, maybe we'd know what the hell was going on with you."

Was he right? Yeah, in a way he was.

Was I going to cop to it? Hell, no.

"Leave him alone, Kev." His wife, Tiffany, placed a hand on his forearm, but he shook it off. "It's your brother's life."

"He's a selfish asshole," Kevin said and dared me to contradict him.

"Hey, little brother, you're the one who went off to Rome for three years," I shot back.

"That was work."

"So was this."

Kevin mumbled something under his breath and I felt like knocking him on his ass.

"You got something to say to me, say it." I sounded like an outtake from an old Clint Eastwood movie.

He shot me the same look he used to aim at me when we were in high school and competing for a spot on the football team. I liked it even less today than I did then.

"Still an asshole," I said, shaking my head. "Good to know some things never change."

"Put a sock in it," my father said, not missing a bite, "or you idiots won't have anything left to fight about on Christmas."

Everyone but me laughed.

"This was supposed to be a friendly family get-together," I said, still steaming, "not an inquisition. Lay off the questions when Chloe comes back, okay? If you want to know something, ask me."

"In-qui-si-tion," Ronnie said dryly. "Four syllables. The boy must be pissed."

"Pissed? Yeah, I'm pissed. She's nine months pregnant and we drive down here in a friggin' snowstorm so you can grill her like a slab of bacon? I told her this wasn't a good idea. Thanks for proving me right."

"She didn't look that upset to me," my father said, stuffing his face with blueberry pancakes dripping with maple syrup.

"She was," I said. "Trust me on that one."

"She got up and went to the bathroom. What's the big deal?"

"Not every woman's a yeller, Dad," Ronnie's wife, Denise, jumped in. "She looked the way I felt the first time I ran the MacKenzie gauntlet."

"Tell me about it," Tiffany said with an eye roll. "I still have nightmares."

"A couple MacKenzie family outings should get her up to speed." This from Jenny's husband, Paul, who still had his own set of scars.

Not only didn't they get it, they weren't even close to getting it. I had seen her deal

146

with her very human customers and their nosy questions and she never once tripped over the dividing line between the public story and the truth.

But those times her emotions hadn't been involved.

Pregnancy and magick were a dangerous combination. Spend nine months living with a pregnant sorceress and you would know what I'm talking about. I'd seen the telltale signs of imminent flamethrowing and figured she was soaking her hands in a basin of cold water to keep it under control. Either that or she was burning down the outbuildings in the back.

I pushed back my chair and stood. "I'm going to see how she is."

"Oh, no, you're not." My mother fixed me with a steely glance. "You'll get in that truck of yours and we won't see you for another two years."

"I'm not looking to sneak out," I lied.

The laughter wasn't pretty.

"You haven't seen your family in a very long time," she said over the catcalls. "Stay put. I'll check on Chloe."

"You stay put, too, Mom," Kim ordered. "You grill Luke about why they aren't married while I handle reconnaissance."

I shot Kim a look, which didn't exactly

stop her in her tracks.

"You're seriously telling a pregnant woman she can't use the bathroom?"

I could think of a thousand reasons why she shouldn't, but short of tackling my pregnant sister, there was nothing I could do to stop her.

The day just kept getting better.

CHLOE

By the time I ducked into the ladies' room I looked like a giant Fourth of July sparkler and had to submerge my hands in water in an attempt to control the collateral damage. As it was, the door around the handle looked pretty scorched and I wasn't so sure the carpet in the hallway had escaped unscathed.

The first thing I did was turn one of the faucets on full blast and plunge my fiery hands into the cold water. Steam billowed up around me and I was glad my mascara was waterproof.

"I told you so."

I let out a strangled shriek as Elspeth dog-paddled her way across the sink.

"Get out of here!"

"You got yourself in trouble, missy, and 'twill only get worse. The warning signs came to me even through the dimensional

148

barrier. 'Tis time for you to go home before it be too late."

"It's time for you to get lost. You promised, Elspeth. You know you can't be here."

This was a public bathroom. I'd bet my entire stash that either Bunny or one of the sisters marched through that door within the next ninety seconds. If Elspeth would shut up for two seconds maybe I could pass her off as a runaway garden gnome, but other than that I was screwed because there was no way in the heavens or on earth that I could explain a troll to the MacKenzies.

She did a choppy backstroke around my hands. "My only promise was to Himself and that was to see you through to your time and see you through I will." Her loyalty to Samuel was starting to be a pain in the butt.

I had lost the assistant midwife battle with her months ago when she petitioned Brianne and Lilith to attend the birth. She claimed it was to ensure the continuity of Aerynn and Samuel's line, but I figured she was just yanking our collective chain.

"Go back to whatever dimension you were hanging out in. We'll meet you at the truck later."

"The things that protect you from harm cannot protect you here," she said, ignoring my protests. "The wee one is in danger until you return home."

"I'm not due for another three weeks," I said, cradling my belly in the time-honored way of all pregnant women. "We'll be home before you know it."

She aimed a baleful glance in my direction, then, holding her nose between two gnarled fingers, circled the drain and disappeared.

If only.

Luke was right. That constant talk of doom and danger got old very fast. Nine months is a long time. I had spent most of my pregnancy so far worrying about all the terrible things that could go wrong along the way. None of them had happened, thank the gods, but I wasn't at the finish line yet.

"There isn't a finish line," Janice had told me over lunch the week before. "You think your worrying ends once you have that beautiful baby in your arms, but, honey, it's only just beginning."

Lynette claimed that having a child was like wearing your heart on the outside of your body for the rest of your life and this time next month I would find out how true that was. But for right now my heart was doing a pretty good imitation. Elspeth's rantings had sent my imagination skittering along pathways that were dangerous to an expectant mother's peace of mind.

Snow. Icy roads. A three-hundred-year-old troll with issues running wild in the mortal dimension. Not to mention about a thousand MacKenzies talking about me over brunch while I hid in the bathroom and waited for my fingertips to quit sizzling.

Just your average Sunday.

I stepped up to the paper towel dispenser on the far wall. It had one of those motion-sensing devices that required you to waggle your fingers in front of the red light in order to signal it to dispense a length of paper.

I waggled and all hell broke loose. Paper spewed from the machine like lava from Vesuvius. I tried covering the red light with the back of my hand, but that only made things worse. You wouldn't think such a small receptacle could hold so much paper. It was everywhere, entwined around my ankles, drifting across the tiled floor, draped over the sinks and light fixtures.

As if that wasn't enough, the toilets started synchronized flushing. I didn't want to think what might be next. I needed help and fast. I wasn't crazy enough to bring Elspeth back and I couldn't call the Roto-Rooter Man.

That left Janice.

I cupped my hands together and prayed

my blueflame capabilities were still manageable. The last thing I needed was to set Carole's Lakeside Inn on fire.

"Make it snappy," Janice said as her hologram shimmied into view above the row of bathroom sinks. "I'm waxing the entire Griggs family and it's bedlam around here."

"Bedlam?" I said and gestured at the chaos all around me.

"Whoa." She sounded impressed. "I take it you lost your temper."

"Big time," I said and gave her a quick-and-dirty version of what had happened so far, including Elspeth's afternoon swim.

Janice let out a sigh that made her hologram ripple like the surface of a lake on a windy day. "I hate it when I'm right."

"Luke warned me. You warned me. Old Butter Head warned me. But did I listen? Of course not. I just had to meet the Fockers."

Janice snorted. "The Fockers?"

"Worse. You wouldn't believe the questions they threw at me. I'm surprised his mother didn't ask my cup size."

"They're humans. Nosy is in their DNA. You of all people should know that."

Okay, so maybe I had done more than my share of poking around town in search of gossip, but before I came into my powers it

152

was the only way I could find out what was going on. I worked on a need-to-know basis and as de facto mayor I needed to know everything. Being half human put me at a major disadvantage. Everyone else was plugged into some kind of interdimensional Twitter account while I was stuck eavesdropping and peering into medicine cabinets.

Metaphorically speaking, of course.

I burst into tears and the doors to the stalls began to swing open and closed in unison. "They — they wanted to know about m-my father's family and — oh, I don't know what happened, Janice. I just plain lost it." I struggled to rein in the waterworks, but they were as out of my control as everything else in my life. "Next thing I knew, flames were starting to burn my fingertips and I ran out of there."

"I would've just turned them all into stink-bugs."

I have to admit I was tempted, but reason won out over emotion for once. "Don't worry," Janice said. "You won't have any magick at all right after you deliver. It takes a few weeks for those crazy postpartum hormones to regroup with your powers."

"I never thought I'd say this, but I could use a break from magick."

Janice laughed. "You're definitely Sugar Maple's first pregnant flamethrower."

"You've got to help me before his mother or sisters storm the bathroom!"

Magick didn't travel well and trying to launch a spell over blueflame was pretty much destined to fail, but I was desperate.

Better yet, Janice was game. "I'm thinking the seventh variation of the Triad might work if we can sync it up, but only if we supplement it with the third ritual from the Householders ceremony."

"That's your territory," I reminded her. "That ceremony is limited to members of your bloodline."

"Crap," Janice said. "Then we'll have to —"

"Chloe?" Luke's sister Kim stood in the doorway, staring at the scene in front of her. The look on her face was the kind of look you'd expect from a woman who had just walked in on her husband while he was trying on her favorite lacy red bra.

I felt like someone had punched me in the solar plexus. We weren't in Sugar Maple. There was no protective charm shielding the truth of our magick from human eyes.

I waited for Kim to either run screaming from the room or approach Janice's hologram for a closer look, but she did neither.

She just stood there staring at me.

Was it possible to get lucky twice in an hour?

"Which one is that?" Janice asked from within her hologram. "She's either pregnant or hitting the Ring Dings pretty hard."

"Be quiet!" I didn't mean to say it quite that loud.

Kim's cheeks reddened. "Did you just tell me to be quiet?"

Janice snickered and I glared at her, which, thanks to some unfortunate positioning, looked like I was glaring at Kim, whose cheeks grew even redder.

"Listen, I'm sorry things got crazy out there," Kim said, completely oblivious to Janice's intense scrutiny, "but, believe it or not, I'm on your side."

"I didn't tell you to be quiet," I said, struggling to ignore Janice, who was rolling her eyes like an overdrawn cartoon character. "I was talking to the baby."

At that Janice let out a howl of laughter that made the outer edges of her hologram vibrate like a tuning fork gone wild.

"You told the baby to be quiet?" Poor Kim was starting to look scared.

"Get out of this one, Hobbs, and I'll babysit free for the first year." Janice was enjoying this way too much.

"No," I said, doing my best to pretend none of this was happening, "of course not! Be *still*. That's what I told her. Be still! She's been moving around so much today I'm getting seasick."

Kim frowned. "I could swear you said be quiet."

"Acoustics can be very deceptive," I said. "Did you know there's a sweet spot in the Capitol Building where you can hear a whisper clear across the Rotunda?"

"Good one," Janice said, "but I don't think she's buying it."

If there had been a window in the bathroom, I think Kim would have made a break for it. Good thing the swinging doors and mountain of paper towels took her mind off my historical non sequitur as she carefully stepped into the room and looked around.

"What on earth happened in here?"

I struggled to look innocent. "All I did was turn on the faucet and all hell broke loose."

Janice was still laughing as her pixels dissolved and the blueflame connection guttered. Kim, however, continued watching me like I was a runaway convict about to take her hostage. She bent down and untangled a length of paper towels that had ensnared her ankles and tossed the crumpled mess into the trash container near the door.

"I went to jiggle the handles," I said by way of explanation, "but the new toilets don't have handles." I gestured toward the wonky towel dispenser. "Not quite sure what I did to that."

"You should tell the hostess," Kim said in the tone of voice you would use with a troublesome child. "She probably has a list of plumbers or handymen she can call."

"I really hate to bother her." More than Kim could possibly understand.

"Oh, wait!" You could almost see the light dawn. "You're friends with the owner, aren't you?"

"Yes," I said, "business acquaintances, and I'm totally humiliated."

"Accidents happen," Kim said, relaxing visibly as if it was all beginning to make some kind of sense. "She's not going to hold it against you. We'll talk to her together." A smile broke the tension on her face. "I can be your witness."

I made a mental vow to arrange for a group of itinerant working pixies to add Carole's Lakeside Inn to their list of secret stops. An anonymous mea culpa for causing this disaster in the first place.

"So," Kim said, hands splayed across her

burgeoning belly in a gesture I knew very well, "except for the water and the paper towels and my family, how are you doing?"

I curled my fingertips into my palms and willed myself into a no-flame zone. "Better, thanks."

"Sorry about what happened out there. I think the excitement got the better of them. You're pretty much all they've talked about since Ma met you at your yarn shop."

"They're pretty much all we've talked about, too."

"They came on pretty strong, but I guess they figured this might be their only chance to get some answers so they went for it."

I chose my words carefully. "I know Luke's been a little . . . distant."

"We were beginning to wonder if he'd gone into witness protection."

Kim laughed and I smiled along with her. The tingling in my fingertips abated and I found myself relaxing for the first time since I opened my eyes that morning.

"I didn't just come in here to spy," Kim said. "I also came to pee." The toilets had finally tired of autoflushing and she chose the second stall. "If it makes you feel any better," she called out through the closed door, "they're interrogating Luke like he's wanted for murder."

"Actually it makes me feel guilty."

"Guilty!" Her laughter rang out in the small room. "He earned every second of it. You can't disappear the way he did. Families don't work that way."

"A bit of a sweeping statement, don't you think?"

I heard the sound of the john flushing normally, then Kim joined me at the sink.

"We know he went through a terrible time after —" She stopped abruptly and looked down at her soapy hands and regrouped. "After Steffie died, he wasn't himself. Then he and Karen divorced and there was a lot of pressure from my parents to get back together. I guess he reached his limit. God knows, I would have reached it a lot sooner. But at least when he was on the force in Boston we knew where to find him. Once he left, he seemed to cut all ties."

I watched as she grabbed a length of dry towel that was draped over the sink. "Like you said, he had his reasons."

"If Fran Kelly hadn't bumped into the two of you in Salem last spring, we probably still wouldn't know about the baby."

Kim was his sister but she didn't have a clue what made him tick. Another one of my notions about family shot down. Blood mattered, but it wasn't everything. It seemed

159

his friends in Sugar Maple understood him better than his sister did.

"You're right," I said. "He didn't plan to tell you until after our daughter was born. You might not agree with his decision, but you should respect it."

She blinked as if my words had startled her. They definitely startled me. But they were the right words and I was glad I'd spoken them. Luke and our baby came first. Everybody else would have to fall in line behind them.

The baby kicked hard — noticeably harder than usual — and I winced.

"Are you okay?" Kim's image wavered in front of my eyes and I closed them against a surge of dizziness.

"I'm fine." At least I thought I was. "I guess she's tired of waiting for breakfast."

But, as it turned out, breakfast wasn't exactly what my daughter had in mind.

12

LUKE

I was a half second away from barging into the ladies' room to see what was going on, when Chloe and Kim strolled back into the dining room.

"Better watch out, Luke," my sister Jen called out. "Now Chloe knows all your secrets."

Kim gave an exaggerated wink and some of the tension in the room vanished. "You're in trouble now," she said to me. "I gave the woman all the ammunition she'll ever need."

Chloe laughed along with the rest of us, but her mouth was tight and the twinkle in her eyes had gone missing. You didn't have to be a cop to know something was wrong.

"You feel okay?" I brushed her left ear with my lips.

"I think I'm just hungry." She took my hand and placed it on her belly. "She's kick-

161

ing up a storm. It feels like she's wearing cleats."

I studied her face. "What's going on?"

"I don't know," she said quietly, leaning into me for a second. "I just don't feel right."

"Better get yourself some pancakes, Cleo," my dad said, "before I eat them all."

"It's Chloe," my mother said, "not Cleo."

Chloe flashed him a tired smile. "I kind of like Cleo."

"You know what?" He pushed back his chair. "I'm gonna fix you a plate."

"The last time he fixed anyone a plate, Nixon was in office," Ronnie said, to raucous laughter, but my dad was on his feet and on his way to do a little hunting and gathering.

"My mom's a nurse," I reminded Chloe. "You want her to take a look?"

"There's nothing to see. There was a little excitement in the ladies' room, but everything is fine now. I guess I just tire more easily than I realized."

I'd lived with her long enough to know that "a little excitement" was a euphemism for "disturbance in the magickal force field." I also knew that magick had a way of knocking you on your ass. No wonder she was wiped.

162

My dad presented her with a plate piled high with pancakes and bacon and scrambled eggs and a side of hash browns that looked like half of Idaho contributed to it. Chloe gulped hard but thanked him and made a show of digging in even though her appetite was clearly nonexistent.

Okay, now I was worried. The woman I loved was slender, but she could outeat a lumberjack. She was picking at her pancakes like food was an alien notion.

Conversation ebbed and flowed around us. I did my best to keep up with it, but I was mostly focused on Chloe, who was clearly drooping fast.

Finally I made a show of checking my watch. "I think we'd better shove off," I said. "We have a long drive and I'd like to get home before the roads ice over."

The look of naked gratitude in Chloe's eyes told me I'd read the situation right. There were the usual protests, but one look at Chloe's face kept those protests to a minimum.

My mother pulled me aside while Chloe said her good-byes to my dad and the others.

"Why don't you see if you can get a room here for the night?" she suggested. "I don't like the way she looks."

"She says she's fine, Ma, just tired. She can sleep on the drive back."

"She's in her ninth month, Luke. Do you really think she'll be comfortable sleeping in the truck?"

I didn't, but that was where the magick came in. Between Elspeth and Chloe, they'd figure out something.

"I'm concerned," my mother persisted. "I wish I could put my finger on what's different about her."

"This is only the second time you've met," I reminded her. "You don't exactly have a baseline to judge against."

"Talk to Chloe," she urged. "This is a beautiful inn. Tell her you'd like to spend a relaxing day here with her."

Actually the idea had merit. Driving through snow got old pretty fast. Driving through snow with a backseat troll got old even faster. But I knew Chloe wouldn't rest until we were home in Sugar Maple and, to my surprise, neither would I.

You get used to things like protective charms and magick on command. I wanted Chloe and the baby surrounded by every measure of comfort and security possible and I had come to realize Sugar Maple was the place.

Chloe was surrounded by MacKenzies, all

patting her bump and trying to get their two cents into the conversation. I could see she was running on empty.

"Time to go," I said, elbowing my way through the gaggle of kin. I rested my arm lightly across her shoulders. "I want to get us home before dark."

Ronnie clapped me on the back. "Next time we see you, the baby will be here."

"Your mouth to God's ear." My mother quickly crossed herself. "The last few weeks are the longest."

"Especially with the first," Jen chimed in.

"You'll probably go at least a week past your due date," my sister-in-law Tiffany said, "so don't be surprised."

"I just can't believe Meghan would miss this occasion," my mother fretted. "She could have tried harder, in my opinion."

Meghan's "car trouble" phone call had been followed twenty minutes later by an apologetic text message that fooled no one.

Chloe smiled and nodded and clung to me like we were on the *Titanic.*

Another round of good-byes and we were finally out of there.

"It's still coming down pretty steady," Chloe said as we retrieved our coats and shrugged into them at the door. "I was hoping it would stop before we left."

"We'll be okay," I reassured her. "All-wheel drive, snow tires, chains and sand in the back, and Elspeth for ballast. What can go wrong?"

She shivered slightly and pulled her coat tighter. "Don't ever ask that around a pregnant woman."

"Stay here," I said. "I'll pull the car right up to the edge of the walkway."

"I'm not sick, Luke," she snapped. "I'm just the size of a whale. I can walk to the car."

Since when? I had seen her push through a snowdrift to avoid slipping on a shoveled but still icy walkway.

"It's slick out there."

"I grew up in northern Vermont. I think I know how to walk in snow."

And wasn't she the same woman who spent more time on her butt each winter than a toddler learning to walk?

She was smart, funny, beautiful, talented, magical, and stubborn as hell. Nothing short of a wizard or a medium-sized nuclear blast would be able to change her mind.

"Okay," I said. "It's not getting any earlier. Let's go."

We were halfway to the truck when she stopped abruptly.

"I told you it was slick," I said, holding

her steady. "Stay put. I'll get the truck."

"It's not the snow. It's me." She winced, then inhaled sharply. "I wish she'd stop kicking so hard."

"You're in pain."

"Not exactly pain . . ."

"Severe discomfort?"

Her smile came and went in a heartbeat. "Not quite."

"You don't think —"

"Of course not! There is no way I'm in labor."

"Have you been timing the pains?"

"Trust me, Luke, these aren't contractions."

"How would you know if you've never had them before?"

"I'm a woman. I'd know. These aren't contractions. They don't come at timed intervals." She thought for a moment. "It's like I overstretched my muscles and now they're making me pay for it."

That didn't sound like anything I remembered Karen experiencing, but what the hell did I know.

"I've got a great idea," I began. "How about we get a room here and stay the night? We'll catch up on sleep, watch some TV, order room service, and head out early tomorrow morning after the county crew plows and sands the roads."

"I'm going home now."

"Think about it," I urged. "We can get a room with a fireplace and a view of the lake."

She wasn't having any of it. Her jaw was set and that little blue vein in her right temple tapped out a warning.

"I'm going home," she said, her voice climbing into the dogs-only zone. "You can stay here if you want, but I'm going back to Sugar Maple."

We made it another four steps before she stopped again.

"The baby shifted. Let me catch my breath."

"Shifted? Do you mean dropped?" Dropped was a big deal.

"I don't know what I mean," she said, dodging the question. "All I know is that I feel like crap."

I had been down that road before. When it came to babies, anything could happen. I had visions of pulling over to the side of a snowy, slippery road and watching while a yellow-haired troll delivered our baby in the backseat of my second-hand Jeep.

And don't think it couldn't happen. I worked a beat before I became a homicide detective, and believe me, when it came to being born, babies frequently managed to find the worst places and the least convenient times.

I wasn't going to let that happen on my watch.

CHLOE

I was sweating under my down coat by the time we reached Luke's truck, but I would rather choke than admit he was right and I should have let him bring the truck to me.

"I'm not going to break," I snapped at Luke as he helped me settle into the passenger seat. "I'm not made of china!"

"The attitude's getting old," he said with a good-natured grin. "Now shut up and let's put the seat belt on. You can bitch me out later."

"We can't leave without Elspeth."

He leaned close and planted a quick, warm kiss on my lips. "I say we can."

What was the matter with him? He knew we couldn't do that. Even here, far from Sugar Maple, she was still under Samuel's protection and came and went as she chose.

"I sent her a blueflame. She'll be here any minute."

"I thought she refused to use blueflame."

"She's old-school," I admitted, "but I convinced her to make an exception today."

Actually it hadn't taken much convincing at all. Usually Elspeth was hardheaded and as intractable as steel, but she didn't put up any argument at all.

"How long is it going to take the old —"

We both jumped at what sounded like gunfire from the backseat.

"Jeez, Elspeth!" My heart nearly jumped out of my chest. "A little warning might be nice."

She mumbled something, but it was lost as her molecules finished rearranging themselves into recognizable form.

Luke glanced into the rearview mirror, winced, then looked away.

" 'Tis the same Elspeth as before," she said tartly, "no more, no less. Best be on our way before it's too late."

I guess I was feeling a tad edgy because I pounced on her words. "Too late for what?"

"Home is always best," she said, not answering the question.

She condensed herself down to the size of a garden gnome and withdrew into a black hole of silence.

"Not much on conversation today, is she?" Luke asked.

"You're complaining?"

"Not me."

He asked if I wanted the radio on, but I

shook my head. "I like the quiet."

"Enjoy it while you can," he said with a chuckle, "because there won't be much of it after the baby arrives."

Once again I was reminded of the fact that he had been down this road before with someone else. "It's hard to believe a tiny infant can make a lot of noise."

"It's not the volume that gets you," he said as we slowly navigated our way out of the parking lot, "it's the frequency and the duration." A quick, sad smile flickered across his face. "Normally I can sleep through an earthquake, but one little whimper from Steffie and I was —" He stopped himself with a shake of his head. "You know."

I nodded. "I know."

The world could be such a dangerous place. A little girl climbed on her bicycle one sunny day and thirty seconds later she was dead and her parents' world was torn apart.

Elspeth's gloom-and-doom warnings had taken their toll on me. Add them to my own natural propensity for worry, then factor in the scary recurring dreams about missing babies and sick children, and you had one very pregnant sorceress teetering on the edge of a major crying jag.

I wanted to be home. I wanted to be safe inside the protective arms of Sugar Maple. I wanted to know our baby would be born healthy and would grow up happy, surrounded by family and friends who loved her and would do anything for her.

I wanted what every new mother wanted, but mostly as the miles rolled slowly by that afternoon I wanted the pain to stop.

13

LUKE

The only other car on the road was the small dark blue beater that had been ahead of us for at least the last twenty miles. I tried to keep its taillights in view but the combination of snow and dusk made it difficult. Every now and then the driver would slow down enough that I had to ease my foot off the gas to keep a safe following distance.

All in all, not my favorite Sunday drive.

The snow was moderately heavy and steady, swirled periodically by squirrelly winds that made it almost impossible to see.

"Pull over." Chloe's voice broke into the silence.

"There's not much of a shoulder here," I said, scanning the road through the falling snow. We were halfway between Lake Winnipesaukee and Sugar Maple. "Maybe I can —"

"Pull over!"

I had taken my eyes off the road just long enough to see what was wrong, but that was all it took. The dark blue Toyota had stopped moving forward and was skidding sideways across the highway and we were heading straight toward it.

"Brace yourselves." I took my foot off the gas and aimed for the snow-covered shoulder of the road and prayed.

The world downshifted into slow motion. It took forever to travel the fifty yards or so to the shoulder. We went into a minor skid, but the all-wheel drive on the Jeep hung tough and we came to an easy stop, buffeted by a cushion of drifting snow.

"It starts!" Elspeth moaned from the backseat. "All that I foresaw starts now!"

I wanted to leap for Elspeth's pudgy throat, but I flung open my door instead and ran around to the passenger side. Chloe's door was already open. Her seat belt was off. And she was losing her brunch.

Elspeth didn't help matters. She unbuckled her seat belt and provided running commentary on the proceedings, most of which made her sound like Nostradamus predicting the end of days. I tried to block out her words, but they were registering on some cellular level I couldn't control.

I glanced toward the highway, expecting

174

to see the driver of the dark blue Toyota running toward us, but there was nothing but snow. Lots of snow. The car was gone.

Bastard. What the hell kind of person drove away without making sure everyone was okay?

Something was wrong. I didn't know what, but there was definitely a disturbance in the force field and this time the backseat troll wasn't to blame.

Chloe looked like hell. Her cheeks were flushed but her face was pale and her eyes glassy. Morning sickness had stopped months ago, but that didn't stop her from losing the contents of her stomach on the side of the road.

"The flu?" I asked after I helped her clean up and settle back in the truck.

"I don't know." Her voice was weak, subdued. "The pancakes maybe."

"You told me half the sock class yesterday was contagious. I'll bet —"

"Luke, I don't know. I felt sick. I threw up. Enough, okay?"

" 'Tisn't illness," Elspeth proclaimed. " 'Tis the beginning."

I wasn't going to let her drag us down Doomsday Lane. "Nobody asked you, so shut the hell up."

"This isn't helping," Chloe said, then

175

burst into tears.

I don't know how the troll felt, but I felt like a shit. The point had been to keep Elspeth from making Chloe feel worse. Clearly I could do it a hell of a lot faster and more effectively.

I got back behind the wheel and eased onto the empty road. We drove a few miles in edgy silence until I heard a loud bang and the truck pulled wildly to the left.

I gripped the wheel hard and steered into the skid.

I was getting good at this.

"Flat tire," I announced as I found my way back to the shoulder. I added a string of expletives for the hell of it. "Either of you have any magick for changing a tire?" How the hell did we get a flat tire in the middle of a snowstorm anyway? There must have been a nail or some broken glass along the snowy shoulder when we stopped a few miles back.

Elspeth ignored me. Chloe, still crying, gave it a shot, but the best she could do was to make the rear window swing open and closed a couple dozen times.

"Stay in here," I told them both. "Don't get out no matter what. Visibility sucks. You're safer in the truck."

I'd changed probably a thousand tires for

stranded motorists before I made detective. I knew what I was doing. I would set up the flares, the emergency lights, the whole nine yards, and get it done in record time.

But there was a part of me that couldn't help wondering, "What next?"

CHLOE

My water broke while Luke was changing the tire.

One second I was sitting there with my eyes closed, praying the nausea would go away, and the next — well, you can imagine.

"The babe is coming," Elspeth said when I told her. "You are following the way of your Hobbs ancestors. 'Twill be an easy birth and a fast one. The signs are all there."

Easy I liked, but fast? I didn't want fast. We were sitting in a Jeep on the side of the highway during a snowstorm and we were still an hour away from home.

"We can make it back to Sugar Maple, right?" I asked Elspeth as a note of panic rose in my voice. "I mean, fast means five or six hours when it comes to labor."

"Within the earth hour," she said. "You favor the magick now, not the human."

Her words had barely begun to fade when the first wave of contractions hit. The discomfort I had felt at the inn had clearly

177

been the earliest stirrings of labor. Think of a raindrop as the earliest stirring of a Cat 5 tornado and you'll understand. This was definitely Cat 5.

We were too far from Sugar Maple to transport Lilith to deliver the baby. Transporting Brianne from Quebec City was out of the question. If Elspeth's prediction was right, even if we got back on the road right now the baby would be born before we reached the Sugar Maple town limits.

The funny thing about fear is the way it wipes away everything that's unimportant. Suddenly I forgot about Luke's family, the snow, the flat tire, the fact that we were still a long way from home and began to focus on the fact that I would be holding our daughter in my arms within the hour and that meant we needed a plan.

Which, as it turned out, was easier said than done. I buzzed down the window.

"Luke! My water broke. I'm in labor."

"I'm almost done here," he said, sounding calm and in control. "Blueflame Lilith and tell her we'll be there within ninety minutes."

"You don't understand. The baby is coming."

"I heard you," he said, fiddling around with the tire. "This is your first baby. Ask

Elspeth. You have plenty of time."

"We have less than an —" I stopped while a contraction ripped apart my midsection. If this was easy, I didn't want to even think about the alternative. I was grateful for every drop of magickal Hobbs blood I possessed. "Less than an hour to go."

He went whiter than the snow falling around him, then slapped on the cop face. "Everything's going to be fine," he said. "That's why Elspeth is here, right? She's got the baby-delivering mojo we need."

Except, to my shock, she didn't.

" 'Tisn't my place," she said when I turned to her.

"But you said you had eleven children. You have to know something about the process."

"I gathered the eggs, but I didn't create the chicken."

"What does that mean?" I sounded like I'd been poked with a cattle prod. "That's why you're here, isn't it?" My voice climbed up higher with every word. "You're my plan B. You're here to cover in an emergency." And this definitely counted as an emergency. She'd been around since the *Mayflower*. Before epidurals and Lamaze and La Leche. She must have helped deliver dozens of babies over the centuries. "Please don't

179

give me a hard time, Elspeth. I need your help." It killed me to say those words, but I'd ask her to marry me if it meant she would help bring my child into this world.

"Himself chose me to be the protector, not the midwife."

And Samuel had gotten it right. She wasn't a midwife. She knew nothing about delivering babies. All she could do was flap around spouting spells and generally making a pain in the ass of herself.

I couldn't help myself. The situation was so crazy, so totally absurd, that I started to laugh and then I laughed harder and harder until finally I couldn't stop until I was gasping for air. We were stuck in the snow on an almost-deserted highway two weeks before Christmas and I was in labor. If the gods had any more tricks up their sleeves, I hoped they would hang on to them until after the New Year because right now this was about as much as I could handle.

Luke climbed back into the truck as I was riding the wave of another killer contraction.

"How many minutes apart?" His voice was calm and controlled, but the faint gleam of sweat above his upper lip gave him away.

"Five."

In the backseat, Elspeth began to mutter

under her breath. We knew better than to ask what she was saying.

"I fixed the flat. We can find the nearest hospital with my GPS."

"Too late, too late," Elspeth said. "The babe is nigh."

"I don't want to go to a hospital," I said stubbornly. "I thought we had decided against it."

"We're not in Sugar Maple," he pointed out. "Lilith isn't here to help you. Your midwife isn't here. I want you and the baby to be safe."

We wouldn't be safe in a human hospital. My magick had been running rampant. He knew that. Here one minute, gone the next.

Another contraction, this one longer, more powerful than the ones that had come before, and I realized with a start that my magick wasn't running rampant any longer. It was gone.

I'd been warned it might happen, that my particular mix of mortal and magick might go missing temporarily during delivery, but nothing prepared me for the sense of loss that washed over me, the acute loneliness, and I gripped Luke's hand and squeezed hard until I actually heard him suck in his breath.

"There's no time for a hospital," I said

181

when I could speak again. "It's too late for that now."

He smiled at me and the look in his eyes told me that no matter what happened, I wasn't alone.

14

LUKE

Even I could see we were on the fast track now.

Our daughter was about to be born in the back of my used Jeep and I wasn't sure I remembered my own name, much less what the procedure was.

Chloe's magick was down for the count. Elspeth tried to blueflame Lilith for some long-distance help, but the connection sputtered, then died.

We were on our own and I needed help ASAP so I did what any sane twenty-first-century father-to-be would do.

"YouTube?" Chloe asked between contractions. "You're surfing YouTube while I'm in labor with your child?"

Actually I had done the surfing a few days earlier, searching out how-to videos on emergency childbirth procedures. I'm not saying that I was psychic or anything close, but I hadn't been a Boy Scout all those years for nothing. I believed in being prepared. We had blankets in the back, both the traditional kind and the high-tech silver ones. Water. Heat packs for hands and feet. Nonperishable food. All the things any good New Englander knew belonged in a well-equipped car between October and April. I had two flashlights, an emergency medical kit, flares, and a crank dial radio.

Now all I had to do was evict Elspeth from the backseat and we were in business.

"And where will ye be putting me?" she kvetched. "Strapped to the roof like hunter's kill?"

"Why don't you try making yourself useful," I shot back. "Grab the blankets while I drop the rear seat."

That was the good thing about the Jeep. Instead of trying to maneuver on a short and narrow backseat, with a few moves and a little muscle Chloe had a roomy flat surface to lie down on with a thick blanket beneath her to help make her more comfortable.

The one thing I couldn't give her was privacy.

"The babe will suffocate," Elspeth pointed out, "unless she removes her trousers."

I'd seen Chloe naked hundreds of times

so why the hell was my face burning hot at the thought of pulling off her slacks and panties while Elspeth waved her hands and chanted something in what I guessed was Troll?

From the look in Chloe's eyes, I knew I didn't have time to waste.

"Sorry," I said and tossed the wet clothes into the front seat.

Two minutes apart.

I fast-forwarded through the short video, praying I had absorbed the most important points and would remember the rest from police training.

The truck started to vibrate slightly, just enough for me to notice. Since I had turned the engine off to conserve gas, it got my attention.

"Knock it off," I said to Elspeth. "We don't need special effects."

She glared at me through eyes the size of coffee mugs. "If you were half as smart as you are talky, ye would know 'tisn't me what done it."

And it wasn't the wind or a truck roaring past us doing eighty. We were alone out there.

Chloe drifted back to us as her latest contraction faded. "Why is the truck shaking? We're not driving, are we?"

"We're not driving," I reassured her.

Was I crazy or did Elspeth look a little scared? I tried not to think about that as I made sure I had some towels and blankets at hand ready to swaddle the baby. The first month or so of Steffie's brief life was pretty much a blur. Steffie was a crier and I don't think her mother and I clocked more than an hour's sleep a night. By week two we were zombies. By week four we were calling week two the good old days. The only thing that worked to soothe her was wrapping her up like a baby burrito.

Steffie.

The grief cut through my heart, as sharp and devastating as it had been on the first day. Despite growing up Catholic, I'm not religious, but somehow I knew my firstborn daughter would watch out for her little sister. Or maybe that was the kind of thing a man wanted to believe when he was faced with delivering his own child on a deserted highway during a snowstorm.

CHLOE

I was terrified to be without magick. Even though it had been part of my life for only a year, magick had somehow become my safety net, my go-to destination when things got tough. I'd been warned about transition, that it hit magicks harder than humans and in ways nobody could explain, but I refused to believe it would strip me of my hard-won powers and leave me defenseless.

"I can't do this!" I heard myself say. "I want to stop right now."

I heard Elspeth's grunt of disapproval from the front seat. "The humans are weak and fragile as glass."

Luke unfurled a string of epithets that ended with a threat that would have had me thinking twice about opening my mouth again, but it took more than mortal rage to stop a troll.

"Mind your tongue, human!" she roared at Luke. "There be danger afoot, make no mistake about that, and I would be all that stands between herself and doom."

As the herself in question, I wasn't crazy about the word "doom," but Luke's explosion took my mind off it.

"The only danger afoot is the one I'm going to use to kick your —"

Nothing like a good, loud, horror-movie-queen scream to break up a fight. I even scared myself with the volume.

I had never given physical pain a lot of thought, probably because I had never experienced much of it in my life so far. A random toothache or cramps, sure, but Sorcha, my surrogate mother, had taught me the ways of healing and those ways had served me well.

Or at least they had until transition hit with all the subtlety of a rocket launcher. If this was transition lite, then my admiration for full-blood human females knew no bounds.

Rational thought vanished, replaced by terror and the realization that from this moment on it was all out of my control. It was out of everyone's control. Luke couldn't make it go away. Elspeth couldn't cast a spell to ease my pain. I was caught up in forces as old as time and there was nothing I could do now to escape.

The dark, pulsing, rhythmic pain seemed to go on until I couldn't remember my life before I stepped into this fresh hell. Everything I had learned about childbirth went flying out the window. Those endless Lamaze lessons Lilith had organized were downright laughable. Those little doglike panting breaths she had tried to teach me had been replaced by unearthly howls of agony, followed at odd intervals by embarrassing whimpers from what had to be the world's biggest coward.

I can't even remember what Luke and Elspeth were doing while I cursed nature, the gods, and males of every species. Come to think of it, I don't even remember seeing them at all. It was like an impenetrable crimson curtain had dropped down in front of my eyes, blinding me to everything but what was happening inside my body.

The only thing I knew for sure was that my daughter and I were in agreement: we both wanted her born ASAP.

And then the pains stopped.

One second I was being split in two like an avocado and the next I was in a total state of bliss. It wasn't exactly orgasmic but darned close. In fact, the bliss was so blissful that it took me a moment to notice that I wasn't in the back of Luke's Jeep any longer, a fact that probably should have upset me, but I was so happy to be pain free that the fact I was hovering ten or fifteen feet above it, looking straight through the roof at myself giving birth, seemed like business as usual.

Or it would be if something was happening.

I was lying there in the back of Luke's Jeep with my knees up, supposedly in the throes of hard labor, and I looked like I was napping on a sun-drenched beach.

A ribbon of ice curled itself around my heart. Oh, gods, was it possible? I couldn't be dead. I hadn't seen the white light humans talked about or experienced the sensation of piercing the veil I had heard magicks discuss.

Maybe I just hadn't looked close enough. I squinted and peered down at the scene below me. No doubt about it, I was as still as a department store mannequin. My shoes were on the front seat. My black maternity slacks and granny panties were on the floor in a sodden heap.

I would have thought I was dead except Luke and Elspeth weren't moving, either. I wasn't sure if that was a good sign or a bad sign. The whole scene looked the way the TV did when I paused the DVR so I could race into the kitchen for some more Chips Ahoy.

The only problem was the fact that, at least as far as I knew, life didn't come with a pause button.

Or a DVR, for that matter.

A minute went by and then another and by the time I had sung the *Gilligan's Island* theme song twice through in my head I was starting to worry. Didn't transition mean something should be happening? Weren't we supposed to be moving (moving being the operative word) between one phase of labor and the next? Shouldn't there be some serious stuff going on down there, like maybe Luke yelling, "Push! Push!" the way they do in the movies?

My heart did one of those lurches that made my breath catch in my throat. This definitely wasn't the experience humans described. I had watched enough reality shows on Lifetime and TLC to know what happened when a mortal woman gave birth, and nobody had ever mentioned (1) suspended animation or (2) maternal levitation. I think I would have remembered.

Then again, none of my magick friends had ever mentioned those two minor points, either, so maybe it was just me.

I wasn't a big fan of the *just me* option. A cold sweat broke out on the back of my neck as I realized the pains hadn't resumed. Was I still in labor? I didn't feel anything at all.

Maybe there was a secret password I needed to say before we could proceed. Had I somehow missed the memo that explained exactly what I needed to do to give birth to the next generation of Hobbs sorceresses?

"It is as it should be."

I spun around in midair, searching for the source of the musical voice whispering in my ear, but I was the only being on that particular cloud.

Great, I thought. So now I was hallucinating messages from the big Fortune Cookie in the sky.

I gasped as a woman dropped down in front of me like a golden spider dangling from a shimmering silken web. Her face was in shadow, but I knew instantly that it was Aerynn, the sorceress who had led the exodus from Salem all those years ago and created the safe haven that was Sugar Maple.

The Mother of us all.

"Do not be afraid."

Easy for her to say. She wasn't watching herself trying to give birth in the back of a Jeep. I tried to speak, but I had no voice in this dimension. To be honest, I wasn't sure if I had heard her words or imagined them.

Was this actually happening? When it came to the world of magick it was hard to be sure. So much of the time reality was up for grabs.

But oh, how I wanted this to be real. This was the sorceress whose life had made mine possible, the young woman who had led the endangered from Salem to the Indian village of Sinzibukwud, which, over time, became known as Sugar Maple.

She drifted closer to me, then closer still. Her scent made me think of starry nights near the ocean and I reached out to touch her hand. I needed to make contact with her. I needed to make sure my daughter was connected with all who had come before, but no matter how hard I tried, Aerynn remained out of reach.

I caught movement along the edge of my peripheral vision, but when I turned to look I saw nothing but shimmery fog. For a moment, a nanosecond really, a sense of foreboding rose up inside my chest, a feeling so intense the world threatened to go dark. I felt exposed in a way that had nothing to do with nakedness but with fear. I quickly turned back toward Aerynn, but she was gone and I was in the back of Luke's Jeep with my knees pulled up to my chest and my hands grabbing the seat restraints while our daughter tried to push her way into the world.

15

Luke

"One more push!" The baby's head was crowning. "Just one more, Chloe!"

Elspeth was spinning in crazy circles up and down the length of the dashboard, muttering more of those Troll incantations. Hey, whatever. If it was keeping us all safe, go for it.

Chloe clutched my hand in a death grip. Her eyes locked with mine and then she let out a scream they probably heard back in Lake Winnipesaukee.

"She's coming!" Chloe cried. "Oh, gods, she's —" The rest of the sentence was lost in a long, low groan as our daughter emerged in a slippery rush of blood and fluid and pulsing cord.

There was nothing that could prepare you for the sight of your own child being born. This was my second time and I was still overwhelmed by the miracle of watching the woman I loved deliver the baby we had created.

She was long and skinny like her mom, with a full head of silky blond hair, also like her mom, and I knew I would give my life to keep her safe and happy. Same as I'd do for her mom.

"Ten fingers," I said, laughing through tears as our daughter let out a howl any baby would be proud of. "Ten toes."

I let out a yelp as the umbilical cord sealed itself, then disappeared, along with the afterbirth and all signs of delivery.

"I warned you this might happen," Chloe said.

" 'Tis our way," Elspeth concurred.

Chloe was right. She had warned me this was done to keep the magick from falling into the wrong hands and I understood that, but trust me, it was still unsettling as hell. But right now I was too freaked out to ask questions. I had a newborn to tend to. I swiftly wiped her down, then wrapped her like a baby burrito in the softest blanket I could find.

She was so damn tiny, so helpless. And even though I had some experience handling infants I was scared just the same. My hands felt like big clumsy boxing gloves as I delivered her to her mother.

Chloe opened her sweater and I placed the squalling, hungry infant against her chest. And yeah, I'm not ashamed to tell you I cried.

"Oh, look at you . . . ," Chloe crooned in a voice I had never heard her use before. "You're here . . . I can't believe you're here. . . ."

Chloe shifted position and undid the front hooks on her bra, then guided our daughter's tiny mouth to her breast. The baby made suckling noises, then suddenly latched on, and Chloe laughed out loud.

"She's a genius," she said, looking up at me with an expression of such pure, unguarded love that I could only nod my head in response.

The lump in my throat was the size of a hubcap. The rush of love I felt for Chloe and our daughter almost brought me to my knees. If you had told me this time last year that in twelve short months I would meet the woman of my dreams and that together we would bring a beautiful baby girl into the world I would've asked you what you were smoking. If you'd told me happiness was right around the corner I would've said you were in the wrong neighborhood.

And if you'd dropped the words "magick" or "sorceress" into the conversation, I just might have hauled you in for questioning.

Now I knew that anything was possible. Even building a new life from the wreckage of my old one.

Elspeth was still spinning in happy circles atop the headrest. Hell, I felt like doing the same thing.

"I think she looks like you," I managed over that lump I mentioned.

"She definitely has your mouth," Chloe said. "Maybe your nose, too."

There were so many things I wanted to say to her, to our daughter, but they would have to wait until we were home and warm and dry.

Except we were warm and dry, even though the back of the truck was wide open to the snow and the fifteen-degree wind chill. Chloe's magick had abruptly gone AWOL, the baby was still trying to master sucking, and the best I could do was rub two sticks together and start a fire.

Elspeth was the likely culprit.

Two things occurred to me as I helped Chloe and the baby into a less comfortable but safer position for the drive home.

The first thing was maybe the foul-tempered troll wasn't all bad.

And the second was maybe now she would go back where she came from.

I was smiling as I slid behind the wheel for the trip home.

It had been one hell of a good day after all.

CHLOE

The baby slept the whole way home. Her tiny face was pressed against my breast while her impossibly small fingers curled themselves around the edge of my sweater and held tight. She smelled sweetly familiar and I let myself get drunk on her scent as we rode through the gathering dark.

I felt like I had lived an entire lifetime in the space of an afternoon.

I was a mother now. The baby sleeping against my chest was my daughter. I would never again draw a breath without worrying how it would affect her, without wondering if she was safe, without praying her life would be blessed with everything wonderful.

Luke drove slowly, casting frequent glances at us through the rearview mirror. He looked exhausted, elated, and everything in between and I couldn't wait until we were back at the cottage and we could start being a family.

Elspeth was sitting on the spare tire, her small dark eyes focused on the road rolling by us. I had no idea what she was thinking or, to be honest, why she was still here. Her promise to Samuel had been fulfilled. She had watched the next generation come into this world. She had even cast a spell to keep the baby safe on the car-seat-less snowy drive home. The next descendant of Aerynn had been delivered into the world and, as I understood it, Elspeth's job was finished.

I mean, it wasn't like she had to check the train schedules or snag a rental car. Some deep concentration, a muttered incantation, and she would be back in Salem literally within a heartbeat.

But then my daughter shifted position and Elspeth, along with everything else, vanished from my mind. The only thing that was real, the only thing that mattered, was the beautiful baby girl cradled against my chest.

I must have dozed off because next thing I knew we were pulling into the short driveway next to our cottage. It had snowed here, too, and the thick blanket of white glittered in the rising moonlight. Home had never looked more beautiful.

"Someone shoveled the walkway for us," Luke said as he turned off the engine. He looked surprised and pleased.

"I'll bet Paul Griggs sent one of his boys

over," I said, deeply moved by the kind gesture.

"Pish," said Elspeth, unfolding herself from her perch atop the tire. "Two words, no more, the blink of an eye, and the snow be gone. 'Tis child's play for them that can."

Trolls are not known for their sentimental hearts.

Luke and I both struggled to keep from laughing out loud as he helped me from the Jeep with his right hand while he cradled the baby in his left arm.

"Ouch!" I winced as I straightened up. "It'll be a while before I go bike riding." Even with the blessing of magick on my side, I felt sore and stiff and deeply awed by women who gave birth to twins and triplets without blinking an eye.

"We'll take it slow," he said and I leaned against him as we walked to where Brianne and Lilith were waiting for us.

The women were waiting on the porch, beaming smiles that warmed me despite the cold.

"How did you know?" I asked as we entered the cottage.

"Elspeth," Lilith said.

I glanced down at the surly yellow-haired troll. "I thought your magick wasn't working any better than mine."

She ignored me and disappeared into the kitchen.

Lilith put her arm around me while Brianne, the midwife, reached for the baby. Luke took a step backward.

Luke met my eyes and I nodded. "It's okay," I said. "They're going to make sure all is well and settle us in."

He hesitated for a long moment, then reluctantly handed our daughter into Brianne's care.

"Don't worry, papa," the soft-voiced midwife said with a chuckle. "Your family is in good hands."

He didn't look like he believed her. He looked like he wanted to spend the rest of his life protecting our daughter, protecting us, from whatever the world threw our way.

I thought I already loved him more than it was possible to love a man, but I was wrong. What I felt for him at that moment was off the chart.

"They'll be gone soon," I whispered as Lilith and Brianne glided down the hallway to our bedroom. "They just need to make sure we're okay. It's just a precaution."

He pulled me to him in a full-body hug that was as gentle as it was fiercely protective. "I'll see if I can get rid of the troll. Tonight should be family only."

Family!

The word poured over my heart like hot chocolate on a cold winter's night. Everything had changed. When we left this morning we were just Luke and Chloe, but now we were a family.

"She needs a name," he said as I leaned my exhausted self against him, drawing his warmth deep into my soul. "We can't keep calling her the baby."

I nodded, but suddenly I no longer had the energy to utter a sound. I must have swayed a little on my feet because the next thing I knew Luke swept me up into his arms and carried me down the short hall to our bedroom, where Lilith and Brianne were waiting.

The two women exchanged amused glances as Luke settled me on our bed next to our naked, squirming baby girl.

"Now out with you, Luke!" Lilith made gentle shooing motions with her delicate hands. "We have women's work to attend to."

They shooed him out of the room, then closed the door behind him.

Brianne did a thorough examination and declared me fit on both the human and the sorceress scale.

"And my magick?" I asked.

"Don't worry," she said with a smile. "Rest. Sleep. It will come back better than ever in a few weeks."

Lilith, who had been conducting an equally thorough exam of the baby, looked up at us and smiled. "And I'm happy to confirm that baby girl MacKenzie-Hobbs scored a ten on the human Apgar test. She is as perfect as she is beautiful."

I was so proud you would have thought my newborn had qualified for Mensa membership.

"She really is beautiful, isn't she?" I crooned as I gathered the freshly swaddled bundle into my arms. "She looks just like her daddy."

"She looks like you," Bri said with a chuckle.

"A wee version, to be sure, but definitely her mother's daughter," Lilith agreed.

What did they know? They were both clearly blind as bats.

The MacKenzie bloodline was well represented in our six-pound, twelve-ounce baby girl.

"Any signs of magick?" I asked, even though I knew the answer already.

"Oh, honey, it's way too soon for that," Lilith said. "She's three-quarters mortal. It will take a long time for the magick to overcome all that is human in her blood-line." She paused for a moment. "Besides, you remember how it was with you. Your magick didn't show itself until you fell in love."

"She'll be very vulnerable," Brianne said. "I don't mean to frighten you, but were I you, I would see to it that she is protected by the strongest magick you can weave around her."

That wasn't what I wanted to hear. A few weeks ago I had spent an afternoon deep within the Book of Spells searching for what I could expect in the way of traditions and rituals surrounding the birth of a descendant of Aerynn.

Turned out there wasn't all that much. Most of it was pretty much the sort of thing we did whenever any of our citizens welcomed a new member of the family. On the seventh day after birth, the newborn was presented to the community on the green near the memorial lighthouse monument. This was followed by the blessing from the ancestors, performed by the choir from Sugar Maple Assisted Living, and that was followed by a great party afterward. Touch those three bases and everyone was happy.

But this was different. Our baby was more human than magick. Would the magick latent in her soul be powerful enough to protect her from those who might do her harm until the time came when she learned the ways to protect herself? We wouldn't know the answer to that question for a long time, which meant it would be up to Luke and me and the entire population of Sugar Maple to keep her safe.

And here I thought giving birth was the hard part.

The truth was the hard part had only just begun.

16

LUKE

Elspeth was sitting on the kitchen table eating a stick of butter when I walked into the room. She looked up at me, her face streaked with cholesterol, then bit off another couple tablespoons while I threw up a little in my mouth.

"Try a chair, why don't you," I muttered as I stormed over to the fridge to see what we had on hand. "Only the cats sit on the table."

And, as a dog guy, I was still having trouble with that one.

The troll ignored me. She was good at that. I could've flopped to the ground in front of her in the throes of a massive coronary and she would have continued lapping up butter and staring into space.

I pulled out some eggs, milk, and a bowl of chilled, boiled potatoes, then hunted around for onions and a stick of butter that

Elspeth hadn't manhandled. I was reasonably sure Chloe would be providing our daughter's dinner.

I rummaged around in search of the frying pan, crossing back and forth in front of Elspeth. I might as well have been invisible. Who the hell knew butter was a narcotic? The troll looked stoned on churned cream.

She also didn't look like she was in any hurry to go back to Salem.

"Big day," I said.

Nothing. Not even a grunt.

"Guess I'd better finish putting the crib together."

You would think I was reciting Red Sox scores, the way she ignored me.

Subtlety was overrated. I laid it right out there.

"So now that the baby's here I guess you'll be going back home."

Elspeth didn't move. She didn't blink. I'm not sure she was breathing.

A loud buzzing sounded near my left ear and I jumped. "What the hell?"

She took another hit of butter.

"Damn!" I felt a sharp sting under my lobe and I swatted at the air even though I couldn't see anything. "Knock it off, will you?"

She licked some butter off her desiccated

207

lips and leveled me with a glance. " 'Tisn't me what's doing that."

"The hell it isn't."

"You'll mind your tongue if you know what's good for you. The world's a dangerous place, human, for all of your kind."

I'm a cop. Tell me something I don't know, Butter Face.

She had made her point and the buzzing stopped. Coincidence, right? I was seriously pissed.

"Samuel sent you here to see Chloe through her pregnancy. Well, the baby is here. Chloe and our daughter are both fine. We can handle things from now on. There's nothing holding you in Sugar Maple any longer. You should —"

She was there and then she wasn't. No fireworks. No shimmer of smoke. Not even a "see you around." She was there and then she was gone, leaving only a crumpled-up butter wrapper behind. She didn't even say good-bye. Not that I was complaining, you understand. Gone trumped good-bye any day.

"MacKenzie the Troll Slayer," I said to Dinah and Blot, who strolled in to see if there happened to be an open can of Fancy Feast lying around. "At your service."

They didn't get the joke. I knew only one

person who would and that was my kid sister, Meghan. I had to start calling the family anyway, so why not start with the one who'd skipped the brunch?

I started the onions in the frying pan, then grabbed my phone from the counter.

She answered on the first ring, sounding more than a little crazy. "The bed's getting cold, James, and I'm —"

Better head that conversation off at the pass. "It's not James."

"Oh, shit! Luke?"

"Where the hell were you today?" I demanded, pushing the onions around in the buttery pan with a plastic spatula. "Even Kevin showed up."

"Didn't Ma tell you? I'm snowed in."

"I checked the weather report, Meggie. It's clear and sunny in New Jersey."

A slight pause. "I'm not in New Jersey." A longer pause. "I'm in Massachusetts with a friend."

It was my turn to pause. She had too many friends and most of those friends ended up breaking her heart. Too bad it was none of my business. "James?"

"We came up here for a long weekend and got snowed in."

"If you're snowed in, why isn't he there with you?"

"Back off, Detective MacKenzie," she said with a definite edge to her voice. "I don't have to answer to you."

"So where is he?" I persisted. "Splittin' firewood out back?"

"He went out to get some supplies before they close the roads."

"And how long have you known this Boy Scout?"

"We met last week."

"Last week and you're already holed up in a cozy cabin in the middle of nowhere?" This was how trusting women ended up on a slab with a toe tag fucking up their pedicure. "What the hell do you know about this guy anyway? Tell me he's at least the friend of a friend."

I heard the sound of a long, calming breath being sucked into her lungs. And then another. And another one after that.

"Okay," I said as I cracked some eggs into one of Chloe's spatterware bowls and whisked them with a fork, "I get it. You're thirty years old. You're not my baby sister any longer. You don't need me to vet your boyfriends for you."

Silence.

"C'mon, Meggie," I said in a conciliatory tone. "Don't you at least want to know why I'm calling?"

210

"I already know why. To bust my chops because I didn't show up at the family shindig. Ma probably put you up to it."

"Wrong," I said, enjoying the moment. "I'm calling to tell you that you're an aunt again."

. . . *four . . . three . . . two . . .*

I was pretty sure you could hear her shriek in the Maritime Provinces.

"Oh, my God, Luke, it's true! Ma told me she saw you with some pregnant shepherdess or something, but I half thought she was yanking my chain to rope me into showing up for some family thing where they could all — oh, God . . . a baby . . ."

There was no mistaking the sound of her crying. Hell, I felt more than a little misty myself as I relayed the baby's vital statistics.

"Meggie," I said, grinning like an idiot as I buttered some toast, "quit bawling. This is good news."

"But when — how did it — I mean, did she —"

"Chloe."

"Did Chloe give birth at brunch?"

"Pretty close." I gave her the condensed version of the story.

"You didn't go to a hospital afterward?"

"Why?" I countered, aware I was moving into dicey territory. "Chloe was fine; the

211

baby was healthy. We were practically in a blizzard, Meggie. The safest thing was to drive on home."

"But you've seen a doctor."

"Two midwives were waiting for us on the front porch."

"But you have to see a doctor," she persisted. "Babies need all kinds of shots and stuff, don't they?"

"And we'll take care of everything," I said, sidestepping her questions with what I thought was a damn fine Fred Astaire kind of move.

"Is she beautiful?" My sister sounded wistful. I wasn't sure I had ever heard her sound wistful before.

"Silky blond hair. Can't really tell about her eyes yet. Long skinny arms and legs. Chloe says she has my mouth, but I don't see —" The words were trapped behind the lump that had formed suddenly in the middle of my throat.

"She sounds just like Steffie," Meghan whispered.

"So when are you driving up to meet your niece?" I asked when I found my voice again.

"Soon," she promised. "Send me a picture of the baby tonight, okay?"

17

MEGHAN

A baby.

She couldn't wrap her brain around the news.

Luke was a father again. That whole circle of life thing she'd cried over during *The Lion King* had fresh new meaning.

A baby.

She poured herself another glass of Shiraz and crawled back under the eiderdown quilt to watch the flames dance in the hearth. Steffie had been a wonderful kid. Why hadn't she spent more time with her niece? Why hadn't she understood that life could change forever in a heartbeat?

She started to laugh into her wine. Why hadn't she thought to ask Luke the name of his newborn daughter?

Aunts were supposed to know things like names and birthdays and Christmas lists. She had missed Steffie's last birthday. Greg

— or was it Mark? Well, whoever it was, he had shown up one day at work with a pair of tickets to Jamaica and Meghan had run home to pack, completely forgetting the birthday party that weekend at Luke's place.

"I'll make it up to her next year," she had told her angry brother. "I'll fill her room with Barbies."

But there hadn't been a next year.

She polished off the glass of Shiraz, aware of the pleasant buzz moving its way through her body.

When she opened her eyes later, he was curved against her, his breath hot against the back of her neck, his body hard and ready.

"You were gone so long," she whispered as he moved against her. "I was worried."

"You were asleep." She wasn't sure if he sounded angry or amused. He could shift moods like a magician.

She had been worried, although maybe not about him. She remembered a dark feeling of unease that had swept over her as she sank into sleep. Guilt, that's what it was. Punishment for being a lousy aunt, for blowing off the family get-together and opting to spend another day in bed with a man she barely knew. For being who she was.

He whispered something in her ear and

instantly she was on fire.

"No," she said. "Not that."

He said it again, but this time he didn't whisper and a thrill of fear tore through her like a virus.

She tried to pull away, but his arms were like iron bands around her middle.

"I can't," she said.

"You will."

He rolled her over, pinning her to the bed. "My game," he said. "My rules."

She didn't like rules, his or anyone else's. She tried again to pull away, but he overpowered her.

"See?" he whispered against the curve of her ear. "I always win."

She liked that in a man.

18

LUKE

"She's gone," I said as I settled the bed tray across Chloe's lap.

Her sleepy eyes widened. "Elspeth?"

I snapped my fingers, then winced as the baby whimpered softly. "Just like that," I said, in a whisper. "I'm hoping it was something I said."

"She may not be really gone," Chloe reminded me. "You know she's always doing that cloaking thing."

"I think she's gone. No more waffle stink."

Chloe let out a long, luxurious sigh. "It's been so long since we had the cottage to ourselves. I mean, really to ourselves."

I gestured toward our sleeping infant. "We're not exactly alone anymore."

"She's family," Chloe said, her smile lighting the room. "That's different." She took a sip of orange juice. "Speaking of families, have you told yours that the baby's here?"

I grinned and reached for my coffee. "The screams blew out my right eardrum."

"They're excited."

"You could say that. Bunny went into question-machine mode. My old man got choked up. I asked them to spread the word." I took another sip of coffee. "I had to convince my mother that we didn't need visitors tonight."

"Or tomorrow," Chloe said, eyes wide. "You did tell her that, didn't you?"

"I said we needed a week."

"A week is good," Chloe said. "Two weeks would be better."

"There's no way they'll wait two weeks to see their newest grandchild."

"Next weekend is the Presentation ceremony."

I went blank and it showed.

"We take the baby to the green, where she's welcomed into the magick community."

"That's it?"

"Well, there's some singing involved and a little bit of speechifying, but that's pretty much it."

"Nothing weird?"

"Maybe a little weird," she admitted. "Midge will probably read 'Desiderata' while George accompanies her on the recorder. That's when our equivalent of a godmother is chosen."

"Now you're getting a little too *Rose-mary's Baby* for me."

She grinned and ate some more toast. "There's cupcakes."

"No presents?"

"Hello," she said. "Remember the baby shower on Halloween?"

"So when is this singing cupcake party going to happen?"

"Sunday." She paused for a moment. "Oh, no! Don't tell me. That's the day your family is coming."

"You guessed it."

"When?"

"Around noon."

I could see the wheels spinning inside her head. "That should work out. The Presentation is always at sunrise. We should be finished by then."

"Sunrise is around seven," I said. "How the hell long is the Presentation anyway?"

"You don't want to know," she said with a quick smile. "Let's just make sure we keep our worlds from colliding."

But I think we both knew that collision was coming at us fast.

I told her about my conversation with Meghan.

"I wouldn't be too hard on her if I were you," she said, sipping at her hot, sweet tea. "Your family can be overwhelming."

"To an outsider," I said. "Meg should be used to it by now."

"Give her a break," Chloe persisted. "From what you've told me, she isn't very happy."

"Not happy?" I started to laugh. "I love her, but Meggie does what she wants, when she wants to do it, and expects everyone else to stop everything and pick up the pieces."

"Okay." Chloe shrugged. "Forget I said anything, but I still think you need to cut her some slack. She's a grown woman."

"Who said I lectured her?"

"Lucky guess."

We ate for a while in silence. I'd already scarfed up a half dozen slices of toast while I was putting together the meal so I paced myself while Chloe devoured a heaping plate of scrambled eggs with hash browns and toast.

"The family wants to know her name."

Chloe finished a piece of buttered toast with blueberry jam and gave me a quizzical look. "It's Laria. How could you forget?"

"I thought we agreed on Sarah."

"Too common," she said, wrinkling her

nose. "As soon as I saw her, I knew she was definitely Laria."

She pronounced it "Mariah" but with an *L*.

"Is there some kind of . . . magical significance to the name?"

"Nope." She took another bite of toast. "I just like it."

"Do I get any say in this?"

She shook her head. "I don't think so."

"Laria." I let it linger in the air, then said it again. "Laria."

"It's uncommon," she said.

"You've got that right."

She poked me in the side with the back of her fork. "Uncommon in a good way."

I looked down at the six-pound, twelve-ounce, nineteen-inch bundle of controversy sleeping contentedly in the middle of our bed and felt myself melt. A name as uncommon as our sorceress/mortal child. Maybe there was something to it after all.

"Laria," I said again as a grin spread across my face. "I could get used to it."

Chloe yawned against my shoulder and I settled her back down on the pillows.

"You'd better sleep while you can," I advised her. "Babies keep to their own schedule and it's not usually a good one."

I still remembered what weeks of sleep

deprivation did to new parents. It wasn't pretty.

She nodded and was sound asleep before my words faded away. We had already decided the crib could wait a few weeks so I brought the bassinet Janice had dropped off into the bedroom and set it near Chloe. Laria didn't open an eye as I placed her on the mattress. Her tiny mouth moved in what looked like a smile and then she dipped deeper into sleep, like a diver aiming for the ocean floor.

"Just like your mom," I whispered, bending down to kiss her on the forehead. Chloe slept like it was an Olympic event and she was going for the gold and it looked like her daughter took after her.

I was filled with love so strong, so powerful that it knocked the breath from my body. I stood there looking at the two of them and for the second time that day knew there wasn't anything I wouldn't do to keep them safe.

I had felt this way when Steffie was born, but I was younger then. I didn't understand how fragile life was. Even though I was a cop I still hadn't learned that life didn't always play fair, that sometimes shit happened that you couldn't see coming, couldn't stop no matter how hard you tried.

Love wasn't always enough. That was the hard, sad truth of the matter.

Sometimes love just wasn't enough.

Laria had a healthy appetite for someone not even twenty-four hours old.

I was tapped into her frequency and I was up and by her side with each whimper, checking her diaper for activity, then delivering her to Chloe for another meal. I was pretty much running on autopilot at that point while Chloe struggled to wake up long enough each time for the baby to latch on. I caught up with the Pats on my cell phone while Laria nursed, then burped her and returned her to the bassinet.

Neither one of us was sure how much colostrum Laria was actually getting at this point, but Lilith and Janice (and probably every other female in Sugar Maple) would be stopping by in the morning to help Chloe master the fine points of breastfeeding. I wasn't sure if magick made a difference or not. Then again, there was a hell of a lot about the subject I didn't know.

Mostly I stared up at the ceiling, hyperaware of every sound within a five-mile radius. This was Sugar Maple. Walls and windows and alarm systems didn't mean a hell of a lot around here. The protective spell kept human dangers out, but what about evil hidden within? I had firsthand experience dealing with supernatural evil, and let me tell you, it was nothing like what you saw on TV. They fought dirty and they fought to win and there were just so many times a man could get lucky.

I was glad Elspeth was gone, but something about her abrupt departure gnawed at my gut. Let's face it, there was *gone* and there was *invisible* and a world of difference in between.

The troll could cloak better than the Klingons in *Search for Spock*. She could be sitting at the foot of the bed right now, dressed in her yellow-and-white-striped nightshirt, and I wouldn't know it.

Hard to sleep with that image in your mind.

And then there was Chloe's snoring. Nobody could sleep through that.

Okay, so maybe I wasn't going to get much rest after all. I could deal. Sleep was overrated anyway. I'd catch up after Laria went off to college and I could retire the dragons, drain the moat, and invest in heavy-duty earplugs.

Chloe stopped rattling the windows a little before dawn. The baby was full, dry, and deeply asleep. The room was comfortably warm and quiet. My guard slipped and I felt myself sinking into something halfway between sleep and a coma, when a high-pitched cry pierced the fog.

I was instantly awake, but I couldn't move. At least I thought I was awake, but I might have been trapped in one of those dreams that make you think you're awake but you're really not. Whatever it was, I felt like a human panini, being squeezed by an unseen press. There was no pain, no discomfort, nothing except the fact that I couldn't fucking move.

Just beyond reach, Laria's cries grew more frantic while Chloe kept right on sleeping. What the hell was going on? Had I been hit with a massive stroke overnight?

The pressure on my chest and back increased. I could move my fingers and toes. I could breathe on my own. I could see clearly even if I couldn't turn my head. But I was still trapped.

My heart beat fast and hard and I tried to force deep, calming breaths into my lungs. Waffles? I took another deep breath.

Elspeth was somewhere in the room.

What the hell was she doing here? I thought she'd gone back to Salem for good. Was this her way of getting back at me for pushing her out the door?

My adrenaline kicked in and next thing I knew I was out of the bed and at Laria's side.

Her tiny body was rigid. Her face was red and scrunched in a parody of infant outrage. She was still bundled tightly in her burrito blanket, but the soft peach cap Chloe had knitted for her was lying off to the side, exposing her down-covered head to the night air. I touched her gently, running my hands lightly over her, making sure she was all in one piece. I went to place the cap back on her tiny head and noticed something weird. The vulnerable soft spot visible beneath the silky strands of pale golden hair seemed to glisten in the glow of the night light and at the center I saw a tiny red mark.

Had that been there all the time? I didn't remember noticing it, but I had been pre-occupied with things like blood and breathing and counting fingers and toes and I hadn't paid much attention to the top of her head.

I did remember thinking she was perfect when I placed her in Chloe's arms. So perfect she had seemed like an angel, not an (almost) human child. But didn't all new parents think their kids were perfect? The kid could have a pelt like a mountain lion and the parents would be bragging about the thickness of the fur.

I was sure that red dot hadn't been there before, but it was there now and I didn't like it.

"What's wrong?" my mother asked the instant she answered the phone a few minutes later.

I told her in as few words as possible. I was sitting in the kitchen with Laria asleep against my shoulder while I talked.

"Sounds like a scratch," Bunny said around a yawn.

"It's not a scratch."

Silence, followed by another stifled yawn. "Could be an angioma. Sometimes newborns have them. Nothing to worry about."

"It wasn't there when we put her down around nine."

"Or you didn't notice it."

"It wasn't there."

I could almost hear her shift from mother to nurse. "When did you first notice it?"

"About ten minutes ago. She started crying, crazy crying, and I jumped up to see what was going on. Her cap was off and —"

"Well, there you go. Her cap was off. She definitely scratched herself." She yawned again. "Has anyone clipped the baby's nails yet?"

"I don't know."

"She probably scratched herself when the cap came off. Those little nails can be amazingly sharp."

"It doesn't look like a scratch. It looks like a red dot."

I could hear my old man's sleepy grumbling and the sounds of bedclothes rustling. Was I beginning to sound like a paranoid asshole or just a freaked-out new father? The jury was out.

"I'm sure it's nothing, honey," my mother said. "Get some sleep, then take a look in daylight."

"It's something."

"Why don't you e-mail me a photo later and I'll take a look."

"I'll do it now."

"Honey, I don't know how to say this, but I'm not getting up at" — a pause while she checked her bedside clock — "five fifty-three in the morning to look at a photo of a red dot that I am sure is absolutely nothing to worry about. Now put the baby down and get some sleep."

"But —"

"I've raised seven kids, if you don't count your father. I think I know when it's time to worry and when it isn't. This isn't the time. Kiss the baby, kiss Chloe, tell them we love them, and e-mail me a photo later."

She hung up without even saying good-bye.

19

MEGHAN

The sex haze started to lift the night her niece was born, although you couldn't prove it by the bruises on her body from his lovemaking. He was big and powerful. She told herself he didn't know his own strength, that they were love marks that would fade by the time their fling ended, and sometimes she actually believed it.

She also told herself she didn't know how to say no and make it stick.

First James went out in search of provisions, and then her brother called to tell her about the baby, and the next thing she knew the real world was hammering at the door, demanding to be let back into her life.

They had been up at the cabin for almost two weeks now. She had called in sick to Hot Yoga and, while the boss said all the right things, Meghan knew the end was in sight. By the time they got back to New

Jersey, there'd be a new instructor in her place and a small severance check taped to her locker door.

Which was okay. It was time to move on. She hadn't meant to stay in New Jersey this long. But the question of where to go next stretched ahead of her like miles of empty highway leading nowhere.

Meghan wasn't a big fan of reality. Life continued to roll on, no matter what you said or did or thought, so why not roll along with it in a nice fuzzy state of denial? And she was good at it, too. All of that yoga training had taught her how to empty her mind of everything but the moment.

"Put down the phone and come to bed," James said. "How many times can you look at those pictures?"

How much time do you have?

She slipped beneath the comforter and flashed the screen at him. "My new niece is beautiful," she said, beaming in his direction. "Tell me that she's not the most beautiful six-day-old infant you've ever seen."

For a second she thought she saw a flicker of interest.

"She's cute," he said with a shrug, "but it's not like I have anything to compare her to."

"Seriously, this is a beautiful baby. She's the Miss Universe of babies."

He grabbed for her phone and tossed it onto the pile of clothes on the floor.

"Hey!" She made to reach for it, but he was quicker and rolled her under him.

"We're running out of time," he said. "The roads are plowed. We can start back to New Jersey in the morning."

No doubt about it. Some of the sex haze was finally lifting.

"You really want to go back to New Jersey?" she asked as he grew hard against her belly.

"I thought you had to go back," he said, lifting his head so he could meet her eyes. "You said you were worried about your job."

She made a face. "I don't think I have a job anymore."

"Sorry, babe. What are you going to do?"

She wanted to say "Move in with you for a while," but she didn't. She always made that mistake with guys, moving too fast, exposing too much, needing more than she should.

"I was thinking about going up to Vermont tomorrow to see Laria."

"Laria? What kind of name is that?"

"A pretty one," she said. "I was thinking maybe we could drive up there together. We wouldn't have to hang out long with my family, just long enough for me to meet the baby. I looked at Sugar Maple on the map and we could jump right over into Canada afterward if we wanted. Or if that's no good, I mean, we're in Vermont! There are two resorts within ten miles of Sugar Maple. We could get in some skiing before we go back to New Jersey. You said you liked to ski, right? I'm more cross-country myself, but . . ."

She was all over the place and she knew it. Scattering romantic buckshot like a crazed hunter, hoping she'd hit something.

"Hey, listen," she said. "I'm just thinking out loud. Why would you want to drive all that way to see some kid? It was just a crazy idea. Forget I said anything."

Say yes, James. I need you to say yes. Don't make me show up there alone like the loser I am. I know you're not my boyfriend. I know this isn't going to go anywhere. But couldn't you pretend for just one day?

"Okay," he said. "We'll do it."

Her spirits soared. "Are you serious? You'll come with me to see my new niece?"

"Yeah," he said with the kind of smile that could melt gold. "Why not?"

She could think of a thousand why-nots but none of them mattered. "I have a big family," she warned.

"How big is big?" he asked.

"Osmond family big."

"Do they wear name tags?"

She started to laugh. "We should. That would make life a lot easier for the newcomers."

She gave him the basics while he pretended to listen.

"It's not that bad," she said. "Besides, we won't stay too long, I promise."

"Do they know you like this?" He drew his index finger along her rib cage, long, voluptuous strokes that sent shivers through her body.

"No."

"Or this?" The strokes grew longer, more intimate.

"Not that, either."

He gripped her by the waist with those powerful hands and rolled her on top so she straddled him. "Don't worry," he said as he guided her movements. "I won't leave any more marks."

But she wasn't worried. She wasn't thinking about her family any longer.

She wasn't thinking at all.

20

CHLOE

It seemed like I blinked and Laria was one week old.

The days and nights were a blur of diapers and Snuglis and nursing bras and mini comas that tried to pass for sleep. I was tired in a way I couldn't have imagined eight short days ago.

And happier. The fact that I was a mother, that this tiny little being was a part of my blood, overwhelmed me. When I thought about the series of random events that had brought Luke into my life and how those events resulted in the creation of this perfect baby girl — well, if I hadn't been so tired I probably would have cried, but crying took way more energy than I had at the moment.

Fortunately for all of us, Luke was a natural at fatherhood. He didn't just pick up the slack where the baby was concerned, he did everything short of breastfeeding Laria.

The morning of the Presentation ceremony I sent Luke out to get some bagels and other goodies for his family while Janice came over to do something with my hair, which hadn't seen shampoo or a brush since forever.

"You're wearing that?" Janice said, pointing toward the charcoal gray pants and ivory handknitted sweater I had laid out on the bed.

"What's wrong with it?" I demanded, instantly alert. "It will all be hidden under my coat anyway."

"I don't know," she said with a shrug of her shoulders. "I just thought you should have something special."

And with that she made a quick gesture with her right hand and suddenly a magnificent wrap floated toward me.

"Oh, Janice!" I whispered. "It's incredible."

When it came to knitting skills I liked to think of myself as up there near the top, but this surpassed anything I had ever done.

"I've been working on it since you told me about the baby." The wrap was a generous rectangle worked in soft ivory lace-weight silk and spangled with tiny crystals that made the wrap look like it was lit from within.

"I don't know what to say," I said and burst into tears.

Which, of course, made Janice burst into tears, too.

"Get a grip," she ordered, sniffling. "There's more."

A baby blanket as soft as a whisper and worked in the same ivory lace (but without the crystals) appeared and I totally lost it.

"I want to make sure the fashion police don't do a number on my heartdaughter today," she said, grinning through happy tears.

Heartdaughter was our term for god-daughter.

"If they do," I said, "they'll answer to me."

"By the way," Janice said, "it's baby-barf resistant."

Leave it to Janice to think of everything.

"You know who should be here," I said, clutching the precious knitted garments to my chest.

She met my eyes. "Gunnar."

I nodded. "It doesn't feel right without him, does it?"

"Not even close," she said. "He'd be so happy for you and Luke."

"I dreamed about him the last few nights,"

I admitted. "I keep trying to tell him about Laria, but I never seem to get the words out."

Janice sighed. "I dreamed about him a lot after it happened but not so much anymore. I miss that. It felt like a way of hanging on to him."

"I hope he knows about her," I said as I opened my blouse and flipped open the cup on my nursing bra. "I like to think he does."

"Who knows what goes on in the other dimensions?" Janice said. "I guess anything is possible."

Last year he had communicated with me through Penelope, the feline companion who had been by the side of every Hobbs woman since Aerynn. Somehow he had reached beyond his dimension to help Luke's ex-wife and daughter find happiness away from the constraints of the mortal world. If I lived a thousand years I could never repay the debt I owed him. Without Gunnar's original sacrifice, Luke and I would never have created the baby girl I held in my arms.

While Janice worked on my hair I nursed Laria and tried hard not to stare at the tiny red dot on top of her perfect little head.

"Will you stop that?" Janice said as she wrapped a chunk of hair around the curling iron. "It's just one of those little angioma thingies like Brianne and Lilith said, and it's totally normal in human babies. When her hair grows in you'll forget it's there."

"That's what I keep telling Luke, but I don't think he's listening."

"He's a worrier same as you. Worriers need to have something minor to worry about so they don't totally freak out."

"He e-mailed a jpeg of it to his mother."

"Don't make me laugh," she said, laughing. "I have a dangerous weapon in my hand."

"There's more," I said, as I switched Laria from my right breast to my left. "He thinks Elspeth did it."

Janice burst into hysterical laughter. "I thought she was gone."

"She is gone," I said, "at least as far as we know. There hasn't been a sighting since Luke kicked her out on Sunday."

"But he thinks she came back to put a strawberry angioma on his daughter's head?"

"That's pretty much exactly what he thinks."

Janice wound another chunk of hair around the curling iron. "I know Elspeth's a pain in the ass, but why exactly would she do that?"

"Because he threw her out."

"Nobody throws a troll out," Janice reminded me. "She left because it was time for her to go."

"I wish you'd tell Luke that because he's convinced she's lurking in the shadows." I started to giggle. "He said he keeps smelling stale waffles."

Janice made a choking sound. "What is it with trolls and that baked goods smell anyway?"

"Lilith has a nice ginger cookie kind of scent."

Now Janice was giggling. "But her Archie is uncooked pizza dough."

Laria's eyelids were at half-mast and fading fast and we struggled to rein in the laughter. I bent my head and inhaled her amazing baby smell. "I never believed all that talk about newborns, but they really do smell incredible."

"That's a human thing," Janice said with a shrug. "My babies just smelled like milk."

"You have no idea what you're missing."

"By the way, you have a red mark on your head, too." She met my eyes in the bedroom mirror. "Almost in the same spot."

"I do not."

"Actually you do. It's been there as long as I've been doing your hair, which is pretty

239

much forever."

"Why didn't you tell me?"

"It's your head. I figured you already knew."

"How could I know? Are my eyes on stalks?"

"Well, now you do," she said, clearly amused by my reaction. "Whatever it is, both you and Laria have it, so I wouldn't worry too much."

I tried to laugh, but a sudden, unexpected rush of fear raced through me.

"What?" Janice demanded, winding yet another chunk of hair around her trusty curling iron. "Did I say the wrong thing?"

"It's not you. It's just —" I struggled to find the words. "I don't know. This is all so perfect that I keep expecting something terrible to happen."

"Hormones," Janice said over the baby's adorable snuffling noises. "Things will even out in fifteen or twenty years. I promise."

Who else but your best friend could make you laugh when your maternal hormones were running amok?

"I needed that," I said as she put the finishing touches on my more presentable hair. "I was starting to feel like that *Peanuts* character, the one who walks around with a dark cloud over his head."

"You want something to worry about?"

I shot her a look. "Have we met?"

"Elspeth *is* back."

"You're kidding, right?" She had to be. "This is just to make me quit bitching about red dots and Luke's family."

"She showed up last night while I was outside practicing the moon worship dance she taught me."

"She taught you a dance?" The thought of the beachball-shaped troll teaching anyone to dance made me giggle.

"I'll ignore that." She couldn't, however, suppress the sheepish grin. "Anyway, she's back, so don't be surprised if she shows up at the Presentation."

"It makes perfect sense. The Presentation is the baby's welcome to the community. Samuel would want her to see it through."

Janice put the finishing touches on my hair. "Now I'm the one who's surprised. I thought you'd totally freak."

"Talk to me after the ceremony," I said. "If she's not gone before the MacKenzie clan arrives, then you'll see me freak."

LUKE

Per instructions, we were the last ones to arrive at the green for the Presentation ceremony. It was probably the first and last

241

time a crowd would ever part to let me pass, but it happened that day.

Chloe, cradling Laria against her chest, smiled nervously as Lilith, Janice, and the other townswomen glided toward us with arms outstretched.

Nothing prepared me for how I felt when Chloe and Laria stepped into that circle and I felt the love flowing toward them from the entire town. Chloe was their link to Aerynn and Samuel and the past that forged Sugar Maple. Laria was the promise that the Hobbs link would remain strong for another generation and Sugar Maple would thrive.

Chloe was their present, but Laria was their future.

It seemed like everyone in town had shown up for the Presentation. The village green was crowded with familiar faces, entire families who had bundled up against the winter cold to mark the occasion. Arranged in a circle in front of the lighthouse stood the women most important in Chloe's life: Janice, Lynette, Lilith, Renate, Midge Stallworth, Verna Griggs, and Bettina. They were all dressed alike in flowing burgundy velvet robes with hoods trimmed with dark fur. If I didn't know better I would have thought I had stepped back in time to another century.

Janice glided forward and motioned for Chloe and Laria to join her at the center of the circle.

Chloe's expression was simultaneously solemn and joyous as she and Laria joined her friend. Janice said something I couldn't make out. Chloe nodded, then placed Laria in Janice's arms.

Janice smiled, placed a kiss on the baby's forehead, then took her place in the circle between Lilith and Lynette while Chloe watched from the center.

A choir began to sing from somewhere behind the gazebo. The tune was plaintive, their voices sweet and hopeful, and I choked up despite my best efforts not to. It was tough to be cool when that was the woman you loved being honored and your baby daughter being welcomed into the community with so much genuine affection and caring.

"Waste of time, if you ask me," a grating male voice intoned a few rows behind me. "The kid's more human than magick. She'll never fulfill her promise."

"Darn right," a female voice agreed. "Sugar Maple's about to get screwed all over again."

There's an asshole (or two) in every

crowd. I turned around to glare at the big mouths, but the voices were unfamiliar so I didn't know where to direct my ire.

I took a deep breath, counted to fifty, and then redirected my attention to the Presentation ceremony. The singing stopped and Janice turned toward Lynette, who opened her arms and accepted Laria into them. She whispered something that made Chloe wipe her eyes with a swift swipe of her right hand, then placed a kiss on the baby's forehead same as Janice had done.

One by one the women who were important in Chloe's life took our baby into their arms with whispered words and a gentle kiss. Not a bad way to start life. I had half expected Laria would sleep through the whole thing, but she was awake and very still, watching the proceedings with interest. Being passed from woman to woman didn't seem to bother her a bit. Most infants would be screaming their lungs out, but not my kid. She was a trouper.

Finally Lilith held out her arms for the baby. She whispered something to Laria, same as the others had, but this time the baby seemed to pull back. Lilith didn't react. She smiled sweetly and placed a kiss on Laria's forehead, then returned her to Janice's arms with the words, "A wise woman sees the future in the eyes of a child."

Janice nodded and held her heartdaughter close to her chest and if I didn't know better I would think the wisecracking hairstylist was crying.

Hell, I practically was myself.

Music started up again from behind the gazebo and the sound of the children's voices raised in song joined in. I didn't understand a word, but nothing new about that. There was a common language among magicks and it definitely wasn't English.

I sneaked a peek at my watch. Not because I was bored but because my folks were due to arrive around noon. We still had time, but they needed to move this thing along so I wouldn't have to explain it to my staunchly Irish Catholic family.

The music stopped again. The children's voices faded away.

I was half expecting a *Lion King* moment, but Janice continued to hold Laria close against her chest as she spoke to the crowd assembled on the green.

"A new soul is a blessing to us all and in return we bestow our blessings on Laria, child of Aerynn through Chloe. May she know only joy. May she live in the light of love and peace."

Janice turned toward Chloe, whose beautiful face beamed with pride.

"Come forward, Chloe, and be mother to the child Laria."

Chloe looked toward me, and damn, it was hard to see her through the sudden tears that filled my eyes. Whatever residual longing I might have still had for the world outside Sugar Maple faded away. I was where I was meant to be.

I nodded. Chloe smiled and took a step toward Laria and Janice. Before I could grasp what was happening, she let out a sharp cry of surprise and flew backward into poor Midge Stallworth and the two of them fell to the ground in a tangle of arms and legs.

I was halfway to Chloe when she suddenly leaped to her feet, brushed the snow from her black coat, then helped Midge up from the snowdrift they had landed in.

"Well," she said with a self-deprecating laugh, "it's not like you guys don't know I'm a klutz."

The assembled crowd laughed with her in sympathy, but the buzz of whispered comments began to spread through the crowd like a virus. My fists clenched at my sides as I steeled myself for some snarky cracks about Chloe, but what they said shocked the hell out of me.

. . . the baby has magick . . . one week old . . . it's a miracle, that's what it is . . . no child has ever shown so much power so early . . . and she's three-quarters human . . . can you imagine what a force she would be if only Chloe had mated with one of us? . . .

Didn't they remember their own history? Laria didn't have magick. Serious magick didn't flow into a Hobbs woman until she fell in love and that was a hell of a long way away.

I turned around and shot my best cop look at the crowd in general. This was my home, too. Whether or not they liked it, mortals were here and we weren't going away. Chloe was half human. I was full-blooded. Our daughter was more human than magick. Those were the facts and I was getting a little tired of the constant jabs at our shared lineage.

The buzz faded away and I focused back in on what was happening within the circle.

I figured we were almost at the finish line and was surprised when our newest residents, the Fae contingent from Salem, made an appearance. At least that was what Paul Griggs told me, since as a mortal I couldn't see them at all. They gathered overhead like a giant cloud of glitter in every color of the rainbow, then swooped down, swarming Chloe and Laria, knitting a lacy pattern of pink and yellow and blue and violet glitter chains around them. Chloe's eyes were damp with tears and she looked deeply moved by the gesture. Hard to believe that less than one year ago we had been engaged in a battle to the death with these same creatures.

"And now we have reached the end of our festivities," Lilith said, her lovely face aglow with happiness for us. "Let's all join hands and raise our voices in the Sugar Maple anthem."

I don't sing. And I'd heard Chloe in the shower so I knew she didn't sing, either. But we launched into a rousing version of the anthem anyway, which was followed by "The Star-Spangled Banner," which was followed by cheers and applause and more happy tears from this crazy gathering of faeries and sprites and witches and were-wolves and vampires and shapeshifters and trolls and one very happy sorceress.

And the best part? So far there still wasn't a MacKenzie in sight.

21

MEGHAN

James pulled onto the shoulder a few feet in front of the "Welcome to Sugar Maple" sign.

"This is as far as I go."

Megan heard his words through the heavy fog of sleep. Yawning, she forced herself to sit upright and open her eyes.

"How long was I out?" she asked, running a finger around the corner of her mouth where a patch of dampness had accumulated. Drool. Yeah, that was hot. She hoped he hadn't noticed.

"Long enough," he said. "You missed breakfast."

That woke her up the rest of the way. "You ate breakfast without telling me?"

"I tried, babe, but you were out for the count."

She glanced up at the welcome sign. "Why are we stopped here?"

"I told you. This is as far as I go."

She waited for the punch line, but there wasn't one. He didn't say a word.

Even in unforgiving daylight he was perfect. Chiseled face, even features, thick glossy hair, seductive icy blue eyes, body to die for. A little self-absorbed, but that was to be expected. Most gorgeous men of her acquaintance spent a fair amount of time at the mirror and James was no exception.

"Okay," she said carefully. "I get it. You need to gear up before you meet the family. We can wait a few minutes before we jump in. I don't know about you, but I could use a drink or ten before I meet the family, and I'm related to them."

Still nothing.

She tried again. "They probably have a bar in town. We could stop and get some fortification."

She might as well have been talking to the welcome sign. Funny how chiseled features could turn to stone when you weren't looking.

She struggled to keep her voice even. "I really don't want to be the last one there."

He turned to her, his piercing blue eyes hooded and unknowable. "You're not listening. This is as far as I go."

"We didn't come all this way for us to stop here."

"Nobody is stopping you from being with your family."

"Wait a second." She tried to collect her thoughts, but they had scattered like scared mice. "This isn't a joke?"

"It's no joke."

"You're just going to leave me here."

"Afraid so."

"You won't even drive me to Luke's place?" She had a lousy sense of direction. She'd be wandering that stupid town for hours.

"For the fourth time, this is as far as I go."

"And you waited until now to tell me."

"I didn't know myself."

"Okay," she said, relaxing, "now I know you're kidding." Nobody sane would drive across two states on a Sunday morning in December to pull a stunt like that.

"Listen," he said, drumming his strong fingers on the steering wheel, "either get out or come with. Your choice."

There was no choice. Not anymore. She gathered up her stuff, slid out of the car, then slammed the door shut behind her.

"Want me to come back for you in a couple hours?" He looked as relaxed as if he had spent a day on the sofa watching football. "We could head up to one of those ski resorts you were talking about."

"What I want you to do is go fuck your-self."

"I'll come back," he said, laughing, "and when I do you'll be here."

Throwing her tote bag at him as he drove away was a ridiculously stupid thing to do, but it felt good even if it did miss the car by a mile. This was why she didn't believe in owning guns. If she'd had a firearm on her, he would be lying dead right now in a pool of his own blood and she would be dancing around his corpse.

Maybe not dancing, but it would definitely be a while before she felt any remorse.

The son of a bitch had her car.

22

CHLOE

I was so busy congratulating myself for making sure the Presentation ceremony was over before the MacKenzie clan descended on us that I totally forgot about the buffet Janice and Lynette were hosting at town hall in less than an hour. The entire village had been invited and, trust me, the entire village was going to show up.

The residents of Sugar Maple never missed out on a free meal and if there was the slightest possible chance that some good gossip might break out — well, try to keep them away.

"We're screwed," I said to Luke as we raced around the cottage, picking up laundry, scanning for dust bunnies, making sure the litter boxes were clean. Not to mention seeing to it that Laria was changed, fed, burped, and dressed in her most adorable handknits. "Our worlds are about to collide!"

253

"I thought they'd already collided at the shop after Thanksgiving."

"Not like this they didn't. Every single resident of Sugar Maple is going to make sure to show up and check out your family and I can't do a thing to stop it."

He looked like he was enjoying himself, which only upset me more. "Another blizzard?" he suggested. "Or you could take out the bridge. That usually works."

"Don't be a wise guy."

"I was trying to be helpful."

"If you really want to be helpful, see if you can find the BSJ Janice made for the baby."

He stared at me like I was speaking a foreign language, which I guess I was. Knitting does have a language all its own. "The pink-and-purple-striped sweater with the fancy buttons." I spared him the story of Elizabeth Zimmermann and her amazing one-piece garter stitch jacket that had been delighting knitters for decades.

Wonderful handknits had been arriving from just about everywhere. Long-time customers, newbies, old friends, and even some people I didn't think liked me all that well — they had taken up their needles when they heard I was pregnant and created garments that literally took my breath away.

Laria would be the best-dressed infant in New England and maybe the Mid-Atlantic and Canada, too. She had received sweaters, socks, caps, heirloom-quality blankets, squishy stuffed toys, soakers, mitts so tiny they made me laugh every time I looked at them. And no wimpy baby pastels for my daughter! She would be garbed in every color of the rainbow if my friends had anything to do with it.

Luke came back with the BSJ, a pair of adorable purple angora booties, and a soft cap that somehow captured all of the colors on a very small scale. We struggled a little getting those tiny arms into the equally tiny sleeves of the jacket and our eyes met over our daughter's squirming body and for a moment I swear time stopped. Not in the magick way, but in my heart.

"I know," he said, as my eyes filled with tears. "I feel it, too."

"I keep thinking I'm going to wake up and find out this is all a dream."

"This time last year we were just getting to know each other."

"And falling in love."

"You took some convincing," he said. "I fell in love with you the moment I saw you."

"You said I was asleep on the sofa with my mouth open, snoring like crazy."

"So maybe I like women who snore."

I could feel my heart growing two sizes larger inside my chest, like the Grinch's heart on Christmas morning.

It was a good feeling, but there was no time for sentimental walks down memory lane. We had a baby sorceress to finish dressing and a human family about to descend on us any minute.

"I'm going to send out a group blueflame," I told Luke, "and make sure they all know your family will be at the party. I don't want anyone getting crazy and doing something I can't explain short of shock treatment."

My head spun at the thought of how many things could go wrong. The group blueflame was my last chance to head trouble off at the pass and keep some of our more colorful residents from putting on the kind of show not meant for human consumption.

I had barely doused the flame when Renate's youngest daughter exploded into the room in a spray of bubblegum pink glitter. Not exactly what you'd expect from a teenage goth queen, but the Fae had no choice over their identifying colors. Nature made the choice for them and it was theirs until they pierced the veil.

"Mom says it's an emergency," she said from her perch atop the diaper bag. When it comes to displaying boredom and disdain, Fae teens were the same as their human counterparts. "Some girl knocked on the door looking for you and Luke."

"Some girl?" Luke appeared in the doorway. "What girl? We need more information, Calli."

She shrugged her narrow little shoulders and bounced up and down on the quilted fabric. "All I know is what my mother told me. There's a girl at the door and she's looking for you." She gave Luke a quick but coy look. "Mom says she's a human, too."

And then she was gone in a giant burst of glitter and angst.

"It's got to be Meghan," Luke said when we were outside, as he positioned Laria in the car seat. "She's the only MacKenzie who doesn't travel in a herd."

"I'm not going to get hysterical yet," I announced to the world in general. "We're lucky she showed up at the Sugar Maple Inn to ask for directions and not the Stallworths' funeral parlor." The thought of Midge, a cheerful but bawdy vampire, being Meghan's first contact with Sugar Maple made me dizzy. "Don't even think it."

The Weavers knew how to deal with humans. Their Sugar Maple Inn did a thriving restaurant business, but, when outsiders inquired, their guest rooms were always mysteriously "filled." If Luke's sister had to turn up somewhere unexpected, at least she had picked the right place.

My cell phone vibrated and I peered at the message on the screen.

"Renate says we should go straight to the party. She'll walk over there with your sister."

He started the engine and looked over at me. "At least Elspeth's not here. That's something."

"I hate to break it to you, but she was at the Presentation ceremony. I'm surprised you didn't see her on top of the lighthouse." Then again, when it came to cloaking, Elspeth was Olympic gold.

"Shit." He smacked the steering wheel.

"Luke!" I tilted my head toward the newborn asleep in her car seat.

"She doesn't understand."

"It's never too early."

He gave me a look that was somewhere between amused and exasperated. "So Elspeth didn't really leave."

"That's what it looks like."

"What the hell is she doing hanging

around? Is she going to stay here forever?"

"She hates it here," I reminded him. "She probably had to stay until the Presentation and Laria's formal acceptance into the community. I'll bet she's back in Salem right now bothering someone else."

Luke grunted something, but I didn't pursue the topic. We had more than an irritable troll to worry about today.

To my surprise it looked like everyone in town had chosen to walk to town hall instead of utilizing less traditionally mortal forms of transportation. The sidewalks were packed with werewolves, trolls, spirits, witches, myriad branches of the Fae, and shapeshifters and all of them in human form.

My eyes filled with grateful tears. "Wow," I said, waving at Lynette as we moved slowly past the Pendragon clan. "They're really going all out to make this work."

"Looks like the damn Easter Parade," Luke said as he beeped hello at half the residents of Sugar Maple Assisted Living, who were careening up the block on their motorized Rascals.

"Oh!" I spotted the Weavers near the parking lot. "I think I see your sister. Is she kind of medium height with curly light brown hair?"

He glanced in the direction I pointed. "That's her."

"You're not going to stop and offer her a lift?"

"She's fifty yards away from town hall. We'll catch up with her there."

"She looks like she's been crying."

"She probably broke up with her latest."

"You don't sound very sympathetic."

"She goes from one bastard to another. It's like she has some kind of radar that zeroes in on the one guy in the room who'll hurt her."

I didn't know what to say. My own romantic history was so limited that I felt like a child at the grown-ups' table whenever the conversation turned to affairs of the heart.

Or of the body, for that matter. I didn't exactly have much of a history there, either.

The parking lot was filled with cars with Massachusetts plates, a Connecticut, two New York, and a Rhode Island. It wasn't so much the fact that they were Luke's relatives that made my stomach turn inside out; it was the fact that they were human.

"Okay," I said as we unstrapped baby Laria from the car seat and gathered up the mountains of stuff newborns seemed to need, "it's time for our worlds to collide."

Our town hall was a desanctified church

that we had turned into our central meeting place. Monthly council meetings, wedding receptions, sweet sixteen parties, even an occasional prom or retirement party. This was our venue of choice.

Today it was the site of my Laria's welcome party.

I positioned the baby in her Snugli. Luke's arms were piled high with blankets, diaper bag, and the cakes we'd baked for his family. We had no sooner stepped across the threshold when a giant cheer rang out and we were surrounded by laughing, crying members of the MacKenzie clan, all of whom wanted to kiss and hug and coo over baby Laria.

"They forgot all about us," I said to Luke as Bunny and Jack beamed over their newest grandchild. "We might as well be invisible."

He shot me a look.

"Kidding," I said, gently poking him in the arm. "This is a no-magick zone today."

"Good to know."

"Oh, crap," I muttered, gesturing toward the other side of the room. "Elspeth's lurking around the punch bowl."

Luke started across the room, but I pulled him back.

"Let's just keep an eye on her," I said.

We watched as she chatted up one of Luke's uncles.

"She's flirting with Uncle Matty." Luke sounded downright outraged.

"It gets worse," I said. "He's flirting back."

"There goes my appetite."

Luke's father joined us. His wide, handsome face was aglow with what looked like total bliss. He started to say something about baby Laria, but his hazel eyes filled with tears and his face crumpled up like a handkerchief. Next thing I knew, both Luke and I were enveloped in a bear hug that bordered on incarceration.

"Jeez, Pop!" Luke said when he came up for air. "Ease up on the Old Spice, will you?"

"He's your father," I chided Luke. "Show some respect."

"I love this girl," Jack said, giving me another hug. "You two should go ahead and get married."

"Pop," Luke warned. "Knock it off."

"You're young. You're in love. Chloe looks like a movie star —" He stopped mid-sentence. "Come to think of it, what's in the water around here? You're a knockout, Chloe, don't get me wrong, but you're practically the plain one around here! Even the olds guys on the scooters look like matinee idols." His chuckle was deep and gravelly. "Hell, I thought I saw Clark Gable near the hardware store."

Luke practically mugged his father to shut him up, but I burst into laughter. Yes, my cheeks were red-hot with embarrassment, but I knew he meant it as a compliment. Well, a sort-of compliment anyway.

"I think my old man's had a few too many rum punches," Luke said. "I'm going to snap some photos while he's still upright."

Jack was far too mellow to protest.

Some of the crew from Fully Caffeinated came forward to congratulate me on Laria's birth and Presentation.

"We wanted you to have this," Camille, one of the younger baristas, said as she handed me a beautiful log cabin crib quilt in every color of the rainbow. "We all worked on it. We tried to have it ready for your shower but didn't quite make it." She flipped it over and showed me the inscription complete with their names and the date of Laria's birth embroidered on the back.

"This is beautiful," I said as the tears threatened once again. "I can't believe you did this for us."

Camille cast a quick glance at her sister baristas and they all laughed. "Well, we can't believe little Laria is showing magick already. That was some display this morning at the Presentation."

"What display?"

She winked at me and lowered her voice to a stage whisper. "Oh, don't worry! You can be a proud mama around us. Who would think a baby with so much human blood would show so much talent so soon?"

Lynette joined us, and Camille and the crew smiled and drifted back into the crowd after I thanked them profusely one more time.

"Laria is all anyone's talking about," Lynette said to me. "They all seem to think she's presenting magick! Can you believe that?"

"That's exactly what Camille said. I didn't see any magick, did you?"

"Remember when you fell at the end of the ceremony?"

"I wish I could forget." My adventures in klutziness were legendary.

"Well, they don't think you tripped."

"Hello. Have they met me? I can trip over thin air." She looked so uncomfortable that I stopped short. "What do they think happened?"

"It's too ridiculous to even repeat."

"Repeat it," I said. "I want to know."

"They —" She looked away for a second

and shook her head. "They think Laria did it."

I started to laugh out loud. "Little six-pound-something Laria pushed me into a snowdrift?" My laughter grew louder. "Now that's funny!"

Lynette wasn't laughing. "They think her powers are coming in."

"She's a week old."

"I'm just telling you what I heard."

"I hope you told them how ridiculous an idea that is."

"Is it?"

I stared at her, openmouthed. "You're kidding, right?"

"I was there, Chloe. I've got to be honest with you: I didn't see you trip."

"Of course I tripped."

Lynette looked like she was a half step away from shifting into her canary persona and flying away.

"Don't you dare," I warned her, sotto voce. "This place is lousy with humans."

"You were moving forward, then suddenly you were airborne and moving backward. That's not how it happens when you trip."

"And when did you get your degree in physics, Mrs. Pendragon?"

"I don't need a degree to know what I saw and what I saw had nothing to do with tripping. I think you were shoved." She paused for effect. "Hard."

"And you're saying they — you — think that Laria somehow shoved me into Midge Stallworth."

"It *is* possible, you know. Not everyone takes as long to come into her powers as you did."

"In case you forgot, a Hobbs woman doesn't come into her full powers until she falls in love."

"And in case you weren't listening, I didn't say full powers."

"And here's where your logic goes off the rails," I said. "Do you realize the skill level required to propel an adult through the air? I'm not sure a full-blood magick could pull that one off at her age."

"Maybe she's gifted."

"Maybe you're delusional."

She shrugged. "Well, you asked." She glanced around the crowded room. "I'd better see what's taking Cyrus so long with that punch."

I couldn't remember the last time I saw Lynette move that fast.

"What's with Lynnie?" Janice asked as she joined me near the refreshment table. "She looked upset."

"We had a little confrontation, but it's all okay."

"I told her not to tell you. It's all ridiculous nonsense."

"About the baby having her powers already?"

"Laria's three-quarters human. She can't even hold her head upright yet."

"Exactly," I said. "I tripped. It's boring, but that's what happened."

Janice shot me a look. "You didn't trip."

"Not you, too, Jan."

"No, seriously. There was definitely magick involved." She leaned in close and lowered her voice. "I saw Simone aiming her boobs in Luke's direction. Maybe she decided to pull a little practical joke on the woman who stands between her and another conquest."

"If you're trying to be funny, I'm not laughing."

"Good, because I'm not trying to be funny."

The thought of Simone aiming her ample, albeit otherworldly, assets in Luke's general vicinity made me wish I could turn my fingertips into flamethrowers and singe Simone's extensions.

"First time this season I've been glad Lorcan is at sea," Janice said. "That woman is dangerous."

Simone was a ghost, but that hadn't stopped her from seducing more married and otherwise attached men than I had stitch markers. We spent a few gossipy minutes exchanging details about Simone's many conquests and bemoaning their terrible taste in bed partner.

"Where's Oprah when you need her?" I murmured and we both laughed like teenagers.

Midge Stallworth wandered over with a convoluted tale of in-law woes while I watched Laria being handed from one Mac-Kenzie to another while each moment was captured for posterity. Or, at the very least, next year's Christmas card.

"By the way, Luke's sister is crazy," Janice said as we poured ourselves some hot chocolate from a giant urn. "The guy kicks her out in the middle of nowhere and she's sobbing and texting him every two seconds."

I followed Janice's gaze and, sure enough, there was Meghan MacKenzie, thumbs flying across her smartphone, while she spilled her story to everyone within a ten-foot radius.

"I don't have a good feeling about this," I said. "First Elspeth is flirting with Luke's uncle and now his sister is confessing to

Verna Griggs."

"I wouldn't worry too much about her. My sister Sandy was the same way before she settled down," Janice said, reaching for a tea sandwich. "The worse a guy treated her, the more she wanted him. She fell in love with a werecat who had three other families and even that didn't stop her. She wouldn't know a good guy if he bit her in the ass."

"Metaphorically speaking, I hope."

"No, really," Janice said. "Werecats bite."

There was something wrong with the logic but I let it pass.

Luke had managed to group all of the MacKenzies together for photos and Elspeth wandered off into the crowd. I tried to keep my eye on her, but really, how much fun is it to stalk a troll?

Janice and I stood there watching and snacking as the MacKenzies continued to pass baby Laria around like a fluffy pink football. Everyone had to have his or her turn cooing over her, debating whom she looked like, and posing for pictures. Luke had snapped so many photos he had to swap out his battery for another one, and the party had only just begun. He must have been a shepherd in another life because he managed to keep his flock of family together and pretty much away from everyone else.

"So far, so good," I said to Janice. "I don't think they suspect anything, although his father did make a comment about the whole movie star thing. Maybe we need to take it down a notch."

"We're on our best behavior," Janice said with a mischievous wink. "Besides, I think we're all afraid of Luke's mother."

With good reason. Bunny was in full matriarch mode, focusing all of her formidable energies on her new granddaughter. She wasn't magick, but she might as well have been. She generated enough power to light the entire town.

"Bunny gave me three books on breast-feeding," I told Janice. "And two DVDs on early child development. I'm expecting a pop quiz by the end of the night."

Janice's eyes widened comically. "What about 'Care and Feeding of Your Baby Sorceress, Stages One through Seven'?"

"Thank gods we have years before we have to worry about that."

"I'll be honest," Janice said as we watched Bunny adjust the cap on Laria's downy head while Luke snapped candid shots of his siblings. "I don't know how you're going to keep the truth from them. There's no way that woman is going to be a hands-off granny."

"I don't know how, either," I admitted with a sigh. "Maybe they'll all decide to move to California and I won't have to worry about it." I could see some heavy-duty concealment charms would be needed before too long.

Bunny's voice floated toward us. "Who's the sweetest little girl in the world? . . . You are. . . . Grandma's sweet baby dumpling . . . you're so beautiful . . . yes, you are . . ."

"Yeah," Janice said with an eye roll, "that'll happen."

I was definitely going to have to dig deep into the Book of Spells to find a way to keep Luke's family close but still in the dark about Sugar Maple and their granddaughter's true heritage.

Suddenly I realized someone was missing from the happy family group.

"Where did Meghan go?" I asked Janice, looking around.

"I thought she was with Verna and her boys."

I tapped one of the baristas on the shoulder. "Have you seen Jeremy Griggs?" I asked.

"Sure," she said with a grin. "He and Adam went outside with Luke's sister to smoke."

We exchanged glances. That was all I needed, for Luke's sister to have a fling with one of Paul Griggs's werewolf sons, no matter how cute they were.

I was out the door at the speed of light.

23

CHLOE

The Griggs boys were nowhere in sight, but Meghan was walking up and down the sidewalk in front of town hall, talking animatedly into her cell phone. She glanced over at me and raised her hand in the universal *just a second* motion and continued talking. I couldn't make out her words, but I could tell by her tone that she was seriously pissed off.

I also noticed that two of the Souderbush boys were drifting right next to her, shamelessly eavesdropping on her conversation.

Fortunately they were both long dead. Otherwise we would definitely have a situation brewing.

I motioned for them to move on, but they refused. They both had been part of the human race many years ago and they relished contact with the living. Luke said they had taken to hanging out at the office with him, whittling and telling stories about New England during the Civil War. I wasn't sure how they managed to be visible to Luke and not to other humans, but as long as they didn't screw up today it wasn't any of my business.

I was shivering in the cold and my breasts were starting to get the buzzy, heavy feeling that usually preceded Laria's cry for milk. Time to herd this last MacKenzie back into the fold.

"Meghan," I said, raising my voice in what I hoped was an authoritative manner, "we need you inside."

She raised a finger and continued talking.

"Luke's on his last camera battery. Come on in and let him take your picture with Laria."

I don't know if she had run out of words or my tone scared her because she stuffed the cell phone into her pocket and walked over to me.

"He said he'd meet me by the 'Welcome to Sugar Maple' sign and drive me back to New Jersey when I was done here, but no way that's going to happen. He can bite me."

"Good," I said. Personally I hated ultimatums. They invariably brought out the worst in me. "No reason for you to be pushed around."

I noticed a light splash of Fae glitter on her left shoulder, a pale leaf-green that I wasn't familiar with. Probably one of the Salem transplants. I brushed it off and pretended it was snow.

Her eyes narrowed as she looked at me. "You think he was pushing me around?"

And you don't? "Sounds like it to me."

She frowned, causing deep pleats across the bridge of her nose. She looked so much like Luke that I almost laughed out loud. "Well, he did apologize. I mean, we've only been together less than two weeks. He said the whole family thing was too much for him. And, let's be honest, the MacKenzie family can be a little overwhelming."

I was proud of myself for saying absolutely nothing. Human females were crazy. No doubt about it. I had never been more grateful for my magick blood in my entire life. I'd take flaming fingertips over this torture any day.

"I heard you exploded at brunch last week."

I stared at her. "What?"

"Exploded," she repeated. "Threw a fit."

"I didn't explode or throw a fit."

"Jen said you told them off, then ran out of the room sobbing."

"I was nine months pregnant. Believe me, I wasn't running anywhere. Besides, I don't sob."

"But you were pissed off."

"The questions were too personal for my taste," I said, "and I told them so."

Her grin was pure Luke and I warmed toward her despite my misgivings. "Jen's a bitch — I can say that because she's my sister. Kim's not too bad. It took her forever to get pregnant so I'm really happy for her. She wanted it so much. Kevin's an asshole, but his wife's pretty cool. Ronnie's our dad's clone. Ronnie was already forty years old the day he was born. Patrick's got his problems. Did Luke tell you he screwed around on Siobhan? That's why she left him. Now he's trying to win her back, but I think she's moved on." The grin morphed into a rueful smile. "For a while Luke was the black sheep, but now that he's returned to the fold, I get my title back."

"Wow," I said with an answering grin. "All that without pausing for breath. I'm impressed."

"Too much, right?" She shook her mop of curls. "That's my biggest problem. Well, one of them anyway. I put it all out there, all the time. People don't like that."

"You mean men don't like that, right?"

She nodded. "You know how it is. There's this connection between you and some guy, and pow! Next thing you know you're in bed and you don't even know his name. It's all great when you're living the fantasy, but the minute it even looks like it might go somewhere they start running."

I swear to you this was better than a Lifetime movie. I could have listened to her all day. I mean, we were the same age, but our experiences couldn't have been more different. We spoke the same language, but we might as well have come from different planets.

"He looks happy," she said, changing subjects without warning. "I'm not sure I've ever seen him look this happy."

"He's wonderful with the baby," I said. "He bonded with her instantly."

"And he's in love with you."

I felt my cheeks flame again. "Well, it's mutual."

"So are you two getting married? Just between us. I won't tell the family."

"I honestly don't know, Meghan. We're pretty happy the way things are."

"Really?" Her eyebrows shot up to her hairline. "That doesn't sound like my big brother. Luke is definitely the marrying kind."

I was saved from having to think of something clever to say when two of the brothers MacKenzie joined us for a smoke.

"You don't mind," Kevin said as he lit up.

I gave him what I hoped was a sunny smile. "I'll let you know if I do."

Patrick bummed a cigarette from his brother and lit up, too, as he considered Meghan. "So why the hell weren't you at the brunch last week?"

"I was snowbound."

The two brothers exchanged glances. They also made that annoying snorting sound Luke made from time to time that was supposed to pass for intelligent commentary.

Meghan looked away, but not before I saw the vulnerable and lonely expression in her eyes.

"The wind is blowing the smoke my way," I said in a pleasant tone of voice. "Maybe you could move over there."

"No problem," Patrick said.

Kevin looked a little testy, but he followed his brother around the corner of the old church.

"Thanks," Meghan said. "I'm not in the mood for their crap today."

It didn't even occur to her that the smoke might really have bothered me.

She started tapping a message on her

278

phone. I never saw a pair of thumbs move so quickly.

"He's not answering," she said. "What is his problem? I'm the one who should be pissed."

I probably shouldn't have asked, but I couldn't help myself. "If you don't go with him, how do you plan to get home?" It wasn't like I thought she should go with him, but I couldn't transport her or anything. I was keeping magick way out of the picture.

"I can hitch a ride with Patrick down to Connecticut or go back to Mass. with the folks." She shot me a look. "Maybe I could hang out here awhile and give you a hand with the baby."

Another houseguest? Time to change the subject.

"Come on," I said, moving toward the door to the old church. "I want a picture of you with Laria."

She shoved her phone back into her pocket and followed me inside.

The room felt different on a cellular level. The emptiness was palpable. My heart started to ache in a way that was totally unfamiliar.

Funny thing how quickly you can scan a room. Maybe it was living with a cop all

279

these months or (more likely) watching cop shows like my life depended on it, but I had developed the ability to look at a room and take in all the salient details without even realizing I was doing it.

Luke, his father, Jack, and Kevin's wife, Tiffany, were drinking coffee and chatting with Paul and Verna Griggs in the corner. Bunny was admiring Lynette's wedding shawl while Midge regaled her with stories about life in a funeral parlor. His sisters were attempting to keep the MacKenzie grandkids from decimating the food table while the uncles and aunts gossiped and tried to pump the townies for info on what I was really like.

"The baby." The words tore from my throat. "Where's the baby?"

Time stopped. Nobody moved. I felt like I was trapped in a nightmare.

"Where's my baby?" I cried.

"Remember when you stopped to change memory cards?" Archie the troll said to Luke. "I think I saw Elspeth take her off to change her diaper."

"Elspeth!" Luke's roar soared to the rafters.

Nothing. Not even the faintest smell of stale waffles in response.

"Elspeth!" I cried. "Please, please don't

do this!"

"Do what?" Bunny's eyes were troubled. I think I unnerved her more than the situation. "She's your nanny. Honey, don't get so upset or you won't make it to Laria's first birthday. It's only a diaper change."

She was smiling, but I wasn't. The sense of dread that had been hovering around me for weeks grew exponentially stronger.

Luke and I burst out of the church. He collared his brothers, who had gone back to smoking near the front door.

"Have you seen the baby?"

"Sure, I have," Kevin said, tossing his cigarette butt to the snowy ground. "You took our picture together, remember?"

Not the right answer.

"We think our nanny took her for some reason," I said, trying not to sound like I was on the verge of hysteria. "Have you seen them?"

"You mean that Betty White lookalike who was all over Uncle Matt?" Patrick asked.

Luke nodded, his jaw muscles working furiously.

"I'm pretty sure I saw her about ten minutes ago." Patrick pointed in the general direction of the cemetery grounds. "She was heading that way."

"Was the baby with her?" Luke asked.

"Hard to tell," Patrick said. "She was all huddled over."

I closed my eyes and, dangerous or not, I sent thought probes out toward the old cemetery. One must have bounced off Luke's sister Jen, because I heard an annoyed "Ouch!" from her direction but too bad. I almost cried with joy when a soothing wave of acknowledgment flowed through me almost immediately. Laria? It had to be. I have to admit I was surprised that a newborn could transmit such a strong signal. Surprised and more than a little bit proud. Laria's response was followed closely by an angry and downright painful buzz that could only belong to Elspeth.

"They're together," I whispered to Luke as friends and relatives spilled from the church onto the sidewalk and into the street. I told him about the thought probes. "The baby is fine and she's definitely with Elspeth."

He said things he would live to regret if they were repeated in a court of law, but he was only human, after all, and very upset. "When I get my hands on that —"

"First find them," I said, trying to quell my own rising panic, "then we'll figure out what to do about Elspeth." I gave him the thought probe coordinates, as best I could, and it definitely sounded like they were at or near the burial ground.

Sometimes Luke forgot exactly what he was dealing with here in Sugar Maple. Elspeth's powers were formidable. The other trolls in town were in awe of her abilities. Even Janice, who was distantly related to her on Elspeth's mother's side, looked at the cantankerous old crone with unabashed awe. I couldn't imagine Luke coming out ahead in any battle he fought with Elspeth.

Jack MacKenzie sprang into action while Luke and I exchanged information.

"Spread out," Jack ordered his family. "Check every street, knock on every door, look behind every shrub. If nobody answers your knock, kick the door down, but find that baby."

"Hold on a second!" Lilith's husband, Archie, stormed up to Jack in high dudgeon. "Kick my door down and I'll kick your ass!"

Lilith put a calming hand on Archie's shoulder. "He's upset, Archie," she said in a soft voice. "He won't really kick down our door."

"The hell I won't." Jack stared at the short and furious troll. "That's my granddaughter we're talking about. I'll burn this town down if that's what it takes."

Definitely not the right thing to say.

The town went berserk. The crew from Assisted Living aimed their scooters straight at Jack while calling out his ancestry in colorful terms.

Poor Jack. He had no way of knowing Sugar Maple's backstory, how our fore-mothers and forefathers had fled persecution in Salem to find freedom here.

But there was a definite upside to the melee.

"Go now!" I whispered to Luke while the MacKenzies and the townspeople squared off. "You can find Laria and straighten this all out before Jack and Archie stop yelling at each other."

He took off at a run for the burial grounds.

I turned to find Meghan looking at me with a quizzical look on her face.

"You take your crowd," I said, "and I'll take mine. We'll hope for the best." As long as magick didn't break out and turn the garden-variety brouhaha into a nuclear meltdown we had a chance.

"Sounds like a plan," she said and we waded into the fray.

"Frank!" I cried. "Manny! Rose! Everyone! Turn off those scooters and get a grip."

"He threatened to burn down the town," Archie the troll cried. "I heard him myself."

"Why are we wasting time arguing?"

Meghan said. "We should be out looking for Laria. She's the only thing that's important right now."

"It's the man's grandchild, Archie," Lilith said in that soothing voice of hers. "You can't blame him for being upset." And if she put the slightest extra emphasis on the word "man" only the magick would notice.

It worked. Archie backed down. Jack scaled back his rhetoric. And two minutes later they all headed out to scour Sugar Maple for my daughter.

"Where did Luke go?" Meghan glanced around at the departing crowd.

"He figured Elspeth might have taken the baby back to our cottage. He went to check." Lies, lies, and more lies. I would have felt guilty, but the stakes were way too high. Besides, she'd never believe the truth.

"Funny thing," Meghan said, looking at me intently, "but you don't look half as upset as you did a few moments ago."

Crap. As far as I knew she had never been a cop, but there was no doubt she had inherited the same detective genes as her brother. "This is a very safe town. Besides, she's with her nanny."

"You mean that weird Betty White lookalike."

"Elspeth," I said, "and I don't really see

285

the resemblance." Definitely time to tone down the Hollywood vibe.

"Five minutes ago I thought you were going to have a stroke. Now you're okay with it. Did I miss something?"

I made a silly face and rolled my eyes for emphasis. "Hormones," I said, falling back on that age-old excuse for crazy behavior by both sexes. "One second I'm happy, the next second I'm crying my eyes out. And here I thought PMS was bad!"

It was a lie. I knew it was a lie and I'm pretty sure she did, too.

But then her new boyfriend texted her and she forgot about my lie, about me, about everything but the words on the screen.

Whoever he was, I owed him a big, fat thank-you.

24

LUKE

I took off for the burial grounds like the hounds of hell were after me. I shot down Osborne skidding on patches of ice and new-fallen snow.

Laria.

I could see her tiny face in front of me, hear those soft, mewling cries.

I'd known from the start that something wasn't right with Elspeth. From the very beginning I could see we were headed down a dangerous road with the elusive, intractable troll Samuel had set on our house like one of the biblical plagues and I couldn't understand why Chloe remained blind to the truth.

Hell, she could be mixed up with the Salem Fae who had settled in Sugar Maple a few months ago. The Salem Fae had pledged their loyalty but centuries-old animosities didn't disappear overnight. Unless I missed my guess, not all of the Salem Fae had been in favor of the decision and it was just a matter of time before trouble started.

Sugar Maple existed and thrived in the world of mortals and you only had to spend five seconds with Elspeth to know her opinion of my species. Elspeth and the more disgruntled members of the Salem contingent? It wouldn't surprise me one bit if they had formed some kind of alliance.

First Elspeth marked my daughter's head with some weird red dot and now it looked like she had spirited Laria off to an old burial ground where nobody except Chloe's father was actually buried.

Nobody was going to take my child to a cemetery and perform some weird mumbo-jumbo rite. I'd had a bellyful of strange-ass shit since coming to Sugar Maple and I had learned to accept what was good and ignore the rest. But hell, Elspeth wasn't even part of Sugar Maple. I didn't give a damn that Samuel Bramford had given her marching orders before he pierced the veil or died or whatever happened to magicks when they left this realm. All I knew was that I was putting a stop to it now.

Elspeth's back was to me as I approached, her cape spread out around her like a giant pup tent. She was crooning something in that rusty-nail voice of hers, more sounds than words, although if they were words they definitely weren't in English. I listened hard for sounds from Laria, but heard nothing, and a hot rush of adrenaline shot through my veins.

I crept up slowly, quietly, careful to ease my feet into the snow rather than crunch my way toward her. Elspeth was magick and magick meant powers humans could only guess at. I had experienced magick for myself last spring and I knew exactly what I was up against. The troll might be old, but her powers were formidable. If she chose to turn them against me I didn't stand a chance.

If she sensed my approach she didn't let on. Maybe she was in some kind of zone. Whatever the reason, I wasn't complaining. I needed time to locate Laria and scope out the situation before I made my move.

Except suddenly I couldn't move at all. I tried to take another step and another. I didn't feel different, but I hadn't moved an inch. I watched in horror as Elspeth slowly began to rise above the ground until she floated a good ten feet off the earth, her gruesome black cape swirling in the snowy late afternoon wind.

"Fool." Her tone was rich with scorn. "The truth lies before your human eyes, but ye cannot see. Go now before you cause unending harm."

She was wrong. I could see, and what I saw was my daughter lying on the slab of stone that marked Aerynn's resting place, surrounded by swirling clouds of color and light that entwined themselves around her tiny exposed limbs and danced across her forehead in shimmering formations that made me feel like puking.

"Touch her again," I said, "and I'll kill you."

" 'Twould be the human answer to everything," she said, "but there be worse that can happen than earthly death."

She swooped downward and cradled Laria's tiny face between her gnarled hands and exhaled loudly into the baby's mouth. My gag reflex kicked in and I came close to losing my breakfast.

The baby laughed, or what passed for a laugh in a one-week-old child, and then Elspeth vanished, along with the clouds and my paralysis.

I lurched forward, limbs strangely rusty with disuse even though only seconds had passed, and dropped to my knees next to Aerynn's memorial stone. A familiar buzzing moved through me, the same feeling I always got when I visited the burial ground. They may not have interred bodies here, but there were enough energies present to light Sugar Maple for centuries to come.

Laria gurgled, her arms outstretched in the loosely wrapped blanket. I noticed a faint damp sparkle smeared across her forehead, but other than that she appeared happy and unharmed. I bundled her up tightly and, holding her against my chest inside my shirt, made my way quickly back to Chloe before anything else happened.

"I know you're following me," I said out loud as I plowed through unshoveled snow. "I can smell you, Elspeth."

There was no response, but the odor of stale waffles intensified the closer we got to the old church we used as a town hall. The crafty old bitch was cloaking, biding her time until she could swoop in and pull another one of her tricks.

Whatever the hell she was up to, it had to stop now before it was too late.

CHLOE

Luke had found Elspeth and Laria at the old cemetery just as I'd hoped. He pulled me aside and told me about the ceremony he had interrupted and although I tried to

291

tamp down his nuclear anger with soothing words about rituals and traditions from the Old World I was seriously freaked out. Who in their right mind would take a lightly covered newborn out in a winter snowfall? And don't get me started on the whole stretched-out-on-a-grave-marker-and-blowing-in-her-mouth thing or I'd really go off.

None of it made any sense. Elspeth was here to protect Laria, not harm her, but the things she had done since the baby's birth often fell into the second category. Was it possible she had a hidden agenda, one that had nothing to do with the reason Samuel had sent her to us before he left this dimension forever? Luke definitely thought so.

Elspeth was a pain in the butt, but there was a part of me that had grown perversely fond of her. Call me crazy, but I didn't want to believe she had kidnapped our daughter, laid her atop Aerynn's grave marker, and set colorful clouds dancing across her body. I mean, would you?

Of course we didn't tell his family what had really happened.

We went with the story about germs and diapers and a maybe-a-wee-bit-too-old nanny who had become overzealous in the performance of her duties and whisked the baby home where she could keep her safe from random sneezes.

Relief spread from one side of town to the other. And to say the MacKenzies were happy is putting it mildly. Their love and concern for Laria was powerful and genuine. She was one of their clan. If something happened to me today, they would be there to help Luke keep her safe.

Well, at least until her magick kicked in.

Meghan stayed around long enough to give Laria a kiss and then announced she was off to meet her new boyfriend.

"I don't like this," Bunny said as Meghan made her quick good-byes to the rest of the family. "Whoever he is, he should drive here and pick her up."

"He doesn't want to meet the family," Jen said with a knowing smile. "That's not a good sign."

Then again, Meghan and her mystery man had been together less than two weeks. Nobody but a Kardashian boyfriend met the family that soon.

But I kept my mouth shut.

And then there was the minor fact that Luke was downright homicidal with anger. According to him, Elspeth had refused to give an inch by way of explanation or apology. She had stopped him literally in his tracks while she finished whatever bizarre ritual she was performing, then cloaked herself without a word.

No doubt about it. The Elspeth party was definitely over, but unfortunately a whole lot of partygoers still remained.

The MacKenzies were like a small army. I'm not sure what I had been thinking when we invited them en masse to see the baby. I'm not sure we had been thinking at all. I'd had some half-baked idea about opening the shop and hiring the house sprites to whip up a buffet spread fit for humans, but the days since Laria's birth were all a blur. The only thing I knew for sure was that I had never gotten around to doing any of it.

I guess I just hadn't realized how many of them would actually show up. There was no way we could fit them all into the cottage and, with Luke in the mood he was in, I was pretty sure they wouldn't want to be there even if we could.

Unfortunately house sprites took off on the weekends to some uncharted place in a different dimension. I knew that Renate frequently employed them around the inn, so I cornered her to ask if she thought they would make an exception in an emergency.

"Not a chance. They disengage with the world on our Saturdays and Sundays." I must have looked distraught because she patted my hand kindly. (Hard to believe we had been at each other's throats a few months before.) "Tell me what's wrong. Maybe I can help."

I did, in as few sentences as possible.

"We can open the restaurant for them," Renate offered. "I'll call in one of the chefs to help Colm, and Bettina and I can handle the front."

"You're a lifesaver," I said, giving her the kind of hug that was impossible when she was her usual tiny Fae self. "I don't know how I'll be able to thank you for this."

"I can't give them rooms," she warned me. "The Spirit Trail is very active right now and we're actually doubling up on accommodations."

The thought of the MacKenzie clan mixing with the Spirit Trail travelers was horrifying. But then, anything that brought Luke's family in contact with the real Sugar Maple sent arrows of terror through my heart.

"We'll figure something," I said, even though I couldn't imagine what.

I pulled Bunny aside and explained that Luke and I had to go home and deal with our "nanny problem" but would join the family at the inn as soon as we could.

"You do what you have to do, honey," she said. "We understand."

I was somewhere beyond exhausted and it was starting to show. I almost fell asleep during the four-minute drive back to the cottage. Not even Laria's hungry cries from the backseat penetrated.

Somehow we all managed to make it home and that was when the fun started.

"Elspeth is out of here tonight," Luke said as he paced back and forth in our tiny kitchen. "I don't know what that bitch is going to do next and I'm not going to take a chance with our daughter's life."

I was sitting on the floor changing the baby and trying to keep curious cats from exploring the newest member of our household. "She was performing a ritual," I explained for the third or fourth time. "She was connecting Laria with her forebears and asking them for protection."

At least that was what Janice said and I wanted to believe she was right.

"Why would the baby need more protection?" he asked. "This entire town is protected against discovery."

"No system is perfect." I reminded him of some of the glitches he had experienced during his brief time in Sugar Maple. "Besides, when it comes to keeping Laria safe, isn't too much better than too little?"

"Sorry, but I'm not buying it," he said, still pacing the room. "I think she's up to something."

I looked up from diaper duty. "What could she be up to? She spent the last three hundred years doing Samuel's bidding. Do you really think she would screw up his last wish?"

Suddenly the room filled with the smell of stale waffles and I saw Elspeth sitting on top of the refrigerator like a gargoyle.

"The babe must be guarded," she said, staring down at Luke with disdain. "The old ways must be followed."

I'm not sure Luke could feel the power vibrating from the rotund troll, but I was stunned by its force. I didn't doubt her loyalty to Samuel, but she was still not a being to trifle with.

"We had the Presentation ceremony," I reminded her as I made sure the baby's diaper was fastened the way it should be. "That's one of our oldest rituals. The baby now has a heartmother to help her move through life."

"There be more what's necessary," she said in that nails-on-the-blackboard voice of hers. She aimed her look straight at Luke. "Danger is everywhere and she must be protected even from the blood."

Luke stopped pacing right beneath the refrigerator. He glared up at her, bringing the full force of his years as a big-city cop into play. A lesser troll might have decided this was a good time to head for home but not Elspeth. She met his fierce gaze with one of her own.

"Enough with the dark looks and mysterious comments," Luke exploded. "If you've got something to say, then goddamn say it. Otherwise get the hell out of here and stay out."

"I say what I say. I do what I do. No more, no less than possible."

"See?" Luke turned to me in exasperation. "How the hell do you deal with that crap? We need an interpreter."

"Are we in danger?" I asked Elspeth.

"That depends."

"Is Laria in danger?"

"The babe needs keeping."

When it came to nonanswer answers, the troll was a genius.

I pulled in a deep breath and tried to calm the tingling sensation building in my fingertips. I did not want to go mano a mano with a troll. Especially not one with centuries of practice under her belt.

"Why are you so worried, Elspeth? Are we

in danger?" Maybe this was some weird troll ritual and I had to ask three times before she would answer.

"What is danger?" she asked with a shrug of her plump shoulders.

"Now she thinks she's Bill Clinton," Luke muttered. "Next she'll be asking us what *is* is."

I shot him a look. Confrontation wasn't going to get us anywhere with Elspeth, but maybe it was time to play my trump card.

"I'm sorry you won't share your thoughts with us, Elspeth," I said with a sad smile and a shake of my head. "Samuel would be very disappointed if he knew you were holding back information we might need to keep Laria safe."

"I do what I do. More can't be done."

I pushed a little harder. "Why did you take the baby today? What were you trying to do?"

She spun around, butter yellow hair flying like the ropy strings on an old-fashioned mop, faster and faster until she was only a blur of motion.

"Elspeth!" I brought my hands down in a slicing motion. "No more!"

I shouldn't have tried magick against her, but I was getting desperate. I'm not saying I managed to stop her entirely (the magick

Samuel had protected her with was too strong), but I surprised her enough that she slowed down. I considered it a small victory.

"Your job here is done," Luke said. "We want you out of here tonight."

Shimmers of heat radiated outward from Elspeth. "No human orders me about."

"Then you will listen to me, Elspeth," I said. "It hurts me to say this, but we don't want you living in our home any longer."

The look she gave me chilled my bones, but I held firm. It wasn't an angry look or a look of hurt or embarrassment. What I saw in her eyes was something that unnerved me more: I saw pity.

"And none of that cloaking shit," Luke said. "I want your ass back in Salem."

I shot Luke a warning look, but I wasn't sure he saw it. Diplomacy wasn't necessarily his strong suit.

"You fulfilled Samuel's request," I said calmly. "Now Laria is my responsibility. The Book of Spells says it is so."

She considered my words for an uncomfortably long time, then nodded her bright yellow head. "So be it."

And with that she stepped into the space between her world and ours and was gone.

"Did you see that?" I asked Luke. "It was

like she parted a curtain."

"Yeah, well, last time she did that she was still here in Sugar Maple watching everything."

"I don't think she's in Sugar Maple any longer," I said. "Something feels different."

He sniffed the air. "I don't smell funky waffles. That's something."

"No, it's more than that." I didn't want to tell him that the energies surrounding Laria had dimmed the moment Elspeth vanished, almost as if a ring of guardianship had been removed. Maybe we hadn't done the right thing after all. "I can feel her absence."

"You think I'm wrong about her." It was a statement, not a question.

"Yes," I said. "I think she was telling the truth about why she took Laria."

"And I think she was lying through her crooked little teeth." Those muscles in his jaw were working overtime again. "What about that mark on the baby's head? Where did that come from? I'm still waiting for someone to explain it."

He wasn't buying his mother's strawberry angioma explanation.

"I told Janice about it and she said I have the same mark on my head."

He looked like I'd told him I had suddenly sprouted a unicorn horn.

"Take a look," I urged him. "It's not like it's something I can see for myself."

He stood behind me, moving my hair this way and that. "Son of a bitch," he said. "She's right. You do have the same mark on your head."

"Feel better?"

He nodded, some of the day's tension draining from his face.

To my surprise, I felt better, too. It wasn't that I thought Elspeth was a danger to Laria, but the sudden appearance of that red dot had unnerved me more than I had been willing to admit. If we both sported it, it was probably some kind of Hobbs birthmark and nothing to worry about.

Then again, Elspeth had been around since the days of Aerynn. Who could say she hadn't placed the mark on my head thirty years ago?

But that was the kind of chicken-and-egg argument I didn't have time for. Not with an inn filled with Fae and family waiting for us.

I fed the baby and we drove to the inn for an early dinner with the MacKenzies.

"Kevin and Tiffany had to leave," Bunny said over the remains of her roast beef with all the trimmings. "They said they'll call."

Jen and her husband and kids were gone.

Ronnie and his family were halfway out the door.

"I'll Skype you this week," Kim said as she finished her dessert. "I want all the details about the delivery."

"No, you don't," Bunny said, breaking into the conversation. "Every delivery is different. You're not planning on giving birth in the back of a truck, are you?"

"No, but —"

"Worry about your own situation, Kimberly, not Chloe's."

Kim rolled her eyes in her mother's direction, but she did it with great affection. "I don't think Chloe planned on giving birth in a truck, either."

"Can't say that I did," I agreed. "I'd been planning on a home birth."

"A home birth!" Bunny sounded horrified. "My God, what were you thinking?"

"She was probably thinking hospitals are germ factories waiting to infect you with staph and who knows what else," Kim said, leaping to my defense. "I've thought about home birthing our baby, too."

"Over my dead body," Bunny said. "I put in over thirty years as a nurse. I know what can happen during a delivery. The hospital is the best place for you."

"You were in cardiac, Ma," Kim reminded

her. "I don't think you assisted at too many deliveries."

"Laria is healthy and happy," I said, glancing toward the baby who was sleeping in her Snugli, tiny face pressed against Luke's chest. "That's the important thing."

"I can't believe you're out and about only a week later," Kim said. "I thought you'd receive us from your fainting couch."

"I can't believe the nonsense you're spouting, Kimberly." Bunny shook her head in dismay. "She gave birth. She's not recovering from surgery. Of course she's out and about."

Conversation ebbed and flowed around me as I picked at my chicken with sun-dried tomatoes. Suddenly I was so tired I wanted to crawl into a Snugli myself and sleep for a week or two.

"That's it," Bunny said, tossing her napkin on the table next to her empty dessert plate. "It's time for you to go home and go to bed."

Luke, who had been dozing himself, awoke with a start while I nodded mutely. Home. Bed. Sleep. What's not to like?

Renate thanked everyone warmly for visiting the inn. She waved off the check, but I would take care of it the next day. I noticed that Jack left a very generous tip, which made me happy. Like father, like son.

After another flurry of good-byes as MacKenzies headed back to their various homes.

All except Bunny and Jack, who walked out to the parking lot with us.

"Better hit the road, Pop," Luke said as he strapped the baby into her car seat. "You've got a long ride home."

"Oh, we're not going home," Bunny said with a chuckle.

Maybe if we hadn't been so tired we would have known what was coming next, but sleep deprivation had dulled our faculties to the point where we didn't know our own names without checking our driver's licenses.

"Darn right we're not going home," Jack said, putting an arm around each of us while Laria peered up at him from her Snugli. "We're staying here with you."

25

CHLOE

"Look at those faces!" Bunny said through her laughter. "We don't mean we're going to stay at your house. We're going to stay here at the inn."

This was wrong on so many levels I didn't know where to begin.

"You — you have a room at the inn?" I asked, knowing that was utterly impossible.

"Well, not yet," Bunny admitted, "but we're going to talk to that lovely Renate and set something up."

"I don't think you can, Ma," Luke said, sounding as shell-shocked as I was feeling. "Last I heard, they were full up."

"Actually they're not," Bunny said. "I checked."

Time to pick my jaw up from the floor. "Renate told you that?"

Bunny made a dismissive gesture with her hands. "I saw it for myself."

Oh, gods, this wasn't going to end well.

"What did you do, Ma?" Luke asked.

Jack rolled his eyes. "What do you think she did?" he said. "She stuck her big nose where it doesn't belong."

Bunny looked defiant and defensive. "I took a little tour of the place," she said. "What's so terrible about that?"

"Does the term *private property* mean anything to you?" Luke asked.

"It's an *inn,* Luke," Bunny said. "A public place."

"Don't look at me," Jack said, hands up in surrender. "I can't control her."

"The rooms are beautiful," Bunny continued, "and every single one I saw was unoccupied."

Luke looked to me for help, but no way was I tackling his mother.

He gave me a look and plunged forward. "And it never occurred to you the guests might be out."

Bunny sighed in obvious exasperation. "Trust me, Luke. I'm old enough to recognize when a room is empty and when it isn't."

One night, I thought, as Luke and I exchanged glances. It wouldn't be that bad.

"We'll check out Christmas Eve morning and drive home," Bunny said with a big smile. "We'd only need a room for a week. I'm sure they can do something for us."

"No time like the present to find out," Jack said. "Let's ask them."

"No!" I sounded like a crazy woman, but I didn't care. "Let me see if I can call in a favor or two."

I raced back into the inn and cornered Renate and Colm in the hallway.

"Tell me there's no room at the inn," I begged.

"There's no room at the inn," Renate said with a chuckle, "but we do have a double available at a good price."

"Luke's parents want to help out with the baby for a few days and they need a place to stay."

"They can't stay here," Colm said with a wink. "Sorry, but we're all booked up."

I ran back outside to deliver the bad news.

His parents looked crestfallen and I felt a little guilty for feeling like we'd dodged a bullet.

"Wait!" Jack's eyes lit up with excitement. "I think I saw a motel a few miles outside of town. We could stay there."

"Bedbugs," Luke said. "Big scandal. You don't want to do that."

"This is terrible," Bunny said, looking like she was about to cry. "You don't have a family of your own, honey, and I think it's the grandmother's place to help her kids with a new baby. I did it for Ronnie and Deni. I did it for Jen. I did it for Patrick and Kevin and I was so happy that I could do it for you."

What was I supposed to say to that? This was what families did. They helped each other.

I took a deep breath and jumped into the deep end of the pool.

"Stay with us tonight," I said, trying to ignore the look of total shock on Luke's face. "We'll figure out what to do tomorrow."

"The place is small," Luke warned. "The guest room has all the baby stuff in it and a lot of Chloe's yarn."

"And spinning wheels," I added. "We planned to have everything straightened out by the time Laria came, but she surprised us."

"We don't mind small," Bunny said with a wave of her hand. "All we want is to be with you and the baby."

"How small is small?" Jack was beginning to sound concerned.

Luke shrugged. "Maybe eight by ten."

"That's small," Jack said, nodding. "If I sneeze, I'll probably blow out a window."

"Jack!" Bunny shot him a reproving look. "We'll be just fine. We're early risers so we can feed the baby while the two of you get a little extra sleep."

"I'm nursing," I reminded her.

"Express your milk so I can give her a bottle."

My head was starting to spin. Maybe I should have urged them toward the hot-sheet motel after all.

"Am I the only one here who's freezing his ass off?" Luke asked. "Let's continue this at home."

My stomach dropped at the realization of what I had done. Our tiny cottage was not made for visitors. Last year Luke's ex spent a few nights with us (which is a whole other story) and I don't think I got a second of sleep the whole time. When it comes to homemaking I'm not exactly Martha Stewart and it takes a yearly visit from my house sprite friends to keep me from drowning in clutter.

"Did you clean the litter boxes this morning?" I asked Luke as we pulled out of the parking lot.

"I changed three diapers. Does that count?"

"I can't remember the last time we changed the litter. I don't imagine your parents are cat people, are they?"

"My mother has plastic covers on the living room sofa."

"This is going to be a disaster."

And don't get me started on the whole magick part of the equation.

At home Luke maneuvered the Jeep alongside my Buick, which left his parents' minivan hanging out on the street. Not that we ever had any traffic, but both Bunny and Jack were starting to look a little stressed out so I asked Luke if he would move the Buick to the street and let his parents pull next to his Jeep.

"Besides," I said, "that'll give me a minute to race through the house and make sure nothing weird is going on in there." A flatware conga line. Mini tornados on the kitchen table. Self-opening roofs. I'd seen it all and wanted to make sure Bunny and Jack didn't get the surprise of their lives.

I was brushing cat hair off the living room sofa when Bunny walked in.

"You have cats," she said.

I crumped the hairy wad of Scotch tape in my hand and stood up. "Four of them," I said. "Five, if you count Penny the store cat." Of course Penelope was a great deal more than a store cat, but there was such a thing as TMI.

"I didn't know Luke liked cats."

"I'm not sure he likes cats in general, but he's pretty fond of our crew."

She nodded and I could see the wheels spinning inside her fluffy blond head.

Pyewacket and Lucy strolled in from the kitchen and began to purr and wind themselves around Bunny's ankles.

"They like you," I said as I dropped the tape into the nearest wastebasket. "They don't like just anyone."

I'm not sure Bunny felt particularly honored, but she nodded and forced a smile.

I took pity on her and scooped the two girls up and deposited them a few feet away just in time for the next kitty onslaught. Blot and Dinah, meowing loudly, entwined themselves around Bunny's ankles where the other two had left off.

"That's exactly how they reacted when they met Luke," I said. "It must be genetic."

"What did you say their names are?"

I gave her a quick rundown on who was who and to my surprise she bent down and gave Blot a cautious scratch behind her right ear. Blot, instantly delirious with joy, flung herself across Bunny's boots and presented her belly for admiration and attention.

"You'll never get rid of her now," I laughed.

Bunny crouched down to do Blot's bidding while I took the opportunity to race down the short hallway to the guest room and shovel a path to the bed. Were the sheets clean? I hoped so, but there wasn't time to find out. Everything seemed in order. Cluttered, but at least there were no signs of any outbreaks of magick as far as I could see.

There was nothing left to do but cross my fingers and hope for the best.

LUKE

"No arguments," my mother said as she shooed Chloe away. "I ran a bath for you. Go! Enjoy!"

"You heard her," I said. "We'll hold down the fort."

She disappeared down the hallway before I finished my sentence.

My mother was sitting in the rocking chair by the living room window, cradling Laria, who showed no interest in sleep.

"You, too," my mother said to me. "You look terrible. Go get some sleep. That's why I'm here. Take advantage of your father and me while you can."

"Laria," I said. "She'll need —"

"I raised seven of these," she reminded me. "I think I have a pretty good idea what

313

she needs and when she needs it."

"Her bassinet is in our room."

"Why don't we put it in the guest room overnight?"

"Have you seen the guest room?" my dad asked. "We're lucky we can fit in there."

"You're going to need a bigger house soon," my mother said over Laria's steady crying.

"The cottage is big enough for us."

"But not for two adults, four cats, and a toddler."

"We have time."

"It goes faster than you think, Luke."

"You two lived in a four-room apartment until just before I came along."

My mother flashed me a smile. "That's how I know you'll need a bigger place."

"Listen to her, son," my dad said. "She knows what she's talking about."

I didn't even try to hold back my yawn. "I'm going to take you up on your babysitting offer and hit the sack."

I made sure my folks had access to food, drink, and baby paraphernalia and took off before my mother had a chance to offer any more suggestions.

"She means well," Chloe said later as she climbed into bed next to me. "She wants everything to be perfect for us."

"She's planning to reorganize the kitchen while she's here."

"The kitchen?"

"That got your attention," I said with a tired laugh.

"There's nothing wrong with the kitchen. I know where everything is."

"She'll probably Dewey decimal your cookbooks."

"I don't have any cookbooks."

"Metaphorically speaking."

"Oh, hush," she said, curling up against my side and resting her head on my shoulder. "I'm too tired for multisyllables."

I grinned into the darkness. "Me, too."

"Do you think the baby is okay?"

"Yes."

"Does your mother know where we keep the diapers and everything?"

"Yes."

She gave me a light sock in the arm. "I'm too tired for multisyllables, not multiwords."

"Got it."

She started to giggle. "I like your parents."

I pulled her closer and stifled a yawn. "They like you, too."

She was quiet for a long moment and I thought she'd gone to sleep. "I miss Laria."

"Want me to get her?"

"No," she murmured through a yawn.

"Bunny and Jack need some time with her."

And just like that we let down our guard and trouble walked right in.

26

CHLOE

I woke up with a start and poked Luke in the side. "Did you hear that?"

"Mmm-mmph," he said, burying his face deeper in his pillow.

"You didn't hear that yelp?"

Maybe he couldn't hear it over his snoring.

Laria wasn't in her bassinet, which meant I wasn't going back to sleep until I found out what the yelping was about.

"Nothing to worry about," Jack said as I stumbled sleepily into the living room. "Everybody's fine."

Laria was lying on the floor in a soft and cozy nest of blankets. She wore a pale peach onesie with watercolor bunny rabbits on it and was happily kicking her arms and legs like it was early morning instead of late at night. I bent down next to her and she clutched at my finger with one tiny hand

and my heart did that crazy lurching thing it did every time I saw her.

"Where's Bunny?" I asked, looking up at a slightly disheveled Jack.

He looked down at his feet and my early-warning system went off. "She's — uh, she's in the bathroom." He met my eyes briefly, then glanced away. "She had a little accident."

"Watch the baby," I said, then raced down the hall.

"Now, don't worry," Bunny said when I burst into the tiny bathroom. She was sitting on the closed toilet seat running cold water over a hand towel. "It was just one of those freak things."

I stared at her in disbelief. "You're getting a black eye." A horrible thought popped into my head. "Did Jack —"

She laughed, then winced in pain. "Actually it was Laria."

"Laria?" It was my turn to laugh. "No, seriously, Bunny. How did it happen?"

"It was Laria," she repeated. "I was tickling her tummy during a diaper change and she kicked me in the face."

I made all the right noises, but I found it hard to believe my week-old infant could kick hard enough to do any damage at all. A poke in the eye? Sure. But Bunny's eye looked like it ran into a small but powerful fist.

Was it possible the MacKenzies really had mixed it up in the living room and Bunny was covering for her husband? I pushed the thought out of my head. Maybe she had had one of those klutzy accidents (the kind I had all the time) that were too embarrassing to own up to and she had substituted a little white lie.

I had no idea, but there was one thing I knew for sure: Laria couldn't possibly have done it.

"You need ice," I said as I took a good look at the quickly bruising area. "I'll be right back."

I dashed to the kitchen, grabbed an ice tray from the freezer, and hurried back to the bathroom.

"I'm supposed to be the nurse," Bunny said with a rueful smile as I wrapped the ice cubes in a damp towel. "I should be taking care of you."

"I brought you some ice cubes," I said with a laugh. "I didn't perform surgery."

"I'm sorry I woke you," she said, wincing as she pressed the cubes against her eye. "You must be wishing Jack and I had stayed somewhere else."

"We're glad you're here," I said. "All three

of us are."

And the strange thing was I meant it. Not the black eye part, but the rest of it.

An hour later Bunny and Jack were safely ensconced in our minuscule guest room. Laria was asleep in her bassinet. And Luke and I were having one of those intense whispered discussions familiar to new parents since time began.

"A week?" he whispered, sounding desperate. "They're going to be here a whole week?"

"They want to help us with the baby," I whispered back. "That's what families do."

"We only have one bathroom."

"I know."

"My father can stay in there for hours."

"TMI," I said.

He drew me into a hug and I curved my body around his. "And here I thought Elspeth was our biggest —" He stopped. "Trolls hold grudges, right?"

"Like you wouldn't believe."

"Maybe Elspeth coldcocked my mother from some other dimension as a way to even the score."

I started laughing and had to bury my face against his side to keep from waking the baby. "She doesn't even know your mother.

Why would she want to punch her?"

"Think about it," he said. "Elspeth was seriously pissed at us, right?"

"No argument there."

"And she hates humans."

"Agreed."

"Why not take a free shot at my mother and screw with us in the bargain?"

"You're beginning to sound like one of those conspiracy theorists. If Elspeth wanted to take revenge against us, she wouldn't be subtle about it. We'd be the ones walking around with the black eyes."

"Okay, then how about what happened to you at the Presentation ceremony?"

"I tripped."

"Backward?"

"Now you sound like Lynette."

"So I'm not the only one who thought it was weird."

"No, you're not. But people have weird accidents every hour of every single day."

"And there's probably a troll behind most of them."

"Welcome to Sugar Maple," I said, then promptly fell asleep.

I woke up just before dawn with my breasts aching and heavy with milk. *Strange,* I thought. Laria demanded food every two and a half hours, night and day. She was like a tiny Swiss clock engineered for total accuracy. Was it possible I'd slept through her cries? Waves of mommy guilt washed over me as I glanced at Luke, who was sleeping soundly next to me. It didn't seem possible that we'd both sleep through her demands and it definitely didn't seem possible that Bunny wouldn't have heard her cries in the guest room next door.

I quietly climbed out of bed and peered into the bassinet.

Okay, now that was even stranger. Laria was wide awake, looking up at me, as peaceful and placid as an infant could be.

Just the sight of her made my milk flow. I scooped her up and carried her out to the living room. I loved to sit in the rocking chair while I nursed and watch the sun come up over the mountain Forbes the Giant called home. Funny how you could spend your entire life in the same town and never take time to appreciate the small daily wonders.

Despite all the drama surrounding her birth and the Presentation ceremony, I had felt more settled and at peace in the last eight days than at any other time in my life. All the puzzle pieces had finally dropped into place and —

"Ouch!" I didn't mean to yell, but Laria had my nipple in a death suck. "Sweetie, let go!"

Her eyes had lost that deliberate look and had gone all unfocused. So much so that I wondered if maybe she had fallen asleep while nursing and this was some painful (to me at least) reflex motion.

The pain increased. We were at nine on a scale of ten and climbing fast and my girl was hanging on like an angry dog with a bone. I stood up and started walking swiftly around the room, hoping to break her concentration, but somehow she managed to take it to yet another level of hell.

I guess I was making more noise than I realized because Bunny ran into the room, hair askew, feet bare, and quickly gauged the situation. I thought I saw a small smile twitching at the corners of her mouth but didn't have time to be annoyed. I was too busy trying not to cry.

"She won't let go," I managed. "I can't make her stop!"

"You need to break the suction," Bunny said, then told me to slip my fingertip between the baby's mouth and my poor abused nipple.

Which turned out to be easier said than done. "I can't get my finger into her mouth,"

I said. "She's latched on pretty good."

"Let me try," Bunny said. "Do you mind?"

At that point I didn't mind if every soul in Sugar Maple gave it a try.

"You're right," Bunny said as she tried to slide her pinky between my screaming nipple and Laria's hungry mouth. "She's like a little vacuum cleaner."

"Please, I can't take any more! Do something!"

"I'm trying, honey, but — wait a second . . . wait a second! Mission accomplished!"

Tears of relief coursed down my cheeks as I freed my poor nipple from Miss Baby Death Grip.

"Go put some ice on it," Bunny advised. "It's going to bruise anyway, but the ice will make you feel better."

"I think we're going to have to change her name to the Terminator," I said as Bunny followed us into the kitchen. "She definitely did a job on the two of us."

Bunny took Laria while I rummaged in the freezer for a bag of peas I could cover with a dish towel. (We'd used up all of our ice tending to Bunny's Laria-induced black eye.)

"You know," Bunny said, placing a kiss on

the baby's forehead, "she feels a little warm to me."

I winced as I placed the makeshift ice bag against my breast. "Maybe I should put on one of her lighter onesies."

"No, that's not what I mean. Touch her forehead."

I pressed my lips to her soft, fragrant skin and frowned. "You're right. She is running a little warm."

"I'm sure it's nothing to worry about," Bunny said. "Babies run low-grade fevers all the time, but let's keep an eye on her."

I peppered her with questions about babies and fevers, when to worry, what to do, who to call, and I started to wonder how new mothers made it through the early weeks without someone to lean on. I trusted my magick friends implicitly, but there was something deeply comforting about sharing my concerns with Laria's grandmother. Her blood kin.

I gritted my teeth and tried to nurse, but Laria was having none of it.

"Her little mouth is probably sore from all that sucking," Bunny said with a chuckle.

Although I didn't mind the reprieve, Laria's lack of interest left me vaguely unsettled.

"Looks like it's going to be a beautiful

day," Bunny said, peering out the kitchen window. "I think I'll change into some warm clothes and go out for a nice long walk. I might even stop at that bagel shop and bring home some goodies for all of us."

As far as houseguests went, Bunny Mac-Kenzie was a whole lot more fun than Elspeth.

Ten minutes later I heard Bunny and a grumbling, half-asleep Jack head out on their early morning constitutional. Laria was lying peacefully in her bassinet, not asleep but content to watch the world go by. Luke had planned to go in to work for a few hours and catch up on things. He was in the bathroom showering. I stretched out on the bed, telling myself I wasn't going to fall asleep.

So much for good intentions. It seemed like a second later that Luke was shaking me awake.

"Wh-what?" I mumbled, trying to pretend I had been awake all along. "I was just resting my eyes."

"Something's wrong with the baby."

27

CHLOE

Instantly I was stone-cold awake and on my
feet. Laria was lying in her bassinet, her tiny
arms and legs outstretched like planks of
wood. Even her spine looked rigid.

My own knees went weak and I grabbed
on to Luke for support. "I think she's having some kind of seizure."

I'd never known fear like that in my life. It
shot through me like lightning headed
straight for the core of my being.

"Where's my mother?" Luke asked. "She
might know what this is."

"She and your dad went for a walk into
town."

Laria's mouth twisted into an expression
of pain mixed with bewilderment that I
hope I never see again.

I cupped my hands and brought up blueflame. "I'm calling Janice," I said to Luke.
"We need help."

"This better be good," she said from within her hologram a second later. "I'm trying to get the kids ready for school."

I quickly laid out the problem.

"I'm on my way," she said and the hologram dissolved.

Luke and I didn't even have time to panic. She was there with us in a heartbeat, not even breathing hard from the rocky transition. She scooped the baby up in her arms, but instead of melting into Janice, Laria grew stiffer and more rigid than before.

"What is it?" Luke demanded. "Say something, Jan!"

"Quiet," I warned him. "She's concentrating."

Janice laid the baby down on the bed and massaged her tiny limbs. Laria began to cry, huge, gulping howls that tore at my heart.

"We need Lilith," Janice said.

Luke reached for my hand and we both held tight.

"It's that bad?" I asked, my voice trembling.

The last thing you want to see on your best friend's face at a time like this was compassion. "I don't know," she said. "That's why we need Lilith."

Lilith came to our side in an instant. She and Janice directed all of their energies, all of their combined skills in the healing arts, toward Laria while Luke and I could do nothing but watch and wait and pray for answers as our baby's tiny body went into what seemed like spasms at irregular intervals.

"I've never seen anything like this," Lilith said finally during one of Laria's quieter moments.

"Neither have I," Janice concurred. "It's some kind of seizure, we're in agreement on that, but that's all we know."

"I think you need to take her to a human hospital," Lilith said, her lovely face awash in worry.

"No!" The word burst from my mouth. "That's the last thing I want to do."

"Honey, you know we wouldn't recommend it if we didn't think it was important." Janice put an arm around my shoulder and gave me a quick hug. "Laria is more human than magick. She needs the kind of help only a human doctor can give."

"At least for the diagnosis," Lilith said, trying to ease our fears. "Once we know what we're dealing with, we can come up with a plan to fight it."

"But until then we're stymied," Janice said.

"But you were able to help me," Luke

reminded Janice, "and I'm full-blooded human."

"Please," Janice said, taking his other hand in hers. "Listen to me. I wish I could do something right now, but I can't. I think you two should get in your Jeep and take Laria to the ER now."

I gasped as Laria's body went rigid once again and her eyes seemed to roll back in her head.

"I'll warm up the Jeep," Luke said and took off at a run.

I was shaking so badly I couldn't dress the baby. Lilith and Janice had to help me snap and button her into her clothes then wrap her in the yellow and white log cabin blanket I had knitted for her over the summer.

"Take her to Good Samaritan," Lilith advised.

I must have looked as blank as I felt. "Good Samaritan?"

"The human hospital. It's not too far from Sugar Maple."

She grabbed paper and pen from my nightstand and wrote down the information.

"Take this," she said. "And if you can, ask for Dr. Albright. She's studied herbal healing with me so she's sympathetic to our ways."

I nodded, but my mind was empty of everything but terror.

"Bunny and Jack are out walking," I said as I hurried toward the front door. "Tell them where we are and give them directions, okay?"

"Your phone!" Janice grabbed my cell from the hall table.

Baby. Phone. Diaper bag. I was running on automatic pilot as Laria and I flew across the snowy yard toward the Jeep.

Luke wasn't doing so well himself. It took two of us to get the baby properly strapped into her car seat. But when he got back behind the wheel he managed to pull it together. Which was a good thing since I was a total wreck.

I gave him directions to the hospital, but other than sharing the information about Dr. Albright, we didn't say a word to each other. What was there to say? Something was wrong with our baby girl. The waves of mommy guilt grew stronger with every second that passed. Should I have seen a human doctor during my pregnancy? Had my stubbornness somehow hurt Laria? Would a medical doctor have noticed a problem early on and handled it in utero?

Was I to blame for whatever was happening to her now?

"Don't cry," Luke said. "She's going to be fine."

I cried harder.

"Kids are always coming down with weird things," he said, the slight hitch in his voice giving him away completely. "My parents spent half their adult lives in the ER waiting for one of us to be examined."

But we weren't your average all-American family and Laria wasn't your average infant. Magick flowed through her veins and we had no way of knowing how or if that magick would somehow make itself visible to a human doctor. But even discovery would be a small price to pay for our daughter's life.

I'm a worrier. The worst-case scenario is always my go-to position. And that was where I went as we raced toward Good Samaritan. By the time Luke wheeled into the parking lot and raced toward the ER entrance Laria was in the throes of what looked frighteningly like a seizure.

Luke slammed on the brakes and I jumped out of the Jeep. I fumbled with the straps on the car seat and finally managed to extricate a struggling, thrashing Laria.

A hospital guard motioned for Luke to move the truck away from the ambulance loading zone.

"Go," he said to me. "I'll catch up."

He didn't have to tell me twice. I'm not sure I was even close to coherent as I tried to tell the admitting nurse what was wrong, but the sight of my baby daughter convulsing in my arms spoke volumes. We were quickly whisked through the swinging doors into the heart of the ER.

The first thing I noticed was that it was much calmer and quieter than the emergency rooms I had seen on television. The second thing I noticed was the smell. Fear? Sickness? Death? I didn't know exactly what it was, but I wouldn't forget it anytime soon. An elderly woman waited attention on a gurney in the corner. I tried not to look at her and wondered why nobody thought to pull a sheet over her exposed limbs. All of these things imprinted themselves on my mind in a nanosecond as nurses and interns swirled around my Laria.

"We need you to stay outside," a red-haired nurse said, drawing the curtain around the space. "One of the doctors will speak with you shortly."

I wanted to rip down that curtain, grab my baby, and transport us back to Sugar Maple where the real world couldn't touch us, but that wasn't an option. I stood there, breathing in the strange smells, when I heard Luke's voice coming from the waiting room.

I dodged an attendant wheeling a cart, then burst through the swinging doors in time to see him hand over an insurance card to the receptionist at the computer monitor.

"They're looking at her," I said as he filled out some forms with a ballpoint pen. "They kicked me out."

I saw him print the name LARIA HOBBS MACKENZIE in block letters followed by his social security number and name.

My stomach twisted as the real world tightened its grip on us. What would I have done without Luke? Despite my half-human heritage, it had never occurred to me that there might come a day when I needed real-world medical insurance. Or that our child might. I thanked the gods that he had provided for Laria.

The admitting nurse got up to adjust something at the printer. Luke bent down and pulled out a familiar bag he'd kept balanced between his feet.

"I thought you might want this." He handed me the knitting bag I kept stashed in the Jeep.

Knitting socks as therapy? Don't knock it if you haven't tried it. At that moment those socks-in-progress were all that stood between me and utter panic.

Finally the paperwork was completed and we marched back into the treatment area. The cubicle where they had been working on Laria was empty and I knew a rush of fear unlike anything I had ever experienced.

"Where's our daughter?" Luke demanded of a male nurse passing by.

Clearly the poor guy needed more information.

"Laria MacKenzie," I offered. "Infant, convulsions — ?"

He looked blank but raised his forefinger. "Gimme three," he said, "and I'll find out."

Three turned into five, which turned into twelve. Luke was ready to storm the hospital in search of our baby, when a middle-aged gray-haired woman in a lab coat approached.

"I'm Dr. Albright," she said, extending her right hand. "Lilith called and told me your daughter was coming in."

I could have cried with relief.

"We don't know anything yet," Dr. Albright said, "but that's actually good news." She named two specific areas that had been mercifully ruled out already through the preliminary examination. She asked permission to run two more tests, neither of which would be invasive, and we agreed.

"It will take a while," she said with a warm smile, "so you might want to set up shop in the lounge on the second floor. Lilith said you're a knitter so I know you'll make use of the great light we have up there. I'll make sure you're kept informed."

And then she was gone.

"I want to run after her," I said as the big doors marked NO ENTRANCE swung shut behind her.

"So do I," Luke said.

"Do you think the baby's scared?"

"She's too young to understand what's happening," he said, squeezing my hand. "That's the only good part about this whole fucking thing."

I bit back hot tears, but this time they weren't for Laria. Luke had lost his first child in an auto accident. His daughter had been riding her bike at the foot of the driveway when a car sideswiped her. He had waited for good news that never came. He had heard the words no parent should ever hear. He had buried his daughter. For the first time I truly understood the depth of his loss and how strong the human spirit really was.

"You'd better call your parents and let them know what's happening," I said. "I'll call Janice."

"You can't use cells inside a hospital. Go to the lounge and I'll meet you there."

"Don't be long," I said. "Laria and I need you."

Even more than I had realized.

28

LUKE

I heard them before I saw them. My dad's rumbling voice, my mother's authoritative soprano, and two other voices I didn't expect.

They were all over me the moment I pushed through the door into the waiting room.

"What's going on?" my father demanded. "Where's Chloe? What the hell are you doing here?"

"How is Laria?" my mother asked, struggling to maintain her professional composure. "What are the doctors telling you?"

Meghan stood near the door looking weepy while a tall, muscular dude took it all in. If I hadn't had more important things on my mind, I would've clocked him just for the hell of it.

Did you ever take an instant dislike to someone? The kind of dislike that makes you want to wipe the smug smile off his face and knock him on his ass? That was the way this guy made me feel the second I saw him. I had to hand it to my sister: when it came to losers, the girl had radar.

I brought everyone up to speed on Laria as we headed toward the elevator that would take us to the visitors' lounge on the second floor.

I separated Meghan from the pack while we waited. "What the hell are you two doing here?"

Probably not the most brotherly response, but I was low on patience at that point.

"Car trouble," she said with a shrug. "I tried calling you and got Ma instead. Great luck, huh?"

"What kind of car trouble?"

She shrugged. "I drive a beater, big brother. I've had all kinds of car trouble."

She said they'd spent the night at the old-school Stardust Motor Court near the county hospital.

"I thought we were going to head up to Canada tomorrow, but he got all antsy and we set out at the crack of dawn."

"Crack of dawn?" My sister only saw the crack of dawn from the flip side.

"Okay, so it was almost nine, but it felt like the crack of dawn." They made it a few miles north of Sugar Maple when the car died and our parents swung by to rescue them and continued on to the hospital.

"You had to bring him with you?" I muttered as the elevator light went on.

"We couldn't leave him on the side of the road."

"Doesn't sound like a bad idea to me."

"Shh," she warned me. "Be nice."

I wasn't making any promises. If the jackass got out of line, I was kicking him out. No questions asked.

Maybe he was smarter than he looked because he nodded at me in the elevator but gave me a wide berth, which was fine by me. My sister might have a thing for bad boys, but I was a cop. I knew that bad boys usually ended up doing twenty-to-life.

Chloe was talking to someone in a white lab coat when we entered the visitors' lounge. She looked tightly strung, pale, and exhausted but slightly less worried than she had before.

"So far, so good," she said as she embraced my parents and shot a quizzical look toward Meghan and her jackass. "They're taking her for a CT scan now, but they don't expect to find anything."

Bunny peppered her with questions that she tried hard to answer but fell short of the detail my mother was looking for. I was happy enough with the news that the seizures had stopped and there was no fever.

"Who's the neonatal?" my mother asked.

"I don't know," Chloe said, "but a Dr. Albright is overseeing everything."

Bunny marched off in search of answers and Meghan took the opportunity to step forward and introduce her friend.

"This is James," she said. "We had car trouble. We tried calling you —"

"Nobody's interested," I snapped and instantly felt like shit when Meghan blushed bright red.

James flashed a toothpaste smile and extended his right hand in Chloe's direction. To my surprise, Chloe nodded but didn't take his hand. Instead she turned to my dad.

"You look like a man in need of coffee," she said, linking her arm through his. "Why don't you sit down and I'll get you a cup?"

"I should be taking care of you," my dad said.

Chloe gave him a tired smile. "You'd be doing me a favor, Jack. Otherwise I'll just sit here and think."

He nodded and lowered himself onto one of the sofas lining the wall.

"Anybody else?" she asked, deliberately

avoiding James's eyes.

"Tea for me, thanks," Meghan said.

I shot my sister a look.

"She *asked*," Meghan protested. "Chill, big brother. You're getting a little intense."

"You want intense? In case you forgot, we're waiting to find out why our eight-day-old daughter is having seizures."

"Luke." Chloe placed a hand on my arm. "It'll be a while until we hear anything more. Help me with the coffees, okay?"

CHLOE

"I wasn't going to lose it," Luke said as we walked down the hallway toward the small cafeteria.

"I know," I said. "I was."

"I saw you didn't shake his hand."

"I couldn't. I was about to turn into a flamethrower." The tips of my fingers were uncomfortably hot and I waved them in the air to cool them down. Was it possible my magick was making a comeback so soon after Laria's birth?

We got on line for coffee behind a frazzled mother of three wired kids who were running laps around the room. My admiration for human mothers took another leap.

"I thought everyone said Meghan liked pretty boys."

Luke shot me a look. "You don't think he's good-looking?"

"Average to plain."

"My mother thinks he should be a male model."

I shrugged. "He'd have to hit the gym a whole lot harder."

"Are we talking about the same guy?" Luke asked. "Chiseled features, blue eyes, guns the size of howitzers?"

I started to laugh as we placed our order. "Maybe your sister should be worried that you're competition."

He turned red, which made me laugh even more. It felt good to release some of the tension that had been building inside us for hours now.

"Not my type," he said as we paid for the drinks. "I like tall, skinny blondes."

We started back to the lounge. "Nothing against Meghan, but I really wish they weren't here."

"Does that mean I can kick his ass out?"

"No," I said. "It means I wish they weren't here."

Bunny and Jack were watching the overhead television when we returned. Bunny was knitting on my sock-in-progress. Meghan was working a newspaper crossword puzzle while James leaned against the window and looked down at the parking lot. Direct sunlight wasn't his friend. He looked older, more jaded, not somebody I'd like to get to know better. Or at all, for that matter.

I have magick, but I'm not psychic. I can't walk into a room and suss out the good, the bad, and the downright evil like many of my Sugar Maple friends can. But this James guy set off a gut-level reaction I couldn't ignore. Even through the dark cloud of worry over Laria the warning bells rang loud and clear.

Okay, so maybe I already knew enough about him to hate him. Cruelty had never been one of my turn-ons and there was no denying he had been incredibly cruel and thoughtless with Meghan. But there was something else at work, something I couldn't identify but sensed just the same, and I wished he were anywhere but here with us.

Luke sat down near Meghan and struck up a conversation. I sat on the arm of the sofa next to Bunny and Jack and tried to muster up some interest in *The Price Is Right* but all I could think of was Laria.

"Hope you don't mind," Bunny said as she handed back the sock. "It looked lonely."

I managed a smile. "Toe-up or cuff-down?"

"Cuff-down," she said, "but I did try two on one circular once. I won't make that mistake again."

I picked up where she left off, willing myself to ease into the comforting rhythm of knit three, purl one ribbing.

Bunny patted me on the hand. "I have a good feeling about this, honey. It's all going to work out fine."

To my embarrassment I totally choked up and could only nod my head in response. I was aware of James's eyes on me, cool and calculating, and I ducked my head against what felt like an invasion of privacy.

Maybe I should have let Luke kick his ass after all.

Time dragged on. I knitted. Bunny bought us sandwiches around one o'clock but I couldn't choke down a bite. Jack dozed intermittently on the plastic sofa while Luke paced a hole in the dark gray industrial carpet. Meghan must have picked up on the unfriendly vibe because she asked James to go for a walk with her so she could "get some air."

Bunny shook her head as soon as they left. "I don't know why she dates men who are prettier than she is. You'd think she'd have learned by now."

Jack snored. Luke grunted something unpleasant. I looked at Bunny in surprise.

"I don't think he's that great looking," I said honestly, then ticked off the ways in which I found him lacking.

"Well, look at you," Bunny said with a laugh. "You look like a movie star yourself. Your idea of average is very different from mine."

"Do you like him?" I asked.

She gave me an *are you kidding* type of look. "He's arrogant, conceited, and stupid. Exactly the type my daughter is drawn to time after time." She sighed and inspected her short, no-nonsense fingernails. "The only good thing is it won't last."

"Will it last the afternoon?"

Bunny looked at me and laughed out loud. "I knew I liked you."

I liked her, too. She was smart, aggressive, and definitely nosy, but she loved her family. By extension I was part of the tribe and it felt good. And to my surprise I saw a difference in Luke, too. His parents might get on his nerves, but their presence at the hospital helped make both of us feel less alone as we waited for news of Laria. Conversation ground to a halt as the hours wore on, but the feeling of being connected to each other by our love and concern for Laria was more powerful than words. I sneaked off to the empty chapel on the sixth floor and quickly blueflamed Janice to let her know what was happening.

"If you need us, we're there for you," she said. "We'll drop everything and transport over. Just say the word."

I tried to tell her how much I appreciated the offer, but Janice wasn't one for big displays of sentiment. She tried to make a joke out of it, but I wouldn't let her.

"Knock it off," she said with a laugh. "Next thing I know you'll be designing a magick line for Hallmark."

Meghan and James popped back in around shift change at three to see if there was any news and then went off again, to the relief of everyone in the room.

Luke and I got to see Laria once between tests and she was her sweet and hungry self. I'd expressed my milk earlier and was ready to feed her, but the doctors were withholding nourishment until the next test was completed.

"She looks fine," Luke said as she grabbed hold of his pinky.

I smiled and kissed the top of her head. "You'd never know anything happened."

"Sorry, folks," Paula, one of the evening

nurses on duty, said, "but Laria has things to do."

We lingered as long as we could, but the nurse was insistent. Reluctantly we turned to leave and found ourselves face-to-face with James Whatever His Last Name Was.

"How long have you been standing there?" Luke demanded, not even taking a stab at being friendly. "I thought you were out walking with Meghan."

"We came back so I could use the john." If the guy was the least bit uncomfortable it didn't show. "I heard your voices on my way back." He smiled and I liked him less than before if that was possible. "I thought maybe I'd get a look at the star of this show."

"No." I didn't mean for it to pop out quite that harshly, but my emotions were pretty ragged by then. "No visitors. It's family only."

Another man might have been ticked off by my confrontational reaction, but he didn't blink. The guy had sociopath written all over him.

"I saw you holding her. She's a beauty."

"Thanks." I was lucky I could manage that much with Luke glowering at me. "We'd better go. They have one more test to run and we're holding them up."

Luke and I started down the hall, but

James stayed put.

"Let's go," Luke said as the moment grew increasingly uncomfortable. "Like we said, family only."

I wasn't sure if the guy was socially awkward or just plain manipulative, but I leaned toward the latter. Luke had been keeping an eye on him before this incident, but now he was watching him like a hawk.

A middle-aged couple came in around four thirty to wait for news of their son, who had been rushed into surgery after a snow-mobile accident. They huddled together in the far corner and I could hear whispered words of prayer rise and fall above the drone of local news on the television.

I found another circular knitting needle deep in the bowels of my tote bag and Bunny cast on for the second sock. She gave me a grateful look that all knitters would understand. At that moment we were definitely process knitters. It didn't matter what came off our needles. It only mattered that we were knitting to stave off the demons.

"I can't take this," Luke erupted around five o'clock. "We've been here all day. Somebody's gotta know something."

"Maybe they forgot you were waiting here," Jack offered from the depths of the couch.

"Did you give them your cell number?" I asked Luke.

"They didn't ask."

"They didn't ask me, either."

"Both of you sit down and take a deep breath." Bunny was exerting her full range of maternal power. "They know you're here. When there's something new they'll tell you. Now try to relax."

"I think we're all starving," Meghan observed. "Why don't James and I see what we can get at the cafeteria?"

Not that we wanted cafeteria food, but the thought of losing James for another few minutes was too good to pass up.

"What the hell is she doing with that loser?" Jack mumbled after they left. "That's the worst one yet."

"Lower your voice," Bunny said. "It's none of our business."

"I've got a good mind to kick that guy's ass."

Luke and I locked eyes and burst into laughter.

"Okay," I said to Luke. "Now I know where you get it from."

Bunny shook her head. "Push her and she'll run straight into his arms. Leave her alone and it will be over this time next week."

I must have been staring at her in something like awe because she reached over and patted my hand.

"Just wait until you have seven of your own, honey. You'll have all the answers, too."

I tried to imagine a life that included a big, boisterous family, but my destiny had been set long ago. Laria would be my only child.

It had been a long day. My emotions were bubbling over and I lowered my head and started to cry. Bunny wrapped her arms around me. "Let it out," she said, patting me on the back in the way of mothers everywhere. "You'll feel better if you just let it out."

So I did. I sobbed my heart out against her shoulder, gasping, blubbering, and thoroughly soaking her pretty red sweater.

"Elsebeth Lavold," I said between sobs. "Silky Wool. Hand-wash only."

Bunny laughed and hugged me tight. "I'll make you one for your birthday."

Nobody ever knitted a sweater for a knitter. The gesture made me start crying all over again.

And just when I thought I had finally run out of tears Dr. Albright walked into the room.

29

CHLOE

Who knew your knees could actually knock?
I stood and took Luke's hand as the doctor
walked toward us. Her smile should have
been a pretty good indicator, but I was so
icy cold with terror that I couldn't even add
up the clues.

"How would you like to take your daughter home tonight?" she asked, her smile
growing even wider.

"She's okay?" Luke asked, his voice thick
with emotion.

"So far everything looks good. Her only
problem at the moment is she's hungry."

I started crying all over again but this time
in a good way.

Bunny stepped up and introduced herself.
She started asking the doctor all the right
questions, taking notes, and generally doing
all the things Luke and I should have done
if we hadn't been so emotionally wrecked.

"Now, just because we haven't found anything and she seems to be one hundred percent at the moment doesn't mean there isn't something to find." Dr. Albright handed me a piece of letterhead stationery with names and phone numbers typed on it. "I'd like you to make an appointment with one of these neurologists and let him or her make an additional evaluation."

"Is Laria in danger?" I asked.

"I wouldn't be releasing her if I thought she was," Dr. Albright said, "but I don't like unsolved mysteries. I'll sleep a lot better at night when we find out what was bothering that beautiful little girl."

And from there we went straight into hyperdrive. Jack went to find Meghan and her terrible boyfriend. Bunny and I went to bundle up Laria for the ride home while Luke took care of the paperwork surrounding her discharge.

All of the tension and stress and worry lifted like clouds after the storm. My happiness was so pure, so intense, that it seemed to light the world. I felt like flying and might have given it a try if there weren't so many humans around. Mostly, though, I wanted to hug my baby and keep on hugging her until she was old enough to vote.

It was dark outside when we left the

hospital and very cold. Laria was warm and cozy in her Snugli, which was more than I could say about the rest of us. It had been a long day and we were all emotionally and physically drained.

Jack was feeling a little under the weather so he and Bunny decided to spend the night in the motel near the hospital instead of driving back to Sugar Maple or going home.

"I'm having a little trouble with these dark country roads," Jack admitted. "My night vision isn't what it used to be." He asked if Luke would lead the way to the motel and we said of course.

Unfortunately this meant we were stuck with Meghan and James for the night.

I suggested they might be more comfortable staying at the motel, too, but Meghan said they had spent the previous night in a motel and now she only had enough room on her credit card to pay for car repairs.

I wanted to ask why her so-called boyfriend couldn't chip in but wisely kept my mouth shut. *One night,* I told myself, *and they'll be gone.*

"Maybe not," Luke whispered to me as we got Laria into her car seat. "Archie found Meggie's Toyota just where she said it was and towed it into his shop. I told him it was an emergency and that we'd pay double his going rate."

"Are you crazy? Archie charges three times more than he should as it is."

Luke inclined his head in James's general direction. "There's the alternative."

I shuddered. "Tell Archie he can have my Buick and the yarn shop if he can get the job done tonight."

The baby and her paraphernalia took up half the backseat. James was a big guy so he took the other half while Meghan squeezed herself into the rear storage compartment. I know it sounds ridiculous, but I couldn't stand that guy being so close to my baby. When he reached out to touch her little hand I had to restrain myself from leaping into the backseat and clawing his eyes out.

Was I overreacting? Of course I was, but believe me when I say postnatal hormones kick PMS ass.

Laria, however, seemed to like him just fine and happily clutched his finger as we made the short drive to the motel.

"She really likes you," I heard Meghan say.

"Babies usually do," he said and I softened toward him.

Just a little.

We pulled into the parking lot of the Stardust Motor Court and seconds later Jack and Bunny pulled in right behind us.

"Do you think they have a bathroom I could use?" Meghan asked. "I can't make it back to your place if I don't find one."

"Try the front desk," Luke said without much enthusiasm. He glanced at James through the rearview mirror. "What about you?"

"I'm cool."

We both tried not to roll our eyes.

Meghan climbed out the back window and trotted toward the main office. Suddenly a bathroom stop didn't seem like such a bad idea.

"Wait," I called out as she dashed away. "I'll come with."

Bunny climbed out as I approached. "Jack can't get his key out of the ignition. Can you believe that?"

"After today I'd believe anything. Maybe Luke can help."

I walked back toward the Jeep and told him about his father's dilemma.

"Hard to believe the old man was in construction," he said as he slid out from behind the wheel and then jogged over to see what the problem was.

I was maybe ten feet away from the truck, waiting for Meghan to come back or Luke to finish helping his father so I could use the ladies' room. There was no way I would leave Laria alone with a stranger.

James looked up and our eyes locked and I swear I could hear the puzzle pieces click into place. *The glitter!* I remembered brushing pale leaf-green glitter off Meghan's shoulder at the party the afternoon before and assuming it belonged to one of the many Salem Fae in the room.

I made a lunge for the car door, but I was too late. With a sickening squeal of tires the Jeep rocketed back onto the highway and out of sight.

Jack was inside the motel front office registering. Meghan was talking to her mother on the front step. Luke was behind the wheel of his parents' car fiddling with the key.

I leaped into the passenger seat and slammed the door.

"Follow him!" I screamed loud enough to be heard in another time zone. "He took the baby!"

This was one of the million reasons you wanted a cop around in an emergency. It took Luke all of maybe three seconds to peel out. His family stared, openmouthed, as the tires spit snow and gravel everywhere, but there was no time to explain.

"He's Fae," I said, heart pounding so hard it hurt.

"You're sure?"

"Absolutely."

"Revenge?"

"Maybe." I was human enough to think so but magick enough to realize that, with the exception of Isadora and her vendetta against my family, Fae motives were usually more complex than simple revenge. Sometimes flat-out cruelty played a larger part than I wanted to acknowledge.

"Elspeth," he said, pounding the wheel with his hand. "That's who's behind this."

"I don't believe that."

"You don't *want* to believe it, but listen to me. She's from Salem. The new contingent of Fae is from Salem. She hated being stuck in Sugar Maple as much as some of them do. A natural connection if you ask me."

"Trolls aren't tacticians," I said. "They're more —"

His cell phone went off and I recognized Bunny's ringtone.

"You'd better answer that," I said. The last thing we needed was for them to bring in the authorities.

"Ma, I can't talk," Luke said without preamble. "The bastard stole my car."

"The baby." I could hear Bunny's voice

loud and clear.

"Fine," Luke lied. "Gotta go, Ma, I need both hands on the wheel."

We screeched to a sliding halt as a family of deer bounded across the narrow road.

"Shit," Luke said. "I still don't see taillights." He looked over at me. "Do you know which way they went?"

"I lost them when they rounded the first curve."

"Best guess?"

Tears flowed unchecked down my cheeks. "I don't have one."

We reached an intersection. "Left?" he asked. "Right?" He sounded desperate. "Magic 8 Ball?"

I tried to tap into something, anything, that would lead us to our baby, but there was no magick for this.

Or was there?

"Do you smell that?" I asked, sniffing the air.

"It's called fear."

"It's called stale waffles."

"You mean that bitch —"

"Say no more, human, or ye'll be a sorry man of snow come morning."

Elspeth, in all her buttercup glory, appeared on the dashboard. Her bright yellow hair was practically standing straight up.

Her usual outfit of black dress and white apron was hidden beneath an enormous hooded cloak that made her look downright demonic. Spirals of pale yellow smoke corkscrewed her round body.

Luke's right hand curled into a fist and I was afraid he was going to do something crazy like grab her by the throat and fling her against the windshield, which, considering the fact that she could probably wipe the floor with him, wasn't a great idea.

Besides, I was clinging to the possibility that maybe she was on our side after all.

"Where's Laria?" Luke demanded. "If you've done anything to her, so help me God, I'll kill you."

She gave him a look that should have scared the crap out of him but didn't.

"Do ye be willing to put your faith in me?" she asked. "Because time is short and her hours are few."

"What the hell does that mean?" Luke exploded. "If you don't quit talking that shit —"

"Shut up, Luke, and let her talk."

I'd apologize later. After our daughter was safe in our arms.

"From my heart and all I know, the wee one will not be harmed," she said, "but she will leave this realm forever if you do not save her now."

Leave this realm? I heard her words, but they tumbled around inside my head like loose coins. After all the battles we'd fought over the past year, all the ground we'd claimed in order to make Sugar Maple the refuge Aerynn had envisioned, was I going to lose the most important battle of all?

"Anything, Elspeth. We'll do whatever we have to do. Just please help us find her before it's too late."

"I can't do it," Luke said as we barreled down the road to nowhere. "This could be a trap."

"What choice do we have, Luke?" I repeated what I had said to him before. I refused to believe Elspeth had stayed by Samuel's side for over three hundred years only to destroy his legacy now by taking Laria from Sugar Maple.

The road ahead was pitch-black. Our headlights illuminated a narrow path. I was a sorceress. I had powers even I didn't fully understand yet, but right now I was as helpless as Luke. Elspeth was our only hope.

"This whole thing makes no sense," Luke railed. "If he's Fae, why is he driving? Why didn't he just magick them wherever they're going?"

Elspeth started spinning madly across the

dashboard. "Questions, questions. Ye should be seeking answers, not asking more questions."

I shot Elspeth what I hoped was a cautionary look, then turned to Luke. "Transition was hard on you and you're a grown man," I reminded him. "Imagine what it would do to a mostly human infant."

Which to my mind definitely proved Elspeth's assertion that, at least for now, Laria wasn't in physical danger. I shivered at the thought of what other dangers might lie ahead for her.

Locals sometimes complained about the lack of new roads in our county, but right now that seemed like a blessing. The fewer choices Laria's kidnapper had, the better our chances of finding him.

"No!" Elspeth shrieked as Luke rounded a curve. "That way, human, that way!"

She waved her hands and the next thing I knew the car veered to the right and headed straight for the dense woods that ringed Sugar Maple.

Luke struggled to maintain control of the wheel, but it was literally out of his hands. "We're going to hit the trees!"

Trust Elspeth . . . trust Elspeth . . . trust Elspeth . . .

We didn't hit the trees. Not exactly. We

went right through them like threading a needle, exploding through massive trunks but leaving no damage behind, and we kept on going, faster and faster, until I saw nothing but a tunnel of trees leading us deeper into the woods.

"Holy shit!" Luke yelled.

But I couldn't yell. I couldn't even breathe. The woods seemed unimaginably dense. We were plunged into primeval darkness, crashing blindly through trees but leaving them whole and untouched in our wake. Even more amazing, we were whole and untouched as well. Maples, poplars, white birch. Nothing could stop us. Not when our daughter's future was at stake.

My magick might have been in remission since Laria's birth, but my maternal instincts were alive and well and telling me my baby girl was very close.

30

CHLOE

We had just come out the other side of a towering pine when Luke's mother called again.

"Bunny will go crazy if it rolls into voice mail," I said. "She'll be dialing 911 so fast our heads will spin."

Elspeth leaped from the dashboard to the console and started jumping up and down on Luke's cell, flipping it to speakerphone mode.

"No!" she screeched. "No! No! No!"

Which of course made Luke answer it.

"Been a long time." A familiar voice filled the car and an overwhelming sense of dread grabbed me by the throat.

"Dane," I whispered. "It's Dane!"

This time last year we had been engaged in a battle to the death with his mother, Isadora, a terrifyingly powerful Fae warrior queen. Only it wasn't Isadora who had died in this dimension, it was her son Dane. Cruel, beautiful, bone-deep-evil Dane. Isadora had launched a death bolt at me and I'd conjured a glass shield to protect myself. The death bolt careened off the shield and went straight for Dane, slicing him in two and forever isolating him from Sugar Maple and the human realm where he had spent so much of his life.

The end of his earthly existence had been an accident but one for which I felt no guilt and definitely no remorse. His only goal had been to do his mother's bidding and she had wanted both Luke and me dead.

And now Dane was back.

Even Elspeth looked frightened.

An unpleasant laugh made the phone vibrate. "Surprised? I thought you would be. I tried to leave a few clues, but pregnancy made you a little slow, Chloe."

Luke muttered something ugly under his breath and I motioned for him to be quiet. Elspeth was frozen in place on the console, one booted foot resting on Luke's cell phone. I was a half step away from hysteria and struggling to hold it together for the sake of my baby.

"So you're behind it," I said. "I saw the glitter. I should have pieced it together."

"It's not too late for you, Chloe," he said

in his silkiest, most seductive voice. "Laria should have her mother with her."

Luke's head snapped in my direction. I saw terror in his eyes.

"Where are you taking her?"

He blew past the question. "You're wasted on humans, Hobbs. Remember that night by the lake? You were so young, so innocent. I —"

Luke picked up the phone and threw it out the window.

"Are you insane?" I totally lost it. "That was our only hope of finding Laria. He was going to lead us to her." Last year Dane's brother, Gunnar, had communicated with me through Penny, my beloved store cat, as a way of reaching between dimensions. Today Dane had used Bunny's phone call as a conduit.

"Sports radio — you gotta love it." His voice surrounded us, spilling from every speaker. I could almost feel it slithering down my arms like warm, poisonous honey. "So how are those Pats doing this year, MacKenzie?"

Luke was a lethal weapon poised to strike, but this time he reined in his emotions and sat still, poised and waiting.

"We're coming for Laria," I said as calmly as I could manage. "You can't stop us."

"Join us," he said again. "I can offer you a world of pleasures you'll never know with the human."

Luke's jaw was so tight I was surprised it didn't snap in two.

"I want my baby," I repeated. "She is a Hobbs. Sugar Maple is her birthright."

"She's one of ours now," he said. "And what promise she has!"

Elspeth motioned for me to keep him talking. We were still deep in the woods. Our headlights quit and we were plunged into utter darkness. I motioned for Luke to keep quiet. Whatever Elspeth was trying to do we needed to give her the best shot.

And then I felt it. A tingling sensation that began at my scalp, then moved down my spine and back up again, faster, stronger, as we pushed deeper into the forest. We were getting closer. I could feel Laria everywhere. My breasts grew heavy with milk.

We darted left, then right, and suddenly our headlights came back on and I saw a flash of pink and movement about a football field away.

I grabbed Luke's hand and held it tight. We were almost there. Laria was almost safe. There was no way in heaven or hell we would let Dane or his minion drag our child beyond the mist.

I wasn't paying any attention to what Dane was saying. I just let him talk while Elspeth maneuvered the car closer and closer to our goal.

We approached a clearing and the flash of pink grew larger.

Laria was lying deep within a cluster of evergreens. She was still in her car seat and snugly wrapped against the cold in her travel blanket. James, or whatever his name really was, stood next to her, staring up at the sky. Our Jeep was tucked deep within a thicket with only its front end visible.

He was beautiful in the staggering way of all Fae. There was no way he could be mistaken for anything else. No wonder Meghan and Bunny had been overwhelmed by his looks. If he had appeared that way to me I would have looked twice as well, but Dane was too clever for that. We knew all about façades in Sugar Maple and he must have allowed me to see what he wanted me to see and not what was really there.

Dane had found his Fae equal in beauty and sent him out into my world to create havoc, beginning with Luke's sister. Stripped of a physical presence in our dimension he needed a surrogate to carry out his plan to snatch Laria.

Could James see us watching him? He

gave no indication. He reminded me of a wax dummy, lifelike in every way but the one that really mattered. He had no soul. He was Dane's perfect creation.

I reached for the door handle, but Luke grabbed me.

"We haven't stopped yet. You'll be hurt."

"She needs me. I have to —"

Elspeth's high scream stopped me in my tracks. She spun from the back of the car to the front, her screams growing higher, louder, more intense, and just when I thought my eardrums were going to burst I saw what she was screaming about.

Dropping through the night sky was a busted-up blue Toyota and it was headed straight for us.

Luke grabbed the wheel and turned it as far left as it would go, but nothing happened.

"Son of a bitch, that's the car that ran us off the road," he said, still struggling with the wheel.

The old blue car that had spun out on the snowy road the night Laria was born. The same car that had taken off without checking to see if we were all right.

His sister's car.

It was all falling into place too late to matter.

"Hold on!" Luke yelled, placing an arm across my chest. "We're gonna hit!"

The sound exploded inside my skull. In the blink of an eye I was six years old again, lying on an icy road while my parents lay dying in what was left of our car.

The car split open like a grape. I was torn from my seat and sent flying across the hood, spinning down toward the ground below. The sickening crunch of metal against metal was followed by a loud grunt from Luke and Elspeth's high-pitched keening.

Twisted metal and glass sprayed everywhere, falling into the trees and cutting into my face and hands as I hit the ground hard. I tried to curl myself up into a ball to protect my back, but I felt the impact in every bone.

I heard nothing from Luke or Elspeth.

The silence was the most frightening thing of all, but it didn't last long. Suddenly the old blue Toyota exploded, sending a fireball over the tops of the trees and into the night sky, where it quickly dissipated.

I tried to stand up, but my right knee buckled and I dropped back to the ground. I regrouped and tried again. We couldn't be more than thirty or forty yards away from Laria, but I couldn't see through the all-encompassing darkness that surrounded me. I would have to rely on instinct.

"Chloe." It was Luke, his voice low and weak.

I followed the sound and almost tripped over his prone body.

"Elspeth," he said. "She's dead." He had seen her hit the ground headfirst, then tumble end over end until she disappeared from his sight.

My sorrow ran surprisingly deep, but, like so many things tonight, mourning Elspeth would have to wait.

"The baby is about sixty yards away. Make a quarter turn to your right and pace it off. He's there with her."

"We can do it," I said. "We can get her back."

"Chloe," he said, "I can't move. Both legs are broken."

Time stopped. I tried to take in his words, but the screaming inside my head wouldn't stop.

"You have to do it, Chloe. You're all Laria has."

"I can't. My magick —"

"It's there. Look at your fingertips."

So my magick really was coming back. My fingertips were beginning to glow like the old-school cigarette lighter in my ancient

Buick. I didn't know why or how it was happening — an offshoot of my adrenaline rush or maybe fear for Laria's safety — but it didn't matter. I needed every advantage I could get.

31

CHLOE

There was nothing left to say. I kissed him, then turned away before I started to cry. Dane's presence was everywhere, a biting edge that made the hairs on the back of my neck lift in response.

"Join us," James said, but I knew the words were Dane's.

I ran toward the baby but yelped as I hit a wall of electricity.

"I need to hold Laria."

"Like any other good mother."

Instantly I realized James was terribly young. As beautiful as he was, and he was shockingly glorious, he was still unformed. As the Fae age, their beauty takes on a complexity that dazzles the heart as well as the eye. James hadn't reached that point yet. He was early spring. The promise of summer still lay ahead.

But there was something more there. I just

couldn't pinpoint exactly what.

"You like what you see." It was a statement, flat and without affect.

"You're Fae," I said with a shrug. "Everyone likes what they see."

Suddenly the expression in James's eyes ignited and waves of heat flowed toward me.

"We have unfinished business between us."

"No," I said, keeping Laria in my line of vision. "Whatever business we had is long finished."

James pulled me into his arms and I heard Luke's cry of outrage from behind me.

Go with it, I told myself. *Find out what he wants before you make a move.*

There would be no second chances.

The look in James's icy blue eyes was Dane unmasked and it took every ounce of strength I had not to recoil.

His hands rested on my shoulders, then moved down over my breasts and lingered.

"I wouldn't do that if I were you," I said. "I'm breastfeeding."

The Fae were hot-blooded, but not earthy, and that reminder of my human side repelled him as I'd hoped it would.

James dropped his hands and stepped away and his eyes once again went flat.

I didn't know much about interdimensional communication, but I did know that it took huge storehouses of energy to maintain the link, which explained this now-you-see-him-now-you-don't rhythm.

Laria started to cry and I felt her distress in every cell. Considering the odds were against me I was surprisingly calm. What were my choices? I could walk away and leave my baby in Dane's hands or I could stand and fight.

But whether I won or lost, I would be with my baby. That certainty helped me to hold it together.

"She likes you," I said, referencing that oddly sweet moment in the Jeep.

James nodded. Was I crazy or did I see a flicker of something behind those dead eyes?

"You're good with babies," I said again. "She sensed that."

Definitely a flicker.

"She's hungry," he said. "He hasn't fed her."

My nursing bra felt damp with milk. I was grateful for the layers of sweater and coat.

"I can take care of that if you could help me get to her."

He shook his head.

"Please," I said, throwing caution to the wind. "I know this isn't your fault. I know he has you under some kind of spell. I know he needs a physical presence in this dimension. Please help me get to my baby. I'm her mother. She needs me."

He's weakening . . . come on, James . . . you can do it . . . let me get my baby and we'll fight him together . . .

He lifted me off my feet and slammed me to the ground, knocking the breath from my body. The wild, white-hot fire was back in his eyes and my heart sank.

"The baby comes with me," he said, his booted foot resting squarely on my still-tender belly. I gasped as he leaned his weight into it. "The rest is negotiable."

The pain radiated through my midsection, sharp, stomach-turning pain that made me dizzy.

". . . And she's the key to everything . . . ," he was saying. "With her powers and pedigree on our side there will be no stopping us."

"Sh-she's an infant," I managed as I rocketed toward the outer limits of my pain threshold. "You know how it is for descendants of Aerynn. She has no powers. It will be years before she's of any use to you."

"And that will give us years to make her one of us." He eased up slightly and the nausea receded. "Years to teach her all there is to learn about our world." He swept me up into his arms and cradled me against his rock-hard chest. "Years for you to mother her the way she deserves."

He put all the power of the Fae behind his words. I could feel his heat burning through the layers of clothing that lay between us. The look in his icy blue eyes was fiery, compelling, desperately seductive on levels I hadn't known existed until that moment.

It would be so easy to let go, to stand down and let Sugar Maple finds its own way, build its own future without a Hobbs in the lead. If I chose the avenue Dane opened to me Luke would be free to step back into the world he had left behind. A world filled with family who loved him, who wanted him to be happy, who would be there for him through good and bad. All the things that loving me denied him.

Elspeth had already lost her earth existence over this. Wasn't that enough?

No matter how hard we tried we would never have a normal life. No matter how much I wanted to be part of the MacKenzie clan, I would always be the outsider, hiding my true self behind walls knitted of secrets and half-truths and lies.

Dane knew me too well. We had grown up in the same small village. He knew my weaknesses. He knew my dreams. He knew I had spent my life longing for my mother's touch and that nothing short of death would tear me away from my baby. His words began to work their magick.

I'd be with my baby. Luke would be free to have the type of life he deserved, with a human wife and lots of kids who could play with their cousins without worrying they might set off some magick bombs.

I couldn't fight it any longer. It seemed I had been fighting my entire life to fit in and always falling short. I had fulfilled the first part of my destiny. Laria was proof of that. Now I needed to guide her toward fulfilling her own destiny. I heard Luke calling my name, but I refused to acknowledge him. I was giving him back his life. He was a mortal man like my father. He deserved a life as open and loving as his heart, a life filled with family and children and a mortal woman who wasn't afraid to take those vows.

I was no match for a Fae at the height of his powers. Dane wasn't even in this dimension and he could still bend Fae and human alike to his will. My powers, at their current level, wouldn't be able to touch him and might only endanger Luke and the baby.

So there it was. The decision had been

made. I opened my mouth to speak and realized Dane was gone and the real James remained. My resolve went out the window and hope filled my soul.

I had one more chance at my happy ending.

"He's been lying to you, James. You don't have to do this."

The flicker of life I'd noticed before grew stronger.

"Help me rescue my daughter and I'll help you make a home in Sugar Maple. He can't touch you there."

"I know about Sugar Maple. That's where his accident happened. The town is deadly for Fae."

I hoped he didn't know I was the one who had banished Isadora from this realm into eternity. That wouldn't exactly help my case.

"Did he tell you he tried to kill me? Did he tell you he tried to kill my baby's father? Did he tell you that he killed my parents when I was a little girl? The problem wasn't with the Fae, it was with Dane and his mother, Isadora."

James didn't answer. He didn't have to. I saw it in his eyes.

"The Salem Fae moved to Sugar Maple this past spring. Do you think they would have done that if Fae were being hunted down there?"

The flicker of life dimmed, then reignited. Any second Dane would take over and I'd be out of chances.

"Humans lie."

"I'm only part human."

"You'd lie to save your baby."

"You're right. I would. But I'm not lying now. You don't have to believe me, but would you believe the Salem Fae if they told you themselves?"

I had him. I could see him wavering. Whatever hold Dane had over him wasn't absolute. There were openings in the darkness where light could still get in.

"Please give me the baby, James. Give her to me. If you want me to, I'll summon the Salem Fae right now and they can tell you themselves."

There was goodness inside him still. I knew there was. Dane hadn't completed the process of turning him toward evil.

"Laria likes you, James. I saw how kind you were to her, but she needs her mother. Please, I'm begging you to bring her to me before it's too late."

I was surprised Dane hadn't reclaimed James by now. Had I made a terrible mistake and somehow played into his hands? Dane was both smart and cunning and it wouldn't have taken him long to figure out what I was up to. Was I really talking to James or was Dane playing the part? All I could do was pray I was right.

"Hurry, James. We're running out of time." *Just give me the baby. That's all you have to do.*

He took a step toward Laria. I swear I stopped breathing. He glanced around, then took another step and another, then grabbed the handle of the car seat with Laria in it. Her eyes were wide and she seemed to be staring straight up at him as he turned toward me.

"Take her," he said.

I stepped forward but was again driven back by the invisible force field.

"You have to bring her to me. I can't get past the barrier." The same barrier he had breached twice already with no ill effects.

I had never before seen a Fae sweat, but beads of perspiration were streaming down James's face. We had that much in common. I had passed into another level of fear entirely.

Don't do it. The voice emanating from James's body was pure Dane. *Deliver the baby to me, James.*

"Don't listen to him," I said as fear threatened to choke off my oxygen. "I'm her mother. You know what you should do, James."

She's human. She lies. We are the same blood. Give me the child.

"James!" I didn't even try to hide the panic in my voice. "Don't take her from me. Please, I'm begging you, don't give my baby to Dane!"

Laria started to cry, her tiny face growing red with the effort. James looked down at her with concern and in that instant I knew I had won.

Don't do it, James. Stop now while you still can.

But he didn't stop. He took another step toward me and then another until we were just a couple of feet apart. Sweat was pouring down his face, beading his eyelashes, actually soaking through his sweater. I could almost smell his terror. But that terror didn't stop him.

"Take her," James said. "I don't want her to —"

Those were his last words.

32

CHLOE

A hole in the sky the size of a baseball opened above the blazing treetops and a lightning bolt shot out and struck James dead center.

I screamed as he exploded into a shower of sparks and opalescent glitter like fireworks on the Fourth of July. The car seat with Laria in it shot straight upward, then fell back to earth.

Without Laria.

"Laria!" My cry ripped from my throat. "Where's my baby?"

The cell phone in my pocket vibrated against my leg. A second later I heard Dane's voice.

"She's with me. I told you I would win. Why did you doubt it?"

Luke answered before I could. "If you hurt my daughter, I'll kill you. I don't give a shit where you are, I'll find you, and when

I do, I'll kill you."

I spun around to see Luke dragging himself slowly, painfully, toward where I stood. "Don't do this, Luke. Stay back." *I have a plan, Luke. Look at my eyes. Just go with it.*

I could feel the energies swirling around me. I knew there was more to come and I wanted to save Luke.

"Here's a proposition for you, Chloe," Dane's voice intoned. "I kill the human and you join your daughter."

"Go to hell," Luke snapped.

"I have one for you, Dane," I said. "Spare the human and I'll join my daughter."

"Final answer?" Dane sounded amused, like a man who knew he had won the war.

"Final answer," I said.

"Make him show you Laria is safe," Luke whispered. "Don't trust him. Make him prove she's okay."

I ignored him. *Let this play out my way, Luke. You've got to trust me on this.*

Dane's powers were obviously limited. Every time he had projected his force into this dimension to take action, he had needed a short time to recuperate. I had noticed it first in his struggle to control James and again after the lightning bolt.

Why did he stop with one lightning bolt when he could have killed Luke with a second strike? The truth was he couldn't. We had to be ready to grab one of those windows of opportunity and act quickly. Then we might have a chance.

"So how do I join you?" I asked after casting a protective spell over Luke.

The wait for a response seemed interminable. "Repeat the joining words and you'll be transported."

"What are they?"

"Not yet, sweet Chloe."

"Will I see Laria?"

"You don't trust me?" he countered.

"When it comes to my daughter I don't trust anyone. Show her to me and then I'll say the words." I counted to sixty and then I counted to sixty again. "I'm waiting, Dane. Is something wrong? Show me Laria and I'm yours."

I heard Luke's sharp intake of breath and I had to force myself not to send him a reassuring look. Dane was everywhere, like a Fae surveillance camera with a three-hundred-sixty-degree view. I had to stay focused.

I was becoming more convinced by the second that Laria wasn't with Dane. Inflicting pain was his lifeblood. If he had her, he wouldn't be able to keep from bragging about his victory. The sight of his baby daughter with Dane would have driven Luke over the edge. Cruelty was as natural to Dane as breathing. There was no way he would have missed an opportunity to twist the knife.

But if Laria wasn't with Dane, where was she?

I didn't believe Dane had the power to move her into his dimension. He had needed James to do that, same as he needed a spoken-words charm to transport me. Something had happened during the explosion that enabled Laria to be taken from Dane's grasp, but what? If only Elspeth were still with us. She had woven all manner of protective spells over the baby. Was it possible one of them had kicked in and saved her?

Instinct told me Laria was close and I had learned in a very short time just how powerful a mother's instinct was when it came to her child.

But first I had to take care of Dane. The solution was so ridiculously simple that I wondered how it had escaped notice all this time. A terrible oversight on my part that had already cost two souls their earthly existence.

I wasn't sure how strong my powers were so I needed every advantage I could get.

Dane had to be open and receptive and totally clueless if this was going to have a chance at working.

I felt Laria's presence in the core of my soul. Her soft skin, the sparse blond tufts of hair, her sweet, milky smell. No doubt in my mind that my baby was close at hand and that we would find her.

"Dane! Please don't leave me here. I'm sorry. I shouldn't have issued an ultimatum. All I want is to be with my daughter. I'm sorry if I made you angry. Please, please talk to me. Tell me the words and I'll join you right now!"

I struggled to mask my excitement as a new opening appeared in the night sky, larger than the last one, iced with the steel blue glitter that belonged to Dane alone.

Help me, Aerynn, I prayed. *Help me, Guinevere and all who came before me. Help me to save our newest daughter, Laria.*

The energies intensified. I could feel them pressing against my skin, nipping, scratching, shooting forks of electricity in every direction.

"Dane!" I screamed. "Help me!"

The phone in my pocket vibrated, then died. His strength was almost depleted. A whoop of excitement bubbled up in my throat and I choked it down.

Just say the words, Dane. That's all you have to do. Just get the words out and I'll do the rest.

They came to me on a small wave of thought. Silly words, in the way magick often was, but their authenticity was undeniable.

I stepped away from Luke and looked straight up at the sky opening and said the words in a loud, clear voice with all the need in my heart.

Steel blue glitter rained down on me as the circle grew wider and wider, lit from behind in a soft silver light. I saw the memory of an image rather than an image itself and I knew this was as close as I would ever get to Dane.

"I banish you!" I cried to the heavens as I should have done last year when I had the chance. "This banishment is inviolable, unassailable through time and space . . ." The words flowed, all of them, and as I talked the glitter faded, the light dimmed, and the hole in the sky shrank in on itself and disappeared.

"Himself would be proud."

I stared in shock as Elspeth, covered in snow and branches, waddled out of the woods toward Luke and me.

"Elspeth!" I did something I never thought

388

I would do: I grabbed the cantankerous troll in my arms and hugged her.

Even Luke looked happy to see her.

"None of that, missy!" She brushed me away with fly-swatting motions and the smell of stale waffles filled the night air. "There be plenty of time afterwards."

"You're right," I said. "We have to find Laria."

Elspeth looked at Luke, then at me, and she smiled.

"What the hell?" Luke muttered.

I don't think either one of us had ever seen the butter-yellow-haired troll smile before and it caused a major disturbance in our personal force field.

She took a good long look at Luke, then passed her pudgy little hands over his legs and nodded.

I gasped as Luke stood up, brushed the snow off his jeans, and kissed Elspeth on the cheek.

I'm not saying she liked being kissed by a human, but she didn't hit him, so that had to count for something. She stepped over toward the empty car seat, clasped her hands together in front of her, and said, " 'Tis time now."

Luke and I exchanged glances. Time for what? We already knew it was time to put everything we had into finding Laria.

And then it happened. The car seat began to glow, faintly at first, then brighter and brighter, and suddenly our baby, our Laria, was back.

I don't have to tell you I cried when I scooped her up in my arms. She fussed as big, fat teardrops fell onto her downy cheeks, but I laughed and cried even harder as I showered her with kisses.

"Elspeth?" Luke asked, his eyes suspiciously wet.

I nodded. "Elspeth."

I looked around for the yellow-haired troll and saw her sitting on the snowy ground, apron pressed to her face, sobbing her ancient eyes out.

"Take your daughter," I said to Luke. They were words I would never tire of saying.

"Elspeth?" I crouched down next to her and placed a hand on her well-padded shoulder. "Don't cry. What you did for us was wonderful. We can never repay you for bringing back our daughter."

"More nonsense!" she erupted, blowing her nose into the apron and glowering at me. "I didn't bring the wee babe back from anywhere."

"You did something," I said, confused and

— I'll admit — a little ticked off. "I saw it happen."

She muttered something Trollish.

"Admit it," I said. "You did something kind. I'll bet you cloaked her, didn't you?"

She made a face. "Ye wouldn't know your nose in a looking glass, would you, missy? 'Twasn't me who done the cloaking, 'twas the babe."

I couldn't help it. I started to laugh.

"I wouldn't be laughing, missy, for I tell the truth."

Luke and Laria joined us and, still laughing, I told Luke what Elspeth had said.

Now he was laughing, too.

The laughter didn't last long. Remember that red dot on the baby's head, the same one Janice said I had on my scalp, too? As it turned out, it wasn't a dot at all. It was a highly detailed rendering of the snowy owl, which happened to be Aerynn's symbol. All Hobbs women bore the mark of the owl, but it usually didn't present itself until the girl reached puberty and began to gain mastery over her powers.

Laria's owl appeared a few hours after birth, which, according to Elspeth, meant our daughter would probably rule the magick universe before she was potty-trained.

The strange rituals Luke had seen Elspeth

performing over Laria were actually teaching sessions. The one on cloaking had probably saved our daughter's life.

I was in something pretty close to shock. "So you're saying our eight-day-old baby cloaked herself, then uncloaked herself. I'm thirty and it will probably be another ten years before I master cloaking."

"Twenty," Elspeth said, nodding her head. "Maybe more."

Luke looked a little shell-shocked himself. "Should make the kids' table at Thanksgiving a hell of a lot more interesting."

He handed Laria off to me and went to check out the Jeep, which James had hidden in the woods. A minute later I heard the wonderful sound of the engine turning over.

He came back for the baby and her car seat and I was happily strapped into the passenger seat and ready to go when I realized Elspeth was standing in the middle of the clearing alone.

Luke looked over at me. I looked at Elspeth. We looked at each other.

"She doesn't really have anyone else," I said. "And she's awfully good with the baby."

He glanced down at his strong, healthy legs and nodded. "And a damn good orthopedist."

"We'll get used to the waffle smell," I said.

"We'll buy Febreze," he said.

"Lots and lots of Febreze," I agreed.

"Hey, Elspeth!" Luke called out the open window. "Hurry up. Don't you want to get home in time for Conan?"

"Stop ye grousing," she said as she waddled across the snow toward the Jeep. "I'll be there when I be there and not a lick before."

"You realize we're going to have to come up with a story for my family," he said.

"And some loaner cars until they call their insurance companies."

"Explaining why James is off the radar might be a tough sell."

"I have the feeling they'll be relieved about that."

"And we'll have to explain Old Buttercup," he said with a grin.

"A nanny with attitude," I said. "I'm not worried. Your family will learn to love her." As long as she didn't cloak or spin her way up to the roof or make the cats do the samba.

"They could be your family, too," he said, taking my hand. "Just say the word."

I looked into those dark green eyes I'd first seen in a dream and said the word I had wanted to say from that very first day.

"Yes."

The console didn't make it easy, but he drew me into his arms and kissed me as white and gold and silver sparks flew from our lips and fingertips and set the inside of the Jeep alight.

"Och!" Elspeth groused as she rolled herself into the backseat. "Spare the likes of me that nonsense. It be too soon for such as that, missy."

"Shut up, old woman," Luke said cheerfully. "If you're going to be part of our family, you'd better get used to seeing a lot of that because Chloe just said she'd marry me."

"A Hobbs she was born and a Hobbs she will die," Elspeth said, unable to hide her smile, "but Himself would be pleased to see you pledge yourselves before the community for all time." She nodded her head. "Pleased indeed."

"For better and for worse?" Luke asked me. "In sickness and in health?"

"Everything but obey," I said. "I have to draw the line somewhere."

"My mother will want to throw a shower for you."

"Let her," I said, feeling reckless and very human. "Let's live dangerously!"

The MacKenzies were a smart and loyal

and nosy crew and it wouldn't be easy keeping our secret right under their noses, but I was willing to give it my best shot. Life was too short, even for a sorceress like me, to miss the chance to be with the people you love. The people who loved you. Family of blood or family of choice, it didn't matter. They were the ones who would always be there for you.

Laria gurgled happily in the backseat as Elspeth fussed with her cap and her blanket. Luke checked his mirrors and eased the Jeep back on the road to Sugar Maple. I plucked my knitting from the console, closed my eyes, and smiled into the darkness.

My family.

We were on our way home.

BARBARA BRETTON: THE SECRET LANGUAGE OF KNITTING

The knitting vocabulary can be confusing to civilians (a.k.a. muggles) so here's a short glossary to help get you up to speed.

Bind Off See "Cast Off"

BSJ Baby Surprise Jacket, probably EZ's most popular design

Cast Off To secure your last row of stitches so they don't unravel

Cast On To place a foundation row of stitches on your needle

DPN Double-pointed needles

EZ Elizabeth Zimmermann, the knitting mother of us all

Fair Isle Multistranded colorwork

FO Finished object

Frog To undo your knitting by ripping back ("Rip it! Rip it!") row by row with great abandon

Kitchener Grafting two parallel rows of live stitches to form an invisible seam

Knit The basic stitch from which everything derives

Knitalong An online phenomenon wherein hundreds of knitters embark on a project simultaneously and exchange progress reports along the way

Kureyon A wildly popular self-striping yarn created and manufactured by Eisaku Noro under the Noro label

LYS Local yarn shop

Magic Loop Knitting a tube with one circular needle instead of four or five double-pointed needles

Purl The knit stitch's sister — instead of knitting into the back of the stitch with the point of the needle facing away from you, you knit into the front of the stitch with the point of the needle facing directly at you

Ravelry An online community for knitters and knitwear designers that has surpassed all expectations

Roving What you have after a fleece has been washed, combed, and carded; roving is then ready to be spun into yarn

SABLE Stash Amassed Beyond Life Expectancy — in other words, you won't live long enough to knit it all!

SEX Stash Enhancement eXercise — basically spending too much money on way too much yarn

Stash The yarn you've been hiding in the empty oven, clean trash bins, your basement, your attic, under the beds, in closets, wherever you can keep your treasures clean, dry, and away from critical eyes

Stitch 'N' Bitch A gathering of like-minded knitters who share knitting techniques and friendship with a twenty-first-century twist

Stranded See "Fair Isle"

Tink To carefully undo your knitting stitch by stitch. Basically to unknit your way back to a mistake-free area

Yarn Crawl The knitter's equivalent of a pub crawl. Substitute yarn shops for bars and you'll get the picture

WHO'S WHO IN SUGAR MAPLE

Chloe Hobbs The half-human, half-sorceress de facto mayor of Sugar Maple and owner of Sticks & Strings, a wildly successful knit shop. As the descendant of sorceress Aerynn, the town's founder, Chloe holds the fate of the magickal town in her hands.

Luke Mackenzie The 100 percent human chief of police. He came to Sugar Maple to investigate the death of Suzanne Marsden, an old high school friend, but stayed because he fell in love with Chloe.

Pyewacket, Blot, Dinah, Lucy Chloe's house cats.

Penelope Chloe's store cat. Penny is actually much more than that. She has been a familiar of the Hobbs women for over three centuries and has often served as a conduit between dimensions.

Elspeth A three-hundred-something-year-old troll from Salem who kept house for

Samuel Bramford. She has been sent to Sugar Maple to watch over Chloe until the baby is born.

Janice Meany Chloe's closest friend and owner of Cut & Curl, the salon across the street from Sticks & Strings. Janice is a Harvard-educated witch, descended from a long line of witches. She and her husband, Lorcan, have five children.

Lorcan Meany Janice's husband. Lorcan is a selkie and one of Luke's friends.

Lynette Pendragon A shifter and owner, with her husband, Cyrus, of Sugar Maple Arts Players. They have five children: Vonnie, Iphigenia, Troy (originally named Gilbert), Adonis (originally named Sullivan), and Will.

Lilith A Norwegian troll who is Sugar Maple's town librarian and historian. She is married to Archie. Her mother was Sorcha the Healer, who cared for Chloe after her parents died.

Midge Stallworth A rosy-cheeked vampire who runs the funeral home with her husband, George.

Renate Weaver Member of the Fae and owner of the Sugar Maple Inn. Renate and her husband, Colm, have four grown children: Bettina, Daisy, Penelope, and Calliope.

Bettina Weaver Leonides Harpist, member of the Fae, occasional part-time worker at Sticks & Strings. Married to Alexander. Mother of three children: Memphis, Athens, Ithaca.

Paul Griggs Werewolf and owner of Griggs Hardware. He is Luke's closest friend in town. He is married to Verna and has two sons: Jeremy and Adam. His nephew Johnny is a frequent visitor.

Frank One of the more garrulous vampire retirees at Sugar Maple Assisted Living.

Manny Another vampire retiree who pals around with Frank.

Rose Frank's and Manny's love interest. She is also a retired vampire who resides at Sugar Maple Assisted Living.

Samuel A four-hundred-plus-year-old wizard who pierced the veil at the end of *Spun by Sorcery*. He was Aerynn's lover and the father of the Hobbs clan.

Sorcha The healer who stayed behind in the mortal world to raise Chloe to adulthood after her parents died in a car crash. Sorcha is Lilith's birth mother.

Aerynn A powerful sorceress from Salem who led the magickal creatures from Salem to freedom during the infamous Witch Trials. A gifted spinner, she founded Sinzibukwud in northern Vermont (later renamed Sugar Maple) and passed her magick and her spinning and knitting skills down to generations of Hobbs women. Aerynn is responsible for the magick charm that enables Sugar Maple to hide in plain sight.

Guinevere Chloe's sorceress mother. Guinevere chose to pierce the veil after the auto accident that took her beloved husband's life.

Ted Aubry Chloe's human father. Guinevere's husband. He was a carpenter by trade.

Isadora The most powerful member of the Fae. She is also the most dangerous. Currently Isadora is banished from this realm until the end of time but who knows what the future might bring.

Gunnar The good twin, he sacrificed himself so Chloe and Luke could be together.

Dane The ultimate evil twin.

The Harris Family They were carpenters in life (c. 1860) but now inhabit the spirit world.

The Souderbush Boys Father Benjamin, mother Amelia, and sons David, William, and John are all ghosts who spend a lot of time on the Spirit Trail, which passes through the Sugar Maple Inn.

Simone A seductive spirit who specializes in

breaking up happy marriages. She usually manifests herself in a wisteria-scented lilac cloud.

Forbes the Mountain Giant His name pretty much says it all.

THE MACKENZIE CLAN

Bunny Matriarch, knitter, retired nurse. Born and raised in the Boston suburbs near Salem.

Jack Patriarch, sport fisherman, retired welder. Also born and raised in the Boston suburbs near Salem.

Ronnie A successful Realtor, father of four. Married to Denise. He still lives in the town where he was born and raised.

Kimberly Luke's oldest sister. Kim is a financial analyst, married, pregnant with her first child by husband Travis Davenport. They have been married eight years. She and Chloe form an easy bond right from the start.

Jennifer Another of Luke's older sisters. She's married to Paul and mother of Diandra, Sean, and Colin.

Kevin Luke's younger brother. He has been married to Tiffany for nine years. They have four children: Ami, Honor, Scott, and Michael.

Patrick Another younger brother. He's

newly divorced from Siobhan. They have two daughters: Caitlin and Sarah.

Meghan The wild card of the bunch. Meghan is the youngest of Bunny and Jack's children and the least predictable. (Her two-minutes younger twin died at birth.) She has the habit of taking up with the wrong guys and paying for it with a broken heart.

Fran Kelly Retired administrative assistant to Boston's police chief. Close friend of the MacKenzie family.

Steffie Luke's daughter, who was six years old when she died in a bicycle accident.

Karen Luke's ex-wife, who sacrificed herself to save their daughter's soul.

Joe Randazzo County Board of Supervisors; a politician who is an occasional thorn in Chloe's side.

JEREMY BREDESON:
THE MAGIC OF FIBER

We've all read the Sugar Maple books (because, um, how would you know where to find this if you hadn't). Chloe's shop has yarn that never knots up. It has amazing colors and perfect substitutions. Literary license goes a long way in making her shop fantastic and fun.

When you take a good, long look at knitting, crocheting, spinning, and dyeing, there's not much to any of them. Color theory, sure. Manual dexterity. The right combination of tension, needles, yarn, and patience, and voilà! You have created something!

Sit down and think about everything that would go into your knitting. (Yes, I'm going to go toward knitting, because I knit. Substitute your Craft of Choice.) On any given project for me, there's searching for the pattern, deciding who it's going to, what color would be best for them, what fiber would be best for them, finding the right yarn, getting the yarn, winding it into balls (because I like center-pull balls), and getting the needles ready. Then there's the cast-on and actual knitting itself. The mechanics of it aren't what's important so much as what you do while you're knitting.

Magic is a matter of raising and forming energy and moving it into what you need it to do. Intent is important when it comes to magic. It's also important when you create something with your hands. For the most part, you're not going to create weapons, unless you're a blacksmith working for a Renaissance fair, and then it's usually only because that's what sells. If you're a fiber artist, though, some of your projects can take hundreds of hours. Those hours will be filled with laughter, movies, talking, cocktails, coffee, friendship, love. Most knitters will tell you, "Don't knit angry!" and most of them will tell you that the minute you pick up your projects while you're mad, you'll mess something up dreadfully.

And really, when you think about it, we take one reeeeeeeeally long piece of string and make it into something completely not-string. It's *magic!*

JEREMY BREDESON: NO MORE MOTHS!

We went shopping one night out at one of our local shopping centers, and we found a store that had, just randomly, things to help protect your clothing from moths. We weren't looking for that, but there it was. Of course, they had the mothballs, but who wants their clothes to smell like those? They also had packages of small cedar balls, so I grabbed a package of those.

We almost walked away right then, but the box next to the cedar balls caught my eye. It looked like it was full of teabags, but when I opened it, the most wonderful smell came out. I was skeptical, because I'd never heard of an herbal mixture that would prevent moths. But my tree-hugging, dirt-worshipper side came out and I knew then and there that I needed to find out what it was. I bought and skimmed the package but it wasn't until I got home and looked closer that I saw what it was:

Peppermint
Rosemary
Thyme
Cloves

Bingo! I can make that! The only thing that I can't grow on my own is the cloves, but I can easily buy those. Anyone can grow peppermint, rosemary, and thyme, and then you just dry them and get yourself some DIY teabags from any organic grocer (I bet even Whole Foods or Trader Joe's would have them) and add a teaspoon or so of each one to the bag and toss one or a few in with your stash. Not only will it keep the moths away, but your yarn will smell good, too!

Incidentally, I keep my stash in plastic shoe boxes and each box has two or three projects' worth of yarn, a cedar ball, and an herbal sachet in it. It makes my knitting that much more enjoyable!

JEREMY BREDESON is a professional administrative assistant (who has very strong opinions about certain fonts — I'm lookin' at you, Comic Sans and Papyrus) and the high priest of one of the oldest cybercovens on the Internet, knits like a fiend, and plays video games

like a teenager in his copious spare time. He lives in Columbus, Ohio, with his husband, Leon, and their very spoiled and pretty, pretty princess dachshund, Belle. You can find him at www.givemamasomesugar.net (though you may want to turn off your judgments; he has very few filters and has a mouth like a sailor) and on Ravelry as technocowboy.

KALI AMANDA BROWNE:
ALL BY HAND,
PUERTO RICAN STYLE

There was a time, not long ago, that when a baby girl was born, she got a handmade outfit, whether sewn, embroidered, or knitted. Generally, a grandmother took care of this. If she herself was not a seamstress, there was always an old lady somewhere who could expertly design and stitch and embroider.

By the time the child made her official debut into the world, she was outfitted like a princess. Lace and satin and delicate designs adorning the precious addition to the family.

Today, because of pressures from work and availability of store-bought ready-to-wear, this is not as prevalent. But the more recent immigrants and those who still have ties to their old country (whatever that may be) keep the tradition alive.

My memories of Puerto Rico are replete with rich, beautiful creations by unknown little old ladies that could rival all the European design houses!

Mom was fortunate enough to have one of these talented ladies growing up in upper Manhattan. Doña Maria, who sometimes babysat for my grandmother, had no children of her own but a deep love for them and my mother soon became one of her favorites.

She combined her passions and made the most beautiful things for her ward. For years, she would lovingly create the clothes and accessories that spoiled Mom to the point that she became the style maven she is today.

In my mother's bedroom there is a photograph of her as a child, standing at the foot of the lake in Central Park. Adding to its sweetly nostalgic essence, the photograph contains more trees in the horizon than high-rises. Front and center is an adorable toddler, all innocence and wearing a pout across her lips, outfitted like a priceless collectable Victorian porcelain doll.

For this park outing, Doña Maria had made a dress. She worked all week, as she did every week, so that she and her husband could have a leisurely Sunday stroll with Mom.

This dress was a magnificent handmade

work of art, with a ruffled A-line skirt, including seven layers of hand-stitched lace. The top of the dress has a doily collar with four layers of lacy ruffles that draped over her shoulders and extended to her little waist.

But it didn't stop there! Doña Maria had also added accessories to complete the ensemble. On the child's head, a sculptured, tulle ribbon had a few smaller but matching lace columns stitched vertically across the fabric. Peeking through the hem of the little dress, she wore a pair of matching lacy panties. On her feet, she wore a pair of knit socks, with hand-stitched lacy borders, matching the ribbon and undergarment, of course.

(Yes, I know. . . . Take a moment to fully picture it and let out that "Awwwww!" you have stuck between your diaphragm and throat.)

Nowadays, you almost always see this only for baptisms in the Latin American community that lives here. Mom and I make it a spectator sport to stand outside the Basilica of Our Lady of Perpetual Help to witness the intricate baby outfits at the end of a baptism.

Traditionally, for all Latin Americans, a baptism not only brings the child into the faith, but it is the formal introduction of the bundle of joy to God and the world.

For Puerto Ricans, of course, this means a party. And a party means food. Not sandwiches, although finger foods are allowed. I mean actual cooked food and a lot of it! We're talking a buffet fit for kings. There is no traditional menu as such, except that it requires sturdy paper plates because there's going to be rice, meat, salad, and some of the aforementioned finger foods piled up on those things and everybody is going be dressed up to the nines — though not as extravagantly as the baby.

Usually there is at least one kind of rice in the offerings; and it will be served with ham, turkey, and probably a rump or shoulder of roast pork — or just salad for those who have (largely) given up meats. (I've never met a Puerto Rican who has entirely given up meat, though there must be six or seven of them somewhere, probably in Los Angeles.)

This is one of our national dishes, but I've tweaked it for busy cooks who don't have time to soak beans overnight. It is delicious and provides a good dose of protein to boot.

416

ARROZ CON GANDULES

RICE WITH PIGEON PEAS

A splash of olive oil
1 medium onion, finely chopped
garlic (to taste; I use 3 or 4 cloves, chopped
  or pressed)
red pepper flakes (to taste)
1 teaspoon dried oregano
1 cup medium-grain rice
2 cups stock*
1 can pigeon peas (15 oz., drained, but
  reserve the liquid)
2 tablespoons small manzanilla olives (pitted
  and stuffed with pimentos)

Heat oil and sauté onions until almost translucent. Add garlic and pepper flakes and oregano (about 2 minutes over medium flame).

Add rice and stir in pan to make sure grains are coated in oil (about 1 minute).

Add stock, increase flame to high, and

bring to a boil. Cover and cook over low heat for 10 minutes.

Add drained pigeon peas and olives. Add reserved liquid if dried out. Cover and continue cooking for an additional 10 minutes.

Fold in pigeon peas and olives into the rice. Taste and adjust seasoning if needed. Let sit, covered, for a few minutes before serving.

* *Depending on your preferences or dietary restrictions, you may use chicken, beef, or vegetable stock (including low or no sodium). Each will add a slightly different depth to the dish. Instead, if you prefer, use water and add one bouillon cube. If this is all you do, the finished product will have a "dirty" rice look. If you prefer a yellow finish, add a packet of sazón (with annatto and saffron).*

The vegetables will disintegrate in cooking and flavor the oil — which the rice will incorporate in its entirety — as well as the stock. Both will plump up and flavor the rice. Also, if you want that authentic old-world taste, you may add a smoked ham hock to the rice in the first stage of cooking. Leftover rice goes well in tacos or to heft up a soup.

¡Buen apetito!

■ ■ ■ ■

KALI AMANDA BROWNE was born in New York City, came of age in Puerto Rico, and has spent her entire adult life in New York. Perverse and twisted, cynical and overeducated, and still a little naïve, she has entirely too much time on her hands. Currently living, cooking, and writing in Brooklyn, she has authored *Kali: The Food Goddess: A Compilation of Delightful Recipes and Memories of Food;* the crime novel *Justified;* and a short story, "Putting May to Rest." Her books are available at several online retailers and through Smashwords at www.smashwords.com/profile/view/ KaliAmanda. She regularly shares her thoughts about her writing life at http://ebooksbykali.blogspot.com, her own life experiences at http://kalistempleofdoom.blogspot.com, and thoughts about food and cooking at http://barbarabretton.com.

ELIZABETH DELISI:
PI OPENWORK DISHCLOTH

Materials

Cotton worsted-weight yarn (I used Peaches and Cream, color #130 Shaded Pastels)

Size 7 knitting needles

Crochet hook or tapestry needle to weave in ends

Finished size

Approx. 9 × 9 inch square

Gauge

Not important

Pi Openwork pattern stitch

Multiple of 3

Row 1 (RS): K2, *YO, K3, with left needle pull first of 3 sts just knitted over last 2 and off the needle; repeat from * to last st, K1.

Row 2 and all WS rows: Purl.

Row 3: K1, *K3, with left needle pull first

of 3 sts just knitted over last 2 and off the needle, YO;

repeat from * to last 2 sts, K2.

Row 4: Purl.

Repeat these four rows for pattern.

Dishcloth instructions

Cast on 43 stitches.

K 6 rows in garter stitch.

Row 6: K5, follow row 1 of Pi Openwork pattern over next 33 stitches, K5.

Row 7: K5, P33 (row 2 of Pi Openwork pattern), K5.

Row 8: K5, follow row 3 of Pi Openwork pattern over next 33 stitches, K5.

Row 9: K5, P33 (WS row of Pi Openwork pattern), K5.

Repeat rows 6–9 until piece is 3/4 inch less than desired length, ending with WS row.

Next 6 rows: Work in garter stitch.

Bind off, weave in ends.

Variation: Use seed stitch for border instead of garter stitch.

Questions? Contact me at elizabeth@ elizabethdelisi.com.

Have fun!

Copyright 2007 Elizabeth Delisi

ELIZABETH DELISI'S time-travel romance set in ancient Egypt, *Lady of the*

Two Lands (a Bloody Dagger Award winner and Golden Rose Award nominee), and her romantic suspense novel *Since All Is Passing* (an EPPIE Award finalist and Bloody Dagger Award finalist) are available from Amber Quill Press. *Fatal Fortune* (a Word Museum Reviewer's Choice Masterpiece), the first in the Lottie Baldwin Mystery series, is currently available from Fictionwise. "Mistletoe Medium" (Elizabeth's novella-length prequel to *Fatal Fortune*) is featured in the paranormal romance anthology *Enchanted Holidays,* available from Ellora's Cave; and "Restless Spirit" is published in the paranormal anthology *One Touch Beyond,* also available from Ellora's Cave.

Elizabeth's two short story collections, *Mirror Images* and *Penumbra,* are available from BWLPP. Her contemporary romance novella "The Heart of the Matter" is featured in the DiskUs Publishing Valentine's Day–themed anthology *Cupid's Capers* (an EPPIE Award finalist). Her contemporary romance novella "A Cup of Christmas Charm" is featured in the DiskUs Publishing holiday anthology *Holiday Hearts 2* (an EPPIE Award finalist), and her romance novella "A Carol of Love" is still available in the series's first anthology *Holiday Hearts* (an EPPIE Award finalist). In addition, Elizabeth has a short story in the holiday anthology *The Holiday Mixer,* available from Haypenny Press.

Elizabeth is an instructor for Writers Digest University. She has taught creative writing at the community college level, and she edits for individuals. She holds a B.A. in English with a creative writing major from St. Leo University. Elizabeth is currently at work on *Deadly Destiny* and *Perilous Prediction* — sequels to *Fatal Fortune* — and *Knit a Spell,* a paranormal romance. For more information, visit Elizabeth's website, www.eliza bethdelisi.com, or her blog, http:// elizabethdelisi.blogspot.com/.

LISA SOUZA:
BIRTHDAY

Many years ago, I read a few lines about a boy asking his infant brother to tell him what God looked like. Somehow, this just resonated with me and I didn't know why until the birth of my first grandson.

I had written about him, calling him the Grandsonfetus from the moment that his parents found out the sex of this ever-growing force of nature. His due date passed, as is more than likely with a first pregnancy, and my psychic friend told me that she got the message that he would be born on the fifteenth of December. The fifteenth passed and my friend was left shaking her head, muttering that she had never been given the wrong information. Somehow, there was something at work greater than what we could know. The birthday of my late stepfather was approaching and *he* had been a force of nature and a noisy ghost. We all waited impatiently and on the evening of December sixteenth, we got the call that our daughter had begun getting some labor pains and, this being her first baby, I figured that we had a couple of hours to think about making that ninety-minute drive to her home. I was so very wrong. My daughter's body kicked into high gear within minutes and the pains were coming faster, which prompted us to throw on our woolly pullovers and head out into the cold December evening, like the cavalry.

That boy was born on the morning of the seventeenth of December, my stepfather's birthday. I was at my daughter's side, holding one of her legs as she pushed the baby out, and as I saw his little face emerge, a flood of emotion washed over me. It was pure and unadulterated Love.

The part of this story that echoes what I read so long ago is that when this little pink being was clean and lying naked on his warming bed, he began to coo and babble while moving his head to several points above him. I will always believe that he was talking to the invisible crowd that had come to see him as his soul slipped into its vessel. I had never witnessed a newborn baby making sounds like these and I mentioned it to my husband, who stood next to me. It lasted only a couple of minutes and then it was as if he began to forget that language and no longer see those faces.

Now my grandson is a five-year-old natural athlete, as was Grandpa Lenny, and he says things that remind me of that older force of nature. Did that baby delay his entry into the world so that Lenny's soul could slip in for one more go-round? I guess I will not know the answer until I slip to the Other Side, where all of my questions will be answered.

LIZA SOUZA studied fine art at the California College of the Arts, became a singer/songwriter for a decade, and then settled into a career in the fiber arts, which had never really left her hands since she could first hold a needle and thread. Once primarily a spinner who created original garments for clients, she has since narrowed her focus to life as a colorist, creating rich palettes of color in yarn and fiber. Her first book, in collaboration with Vicki Stiefel, is *10 Secrets of the Laidback Knitters,* published by St. Martin's Press in May 2011. Find her website at www.lisaknit .com and her blog at http://lisaknit .typepad.com/tiltawhirl/.

FRAN BAKER:
FEATHER & FAN BABY AFGHAN

When it comes to baby blankets or afghans, I'm a "simpler and softer is better" kind of knitter. One of my favorites is the Feather & Fan pattern in Baby Marble by James C. Brett. I love the softness and the subtle shading of Baby Marble. Plus, it washes and dries like a dream. Interestingly, I've found that knitters don't often think of the Feather & Fan pattern for babies, but every mother I've ever given one to has been delighted. And I just love seeing a baby sleeping peacefully under a blanket or afghan I've made.

I don't worry about the gauge with this pattern because I control how many repeats I want. Usually I do 11 repeats, and because I'm a fairly tight knitter, I use a size 7 needle. Below is the pattern as I like to make it. (Note that I use markers to keep track of my pattern repeats on row 3.) The finished afghan comes out to about 40 × 40 inches, give or take.

Materials

Size 6 or 7 knitting needles (depending on how tight a knitter you are)

2 balls of Baby Marble (in the color of your choice)

11 stitch markers

Cast on 208 stitches, which includes 11 pattern repeats and 5 stitches on each end for the border.

Knit 5 rows in garter stitch if you want, marking with a contrasting yarn the first row as the right side.

Pattern

Row 1: Knit (if you've skipped the garter stitch rows, mark this side with a contrasting yarn for the right side).

Row 2: Purl.

Row 3: K5, place marker, *K2tog 3 times, (K1, YO) 6 times, K2tog 3 times, place marker; repeat from * to last 5 stitches, place marker, K5.

Row 4: Knit.

Knit 5 rows in garter stitch if you want. Or skip this step and . . .

Bind off.

Wash and block by hand.

FRAN BAKER is busy writing her four-

teenth novel. Her books have appeared on several bestseller lists and have been translated into more than twenty languages. Fran has conducted a number of writing workshops in the United States and Canada, and she has spoken about writing for publication to local, national, and international audiences. She is a member of Novelists, Inc.; the Authors Guild; and the Society of Midland Authors. She blogs at www.daugh terofthegreatdepression.blogspot.com. Readers are invited to visit her website at www.franbaker.com.

DUSTY MILLS:
TANGIBLE HEREDITY

I'm one of those people with a deep-seated love of all things heirloom. The idea of passing something on to future generations is profoundly weighty for me. Among my favored possessions is an old acrylic afghan that was crocheted by my grandmother years before I was born. You know the kind — with old-school ripple stripes in three shades of blue and doesn't match a thing in the house. . . .

It's now become so holey that I wouldn't offer it to a guest unless it was to save their life, but I still use it every day, and now my young daughter does, too. If I could ever bring myself to use it just a little bit less, my grandchildren might even be warmed by it in years to come!

When we craft something, we don't always imagine that many decades ahead, it will still be used — still be loved — still be cherished, as if it were last Christmas's gift.

433

But the beauty of knitting is that it truly is the gift that keeps on giving. Something of us remains in our crafts long after our needles have stopped clicking and our love pours out of every stitch and right into the hearts of descendants we may never meet.

What I'm saying is this: That blanket you considered knitting for your niece's baby that's due next month . . . cast it on. Knit that lace christening gown or the coming-home sweater that's been in your WIP bag for a month. With each stitch you progress, think not only of the baby before you, but of the babies to come.

Each piece you finish is interwoven with love, hope, dreams, familial ties and anchors, friendship, and history. It's tangible heredity.

DUSTY MILLS is your average, everyday knitter who dabbles with designing knitwear and blogging (www.theknitlife .wordpress.com). She lives in Missouri with her beloved family, not enough yarn or spinning fiber, and a couple of fur-beasts that think they run the show. Dusty would like to invite you to download her mother/daughter hat pattern, Chippewa, for free. Enter the code

STICKS&STRINGS when you check out on Ravelry. You can find the pattern here: www.ravelry.com/designers/dusty -mills.

DAWN BROCCO:
BABY'S FIRST CARDIGAN

This little, easy-to-knit cardigan pattern has two yarn and gauge options — sport and worsted weight — for quick and quicker-yet knitting.

Pattern is written with slash marks separating the directions for sport and worsted (sport / worsted).

Materials

Sport weight: Lobster Pot Cashmere (100% lace-weight cashmere), 400 yd (50 gr) hank: 2 hanks Natural (MC) (used double)

Worsted weight: Cascade Yarns Heritage Silk (85% merino superwash wool, 15% mulberry silk), 437 yd (100 gr) hank: 1 hank color #5659 Primavera (MC) (used double); and either 1 hank Heritage Silk color #5617 Raspberry or 1 hank Cascade 220 Superwash (100% superwash wool), 220 yd (100 gr) hank, color #7805 Fla-

mingo Pink (CC) (used single)
Size 6 / 8 (4 / 5 mm) circular needles, 16–20 inches long
Size 6 / 8 (4 / 5 mm) double-pointed needles
Tapestry needle
Stitch marker
4 buttons, size 5/8 inch / 3/4 inch

Dimensions

Body circumference: 18″. Length: 9″. Sleeve length: 6 1/2″. Sleeve depth: 4″.

Gauge

6 sts and 8.5 rows / 5 sts and 6.5 rows equals 1 inch (2.5 cm) in St st with size 6 / 8 needles or size to give gauge. Take time to check gauge.

Substitute yarn weight: sport / worsted

Abbreviations

approx = approximately
beg = beginning
BO = bind off
CC = contrasting color
ckn(s) = circular knitting ndl(s)
CO = cast on
dpns = double-pointed ndls
k = knit
k2tog = knit 2 sts together
m2 = place 2 twisted loops onto the right-

hand ndl
MC = main color
rnd(s) = round(s)
ndl = needle
p = purl
p2tog = purl 2 sts together
patt = pattern
rem = remaining
rep = repeat
RS = right side
ssk = slip 2 sts, separately, knitwise, then
  knit them together from this position
st(s) = stitch(es)
St st = Stockinette stitch
WS = wrong side

Seed Stitch Lower Edge

With MC and ckn, CO 110 / 92 sts (long-
  tail method recommended).

Set up seed stitch pattern (WS): P2, (k1,
  p1) across, turn.

(RS): K2, (p1, k1) across, turn.

Rep last 2 rows 2 times / 1 time more.

Work 41 / 31 rows in St st (to approx 5
  inches from CO edge), end after finishing
  a WS row.

Right Front

Knit 26 / 22 sts, turn. Purl across.

Work 18 / 12 more rows in St st, end after

finishing a WS row.

Neck shaping (RS): On next RS row, BO 5 / 4 sts, ssk, knit across, turn.

Purl across.

K1, ssk, knit across.

Rep last 2 rows 3 / 2 times more — 16 / 14 shoulder sts rem.

Work 5 / 5 rows even in St st. BO.

Left Front

With RS facing, knit across 26 / 22 left front sts, turn.

Purl across.

Work 19 / 13 more rows in St st, end after finishing a RS row.

Neck shaping (WS): BO 5 / 4 sts, p2tog, purl across, turn.

Knit across.

P1, p2tog, purl across.

Rep last 2 rows 3 / 2 times more — 16 / 14 shoulder sts rem.

Work 4 / 4 rows even in St st. BO.

Back

With RS facing, knit the 58 / 48 back sts, turn. Purl WS row.

Work 32 / 24 more rows in St st (to approx 4 inches from underarm).

Seam fronts to back at shoulders.

Sleeves

With MC and dpns, beg at center underarm, pick up 1 center underarm st, then
48 / 40 sts around armhole, place marker
— 49 / 41 sts. Knit 2 / 0 rnds.

Decrease round: K1, ssk, knit to last 2
sts, k2tog.

Knit 5 / 4 rnds even.

Rep last 6 / 5 rnds 7 / 6 times more. Rep
decrease round — 31 / 25 sts rem.

**Set up seed stitch pattern — Sport
weight only:** K2tog, (p1, k1) around, end
p1 — 30 sts rem.

**Set up seed stitch pattern — Worsted
weight only:** With CC, k2tog, knit around
— 24 sts rem. (k1, p1) around.

Both weights: patt 5 / 3 more rnds. BO in
pattern.

Seed Stitch Right Front Button Band

With MC and dpns or ckn, beg at lower
right front edge, pick up and knit 47 / 37
sts along right front edge (approx 7 sts for
every 10 rows / 3 sts for every 4 rows),
turn.

Set up seed stitch pattern (WS): (K1,
p1) across, end k1, turn.

Rep last row 1 time / 0 times more.

**Buttonhole row (WS) — Sport weight
only:** K1, p1, k2tog, m2, p2tog, (k1, p1)

4 times, k1, p2tog, m2, k2tog, (p1, k1) 4 times, p1, k2tog, m2, p2tog, (k1, p1) 4 times, k1, p2tog, m2, k2tog, p1, k1.

Buttonhole row (RS) — Worsted weight only: K1, p1, *k2tog, m2, p2tog, (k1, p1) 3 times; rep from * 2 times more, k2tog, m2, p2tog, k1.

On next WS row, patt across, working through the bottom strand of each m1. (Insert needle up into the m1 from underneath the horizontal yarn strand. This brings that strand up into the stitch, instead of leaving it to hang down, causing a sloppy buttonhole.)

Patt 2 / 1 more rows. BO in pattern.

Seed Stitch Left Front Button Band

With MC and dpns or ckn, beg at lower right front edge, pick up and knit 47 / 37 sts along right front edge (approx 7 sts for every 10 rows / 3 sts for every 4 rows), turn.

Set up seed stitch pattern (WS): (K1, p1) across, end k1, turn.

Rep last row 5 / 3 times more. BO in pattern.

Seed Stitch Collar

With MC / CC and ckn, beg at center of right front band, pick up and knit 67 / 55 sts around neckline to center of left front band, turn.

Set up seed stitch pattern (WS): (P1, k1) across, end p1, turn.

Rep last row 15 / 11 times more (to approx 1 3/4 inches). BO in pattern.

Finishing

Sew on buttons, opposite buttonholes. Weave in all yarn tails. Wet-block.

MONICA JINES:
TIPS WHEN
KNITTING FOR BABIES

Babies have large heads, almost as large as their chests, so a stretchy bind-off is needed for neck bands. One stretchy bind-off is worked with a yarn over prior to each stitch. A reverse yarn over is worked prior to a knit stitch and a regular yarn over prior to a purl.

For a k1, p1 rib bind-off you would work in this manner:

Reverse yarn over, k1, pass the yarn over over the knit stitch, yarn over, p1, pass the yarn over over the purl stitch, and then pass the knit stitch over the purl stitch. Repeat the process.

Another bind-off:

Knit the first 2 stitches together through the back loop. Pass the stitch on the right-hand needle back to the left needle, then knit that stitch plus the next stitch together through the back loop. Continue this process across your work. For a little different-looking bind-off you can knit through the front loop; you will still have a stretchy bind-off, but it will have spaces between the bound-off stitches.

MONICA JINES: I cannot remember a time in my life when I did not knit. My mother taught me when I was so young I do not remember actually being taught. Although I have gone for short stretches with little knitting being done, I always come back to it. I love knitting all types of projects and also enjoy designing. I have been published in *Vogue Knitting on the Go* and have also designed for the Loopy Ewe and Cherry Tree Hill Yarn. My designs can be seen and purchased on Ravelry at www.ravelry.com/designers/monica-jines and also at the Loopy Ewe and Simply Socks Yarn Company.

RACHAEL HERRON: FIVE THINGS ABOUT KNITTING FOR BABIES

Knitting for babies isn't like knitting for regular grown-up people, and there are several things I have to chant to myself as I go along, or I end up with gifts that are impossible to give, so they end up sitting on my yarn shelves, glaring at me resentfully.

1. Babies have weird proportions. Wasn't it Elizabeth Zimmermann who said they were cubes? You can't consider waist-shaping with a baby, or if you do, give the sweater a Buddha shape, because babies are round, not elongated. And what's more, they stay that way for a long time. The sweater should be wider than it is tall, which will allow the baby to grow sideways into it. (I have begun designing my own sweaters the same way. I'm not getting any taller, after all.)

2. Knitted baby items take longer than you think they will. It's all about the planning, friends. See, I'm a pretty fast knitter. I tend

to knock out sweaters for myself in a month or so. So when I think of something tiny and darling, I also think, "Oh! I'll watch a movie and knit up this sweater tonight!" It's always wrong, and it ends up taking *weeks* to finish something that feels like it shouldn't take more than three hours. It makes knitting for baby showers a dangerous game.

3. Babies are bigger than you think they are, too. I'm not a mother, so I've never really nailed this one. In my head, babies are *wee*. They're tiny little creatures of delight, and a tiny little knitted sweater will be the most cunning thing ever. Right? I once gave a baby sweater to a woman who held it up to her belly and said, "Oh, my God! I'm not having a *kitten!*" It was all I could do to convince her I wasn't trying to wish her into have a preemie.

4. Babies are dirty. If Mom can't throw the sweater, cap, and matching booties into the washer along with the thirty-two other loads she needs to do, our new little prince will wear them once, and that will be the first and final time he will be seen in your finery. If, though, Mom doesn't have to think about it when she's doing laundry? He will wear that sweater all winter, every other day, and there will be a million photos

of him wearing it. Unless, of course, he's a third child, in which case there will be no photos (but that wash-'n'-wear sweater will be even more appreciated).

5. Babies are darling. Oh, that's the part you already knew, right? Me, too. That's the only part I get consistently right.

RACHAEL HERRON received her MFA in writing from Mills College and has been knitting since she was five years old. It's more than a hobby; it's a way of life. Rachael lives with her better half in Oakland, California, where they have four cats, three dogs, three spinning wheels, and more musical instruments than they can count. Visit http:// yarnagogo.com.

JANET SPAETH:
LULLABY

If this is your first child, there is one very important thing you *must* understand before you go one day further.

You are not in charge!

Not anymore. Maybe you once were, but now you are a parent, which means you have given up control of your pride, your sleep, and your sanity. I'm sorry. Someone had to tell you.

My first lesson came when my daughter was a mere four weeks old. My in-laws were going to watch her while my husband and I went to a wedding.

"She'll go down for a nap around three o'clock," I told my in-laws. "The tape is already in the player."

"Tape?" my mother-in-law asked.

Now, tell me this wasn't brilliant: every day when it was her naptime, I played the tape — it happened to be Pachelbel's *Canon in D,* with loon calls and bird whistles.

451

(What can I say? This was my first child. I had no idea.) I figured that she'd soon associate the music with naptime, and eventually, all I'd have to do was play the music and she'd nod off happily.

My husband and I went to the wedding, and the bride walked down the aisle, slowly, very, very, very slowly, to, yes, Pachelbel's *Canon in D*. This was the world's longest aisle, I'll tell you. By the time the bride reached the altar, my husband's eyes were closed, and my head was on his shoulder. We woke up before either of us began snoring, but it was close.

To this day, whenever I hear that piece of music, I start to nod off.

My daughter, however — I swear to you that the girl perks up when the song plays.

And what have we learned from this? That parents are trainable, but children are not. Just accept it. And get some sleep. I have just the thing. . . .

JANET SPAETH is a writer and the mother of two children. Be gentle with her. She's been sleep deprived ever since the tape player broke.

ABOUT THE AUTHOR

Barbara Bretton is the *USA Today* bestselling, award-winning author of more than forty books. She currently has more than ten million copies in print around the world. Her works have been translated into twelve languages in more than twenty countries.

Barbara lives in New Jersey but loves to spend as much time as possible in Maine with her husband, walking the rocky beaches and dreaming up plots for upcoming books.